THE LAST NATION

THE LAST NATION

WAYNE DEERFIELD
with Michael Gordon

Copyright © 2023 by Asia Pacific Missions

All rights reserved.

No part of this book may be reproduced in any form or by any electronic or mechanical means, including information storage and retrieval systems, without permission in writing from the author. The only exception is by a reviewer, who may quote short excerpts in a review.

Printed in the United States of America

27 26 25 24 23   1 2 3 4 5

ISBN 978-1-7356545-9-1

Cover design: Shelby Boyd

Book interior design: Dawn M. Brandon (dawn@ravensbrook.net)

This story is dedicated to front-line workers and their families giving everything to reach the last nations.

PROLOGUE AND ACKNOWLEDGMENT

THIS FICTIONAL STORY came to me over 20 years ago. I worked on it from time to time, but in 2021 after fasting and prayer, I felt led by the Lord to complete and publish it. I'm so thankful for the help of co-writer Michael Gordon—this project wouldn't be finished without him. He filled in gaps and made it a great story. As you read this fictional narrative, remember, we're not trying to create new theology about angels and demons; the goal is to help readers visualize the intense spiritual warfare happening over the remaining peoples worldwide who have never heard the gospel in all human history. Other themes we wanted to surface are the importance of prayer for workers on the battle's front lines and the tremendous sacrifice needed to reach the remaining people groups. Our prayer is that this story will inspire you to pray fervently, give generously, and for some, awaken a dormant call to go.

1

CHRISTOPHER BILLINGS bowed his head and squeezed his eyes shut, fighting back emotions he hadn't felt in years. The soft chords of an acoustic guitar filled the sanctuary, and the words of the preacher gripped his heart.

"Tonight is the night," Pastor Fritz Bernheim barked out to the congregation standing before him. "God is waiting for your reply. Jesus told the rich young ruler, 'Sell all that you have. Give the money to the poor. And then come, follow me.' Jesus was after the one thing this young man didn't want to give up.

"What about you? Is there anything in your life that you aren't willing to give to the Lord? Is there something you're holding back?"

The preacher paused to allow his words to settle. He continued, "In this moment, His question for you and for me is clear: Are you willing to sacrifice that thing on the altar of this church tonight? If so, come. Now is the time."

As men and women all around made their way toward the altar, Chris steadied himself by leaning on the chair in front of him. *What's going on?* he wondered. *God, what is it that You want from me? Is there something I'm holding onto?* He stood still, listening for direction, a word, a nudge from the Holy Spirit.

As he waited, Chris began to feel a deep sense of God's peace, a hunger for His presence — and a dawning realization that after tonight, somehow, everything would change. He turned to his wife, Maria, and the tears streaming down her cheeks told him that God was speaking to her as well. He didn't want to disturb her moment with the Lord, so he slipped into the aisle and moved toward the platform. Chris knew that God's Spirit was just as present in the eighth row as at the front of the sanctuary, but he also felt compelled to go forward, to show the Lord that he was serious about hearing from Him.

Dozens of members of the Lakeside Community Church family were already at the front of the room. Some stood with hands raised, some knelt at the edge of the platform, and a few even lay on their backs. This was a common scene at Lakeside in recent months, especially during the Wednesday night service. Pastor Bernheim's sermons seemed to grow shorter each week, but the prayer time at the altar often extended into the night.

Chris worked his way through the crowd and found some space to the right of the platform. As he arrived, a familiar face greeted him.

"Chris," the pastor said, "God has prompted me to come and pray with you."

"Thanks, Pastor." Chris's voice was barely audible over the music of the worship band. "I'm not really sure why I'm here — I just know I had to come. I feel like God is calling us to something, but I have no idea what it is."

"No idea?"

CHAPTER ONE

"Well, your message tonight. It got to me." Chris cleared his throat, trying to hide the emotion in his voice. "I've heard those Scriptures before, of course, but tonight, for some reason, it felt like you were talking directly to me. I feel there's something more the Lord wants from me."

Bernheim rested a hand on Chris's right shoulder and looked into his eyes. "Chris, the Lord promises in Scripture that if we seek Him wholeheartedly, we will find Him. He doesn't hide from us. That's a promise. Let me just pray with you. Is that okay?"

Chris closed his eyes and nodded.

"Lord," Bernheim said, "I thank You for Chris and Maria and their children. Thank You for the gift they are to me and this church family. Thank You for their willingness to follow You wherever You lead. And now, in the same way You are speaking to so many in these last days, I'm confident You will speak to Chris tonight. Show him what it is You desire him to give to You. Answer him like You did the rich young ruler."

Bernheim gave Chris a reassuring pat on the shoulder and stepped away to pray for someone else.

With arms lifted to the Lord in surrender, Chris took inventory of his life. God had given him so much: Maria, Bethany, Hannah, Timmy, a thriving business, a beautiful home, loyal friends, fruitful ministry in the church. He realized, not for the first time, that he was living the American dream. Point by point, he expressed his gratitude for these gifts and offered them back to the Lord. *What am I holding onto? What am I not seeing?*

Chris lowered his arms and held his hands palms up. "Dear God," he whispered, "everything I have is Yours. I give it all to You. My hands are open. If there's anything You want me to give up, take it. If there's anything You want to place in my hands, I receive it."

Chris grew silent and listened for God's voice. He dropped to his knees and braced his head on the platform. The Holy Spirit brought to Chris's mind a night much like this one over fifteen years earlier. As a college student, Chris had sensed the call of God to serve Him among the nations. He had been willing, but then life got complicated.

Now Chris felt that flame reignite in his heart—but he had so many questions. He didn't know any of the details, but that did not concern him tonight. He was confident that no matter where God directed his family, no matter the trials they would face, the Lord was already there preparing the way. It might be difficult, it might even be painful, but they would never be alone.

When Chris at last decided to return to his seat, he found that he was facedown on the floor and there was no one else around. Instrumental music played through the speakers in the empty sanctuary. Chris checked his watch and saw that he had been praying not for minutes but for hours.

God had met him at that altar, and Chris marched out to the parking lot with new resolve.

He knew what he had to do.

2

THE SUMMONS HAD ARRIVED less than twenty-four hours earlier. It was not an invitation. When the Prince of Darkness called, obedience was the only possibility. And so Nyale had left his island at once, accompanied by two subordinates. They traveled all day and night, arriving in the valley of Megiddo under a red moon.

Coming from a tropical domain, Nyale was surprised by the chill of the nighttime desert. Just another reason to look forward to the end of this convocation. Nyale claimed a secluded place against the wall of the canyon where he could observe the arrivals of the others. Ten years had passed since their last Gathering, and he saw instantly that time had taken a toll. With every day outside the presence of the Most High, their appearances had become more grotesque. The evil inside them had manifested in their visible forms, and the transformation shocked Nyale. Fangs, claws, and scales of every hue now featured prominently on the beasts before him, and he wondered for a second how much he had changed in the past decade.

Nyale snapped out of his musing as the temperature plummeted. Everyone present was aware of what this sudden change meant. They all moved quickly to form a loose circle at the mouth of the canyon, careful to keep their heads down lest they inadvertently make eye contact with their host.

His greeting came in a low but menacing command: "Lift your countenances, faithful ones." The warriors of the army of darkness tentatively raised their eyes, out of both fear and curiosity. What would their lord look like this night? Through the millennia separated from the Creator, his appearance had mutated just as theirs had. Once a glorious angel of light, he had first taken on a yellow and green tint, which gave way over the centuries to red and blue. At their last Gathering, ten years prior, he appeared as a palette of grays with no hint of color.

The sight before them now took Nyale's breath away. If the beast heard his reflexive gasp, he ignored it. Nyale wanted to turn aside, but his eyes locked on the great red dragon. Lucifer had never before shown them this aspect of himself, and the effect was mesmerizing. The seven heads of the dragon leered at the assembled demons.

The middle head spoke: "Look around. I want you to see, I want you to *feel*, the situation we find ourselves in. Go ahead. Look."

When Lucifer convened the first Gathering three centuries before, thousands had obeyed his summons. A mere foot soldier at the time, Nyale had been relegated to the perimeter of the assembly, barely able to catch a glimpse of the Dark Prince or hear his orders. It was only through the instructions of his superior officer that Nyale learned of his assignment, the post

CHAPTER TWO

he held to this very day. But through the decades, their numbers had dwindled at an alarming rate and Nyale advanced closer and closer to the inner circle where his master held court. Traveling to Megiddo tonight, he knew their war council would be smaller yet—but he was alarmed by what he saw in the canyon.

From thousands, they were down to thirty.

"You," the dragon hissed, "are the last line of defense. Need I remind you that we are in a fight for our very survival? Our Enemy is taking territory everywhere around the world, and He will not stop until we are destroyed. Now more than ever, you have one job to do. By any means necessary, you *must* keep your tribes in complete darkness. You *must* succeed where so many others have failed.... I always knew you thirty were my fiercest, most loyal warriors. That is why I chose you for the most important of assignments."

This was a lie, and Nyale knew it, but he tried to push the thought from his mind. He suspected that his master was incapable of reading his thoughts, but he was not certain.

"I am counting on those gathered here tonight to hold the line," the dragon said. "You must hold on just a little longer. When we show our determination to stand our ground, the Enemy's followers will back away from the battle. They are weak. They are lazy. And then the tide will turn. The Enemy does not understand the power of darkness. He cannot succeed. He *will not* succeed."

Lucifer's heads scanned the circle, and the assembled demons once again averted their eyes. The middle head settled on a being that Nyale recognized as the ruler of a tribe in Asia.

"Sheol," Lucifer said, "step forward."

The demon that lumbered to the center of the circle reminded Nyale of an elephant — enormous body, thick legs, even a trunk and fangs that resembled tusks.

"Yes, my lord," Sheol answered as he bowed his head and slime dripped from the edge of his mouth.

"Sheol, my devoted servant. Tell us. How is it that your people, the Zirta, have been kept from the truth?"

These interviews were always precarious affairs for the demons who were called upon. The constant menace in their master's voice made it difficult to discern whether he intended praise or rebuke. Sheol seemed to anticipate the former, so he spoke with confidence.

"My lord, Immorality and Hopelessness have been my steadfast companions, and I have brought them with me this night." He gestured outside the circle to two smaller beings crouching in the shadows. "We have held the Zirta in these twin bondages for all of time. One leads to the other. We have enticed them with the pleasures of sin, but they eventually come to feel the emptiness of such a life. This leads to hopelessness. When they begin to understand their dire state, they try to soothe themselves by returning to self-indulgence. It's a never-ending cycle."

"Well done, Sheol." The seven heads nodded in approval. "Well done."

"Thank you, master. Our hold on the Zirta is unbreakable. Their minds have been brought to the edge of despair with the aid of the corruption transmitters they so eagerly place in their homes —"

"What!?" The simultaneous blast from all seven heads forced those in the circle to stagger backward. "You mean to say...you mean to *tell me* that you have allowed these corruption transmitters to be placed in the homes of unenlightened men!?"

"Well, I, uh, we were very strategic, my lord. The devices are costly, so we were able to limit them to a few locations in order to introduce more destructive levels of corruption and immorality. And—"

"Silence!" the dragon screamed. "You must *never* allow outside influences to infiltrate a tribe where the truth has never been known. It is true that such instruments have been manipulated to great effect everywhere. Our forces have used these boxes to corrupt those who have already embraced the truth and to distort the Enemy's message—but they have also been known to spread it."

The dragon paused and twisted his heads in order to listen to a voice in the distance. He then continued, his volume rising with each phrase:

"Even as we gather this night, my ears echo with the songs of our former brethren. They rejoice in the heavens as we stand here wasting time because these outside influences—influences you permitted by your stupidity and negligence—have broken through. One from your nation now knows the truth. Sheol, we will never utter your name again. You are no longer welcome at this Gathering. Get! Out!"

Immediately, two dark figures swooped into the circle and dragged a stunned and speechless Sheol to his fate. Nyale observed the reactions of his counterparts on the other side of the assembly. Amid the fear and disgust that are always present in Lucifer's shadow, he thought he saw a twitch of delight appear on their faces at Sheol's banishment.

Turning his attention back to the dragon, Nyale was flooded with dread when he saw Lucifer's middle head staring back at him.

"Nyale, my servant."

"Yes, my master."

"Step forward."

Nyale unfurled his jet-black wings, exposing his scorpion-like form. He advanced on all fours, as Sheol had done just moments before.

"What is your report from among the Merapu people?" Before Nyale could respond, Lucifer whipped his middle head forward, stopping just inches from Nyale's face.

Nyale felt the urge to back away from the dragon's fiery yellow eye, but he stood his ground. "My lord, the Merapu are a pitiful people. I have assembled a team to keep them in total darkness. The work of Deception and Black Magic, who are here with me tonight, have kept the people in bondage. And perhaps more importantly, Fear and Isolation have prevented others—including followers of the Most High—from venturing near them."

"Hmm," the dragon growled, pulling his head back from Nyale's. "Go on. Tell us how you intend to maintain this state."

"Master, only one road leads into the territory of the Merapu, and my sentries guard it day and night." The hint of approval on the dragon's heads gave Nyale more confidence. "Because I have long recognized the danger posed by the devices that Sheol—that some—have referred to as corruption transmitters, we have thwarted every effort to expand electricity in our region. Through complete isolation from the outside world, we have eliminated any chance that the Merapu will be exposed to messages that might be detrimental to our cause—especially to our Enemy's so-called good news. As far as the rest of the world is concerned, the Merapu do not even exist. And I will keep it that way."

The dragon exhaled slowly, and Nyale tried to imagine which landmine he had just triggered. But instead of berating or banishing his underling, Lucifer seemed pleased. Nyale was both relieved and repulsed when all seven of the heads faced him and smiled.

"Well done, Nyale. It appears I have at least one general who understands his assignment." Now the heads leered at the rest of the demons in the circle. "I have given each of you everything you need. Powers. Abilities. Dark arts. See to it that you use well the instruments I have granted you. And be sure of this: Your success will keep our kind from the bleak future our Enemy intends for us. In years past, I was not concerned by the shrinking numbers in this Gathering. But now that we are down to the last nations bound by darkness, this mission has become of utmost importance to me. I will not tolerate mistakes or excuses, and my personal agents will be watching everywhere. If there are any brushes with the light, you will be visited by Rephan."

At the sound of this name, a chill spread through the assembly. In ancient days, Rephan had earned a reputation as a robber of humanity's affections from the Most High. The passage of time had made him no less menacing. And now Rephan himself—appearing as a smaller dragon with a single head—stepped from behind Lucifer and advanced to the middle of the circle, relishing the fear and hatred he elicited from the war council.

"When Rephan arrives in your land," Lucifer said, "my wrath is sure to follow."

Rephan glared at each member of the Gathering one by one to ensure the Dark Lord's message was received.

And as the congregation disbanded, one of Lucifer's heads shot out at Nyale. He whispered, "Do not disappoint me."

3

AFTER A LATE WEDNESDAY night at church, Chris Billings hoped to sleep in the next morning, maybe twenty or thirty minutes past his normal six o'clock alarm. But with his brain working overtime—picturing scenarios, posing questions, calculating timelines—there was no use trying to force it. He left a note for Maria on the kitchen table and was out the door by five.

Thursday was Chris's favorite day of the workweek, so he wasn't disappointed to start so early. The rest of the week, he did whatever it took to keep the business running and profitable—sales, marketing, payroll, budgets, calls with suppliers. He liked that part of the job, but he loved Thursdays, when he rewarded himself with a full day in the shop working alongside his employees, working with the wood.

Chris pulled into the parking lot of Custom Clock and Furniture on the edge of Grapevine, Pennsylvania, and completed a careful circuit of the building. Office area near the road, workshop, loading dock, storage units for rent at the edge of the property—everything appeared as it should. Even after all of these years, Chris's pride in ownership remained strong. It had never been his intention to go into his family's business, but after he'd answered their call for help he was committed to making it work.

Every square foot of the building reminded Chris of his grandfather, who had started the business a few years after coming home from Korea. Arthur Bartel was not a great businessman, but over the years he'd earned a reputation as a master craftsman. The quality of his work spoke for itself, and Custom Clock and Furniture had produced a comfortable income for Arthur and a few employees.

All of that changed two days after Christmas during Chris's senior year of college. Chris was home for break, hanging out at the bowling alley with some high-school friends, when he received the message: "Get to the hospital immediately. It's Granddad."

Arthur's stroke devastated his body and his business. He spent months in a rehab facility learning how to walk again. Meanwhile, at the shop, his employees did the best they could—but they were artisans, not entrepreneurs. By the time Chris graduated from college that May, Granddad was finally settling in at home but his family feared the business would never recover. When it became clear that Arthur could not return to work, they got desperate. They turned to Chris.

Although Chris had no desire to join the clock and furniture business, his family thought he would be a natural fit. As a boy, he had followed Granddad around the shop every summer sweeping up sawdust and doing odd jobs. By the middle of high school, Chris was on the payroll, working part-time hours and

CHAPTER THREE

mirroring his grandfather's touch with the wood. And then as a twenty-two-year-old, he earned a college degree in business administration. Put it all together, and his grandmother and mother—not to mention Granddad—saw him as the answer to their prayers.

They knew of Chris and Maria's dream to live overseas as missionaries, so they assured him this was just a short-term fix: "It's not forever," his mother said. "We just need your help until other arrangements can be made. We have to save this business. And you know how proud Granddad would be."

That conversation was now fifteen years in the rearview mirror. Granddad was gone, and no other arrangements had ever worked out. Chris's temp job—*it's not forever*—had blossomed into a lucrative career. He had rescued the company from the jaws of bankruptcy, and it was now more profitable than ever. Custom Clock sent pieces across the country, and Chris earned a salary his grandfather had never even dreamed possible.

Inside his office, Chris set his lunchbox on his desk—one of the first executive desks his grandfather had made back in the late fifties. It was far too nice for an industrial building, just like the rest of the furniture in the space. The file cabinet in the corner, the reception counter out front, the table and chairs in the breakroom—all handcrafted by Arthur from the finest cherry he could afford at the time and all still exquisite six decades later. Even the walls displayed Arthur's artistry and aesthetic: Chris's family photos and business-of-the-year certificates were bordered by frames Granddad himself had made in his basement. And the centerpiece, perched on the wall directly across the room from Chris's desk, was the clock that inspired Arthur to go into this business in the first place, an antique Eli Terry.

☙

As Chris bent over the lathe and applied his blade to a column of cherry, his thoughts wandered to the night before. There was nothing unusual about that church service — a passionate sermon from his pastor, a sense of expectation from the worshippers, dozens of people lingering at the altar, anticipating a personal encounter with the Lord. This might not be typical at most churches, but it was a normal Wednesday night at Lakeside. The only break from the pattern was when Chris himself moved to the front of the sanctuary. He was usually content to pray and worship from his seat, but this time he knew God was calling him forward.

Forward. Movement. Change. How could he explain to Maria what God was showing him? And what would the kids say?

"Morning, boss." Sam Tanner, as usual, was the first of the workers in the shop. And as usual, he had something on his mind. "Did you hear about China? Earthquake. Something like eight on the Richter scale. The news said thousands are dead. Just like that." He snapped his fingers. "It's the fourth earthquake over there this year. Man…what's going on in the world?"

Chris shut down the lathe and took off his safety goggles.

"Wow, Sammy, I hadn't heard that," he said. "I haven't had a chance to check the news yet this morning."

"Yeah, it's pretty scary. And odd."

CHAPTER THREE

"It's hard to imagine so many people dying all at once like that," Chris said. "I hope the survivors get the help they need." He paused. "What do *you* think is happening in the world? Do you remember anything like this?"

Sam was one of Custom Clock's newest employees. He'd driven a school bus for most of his life but had retired just over two years before. It took him all of six weeks to figure out that retirement offered him neither the income nor the social interaction he needed. At his wife's urging, he stopped by the shop one day and asked Chris for a job. Chris, who had known Sammy for years, hired him on the spot to handle cleanup and run errands. He soon found out he'd picked up a news anchor in the deal. Sam devoured the news and was generous with updates as well as commentary.

In response to Chris's question, Sam leaned on his broom and turned his gaze to the corner of the ceiling, as though the answers were written there.

"I don't think I know for sure what's going on, but in all my years I've never seen or heard about so many natural disasters. You?" Chris shrugged, and Sam continued: "Maybe this is the end of the world."

"Really? What do you mean?" This was not a conversation Chris expected to have on a Thursday morning at his lathe.

"Well, I wouldn't call myself a good Catholic or anything, but I know the Bible talks about some of this stuff: earthquakes, weather patterns, pandemics, economies collapsing, small wars everywhere between groups of people I never heard of. Maybe it's the alignment of the planets. Maybe it's God's judgment — the end, like I said. You're religious. What's your take?"

"I wouldn't say I'm religious—"

"But you go to church all the time. You're a good Christian. You know what I mean."

"Yeah, well, it could be that all of these things are signs of the times," Chris said. "The Bible does say that Jesus is coming back, and that's why we all need a personal faith in God."

"It makes you wonder. You know my nephew Robbie? Well, he sends me links to a few internet preachers—not the crazy ones, don't worry. But they're saying we really are living in the end times. It really makes you think about your life. Have you made the most of it? Is it all about a family, a job, a home? Or did God want something from me? You ever wonder about that?"

Chris couldn't believe what he was hearing. He had always prayed for opportunities to talk about his faith with his workers, but Sam had never before given any indication of an interest in spiritual matters.

"Sammy, believe it or not, that's what I've been thinking about all morning. No matter how long I've been a follower of Jesus, I still wonder about the meaning of life. I guess it all starts with saying "Yes" to God before it's too late.... You know, I need a coffee break. Want to go to my office and talk some more?"

"Yeah," Sam said. "I think I need that."

Ω

By the time Chris and Sam finished their coffee and conversation, the shop was humming at full capacity. Chris made his way through the various workstations, offering a quick greeting to each of his employees. They had more than enough work to do—in fact, the company had several months' worth of orders to fulfill—but Chris felt the pressure to keep producing. He never lost sight of the fact that his business decisions affected a dozen families.

When Chris got back to the lathe, his thoughts returned to the questions Sammy had posed earlier. What *is* the meaning of life? Specifically, what was the meaning of *his* life? As a Christian, he knew that his existence on earth was about more than building a business, making money, providing for his family, serving in a church—and then dying and going to heaven. Those were all good things, but wasn't there more? He always said that obeying God was the most important thing, but was he truly living a life of obedience? Or was he just making his own decisions and praying that God would bless them? And what about the business? He had agreed to join Granddad's company to save it from collapse. But now that it was stable, what exactly was he doing here? And where did his call fit into all of this? It was one thing to consider being a missionary when he was in his early twenties—before he was married and had kids—and another thing entirely now that he had a family to take care of.

The rush of questions gripped Chris's attention, and he soon noticed that he had cut too much wood from the column of cherry on the lathe. He groaned, flicked the power switch, and pulled the wood from the machine and threw it into the waste bin. It wasn't a big deal, but he realized he was too distracted to be handling sharp blades and leaning over power tools. He needed some air.

In the parking lot, Chris brushed the sawdust from his sleeves and took a deep breath. He closed his eyes, turned his face toward the sun, and soaked in its warmth. Spring had always been his favorite season—and not just because baseball was back. Spring meant new life, a fresh start. Even as a boy, Chris had been drawn to the idea of rebirth. Looking back now, he saw this attraction as a gospel seed, planted there by God himself. God had been at work within him this whole time. But for what purpose?

Chris prayed and walked, with no particular destination in mind. After a half-hour, he found himself crossing the threshold into The Daily Grind, one of his and Maria's favorite coffee shops in downtown Grapevine. As he stood in line to order a banana-nut muffin, he scanned the room. Most of the customers stared at their phones, as though the devices contained the secrets of the universe. One couple at a table near the door shared sections of a newspaper while sipping from their mugs. But a younger woman sitting alone caught Chris's eye. She scribbled in a leather-bound journal for a minute, stared out the window for twenty seconds, then wrote some more. He had no way of knowing what she was writing, but he was reminded of himself at her age. As a college student, Chris had developed the habit of journaling. He would reflect on his day, list prayer requests, record insights from his Bible reading—really anything he wanted to write. He watched the woman surreptitiously and felt a twinge of regret over dropping his journaling practice years ago. But her writing also gave him an idea.

When he got back to the shop, Chris unlocked the storage room near the loading dock. A couple of years earlier, when

CHAPTER THREE

he and Maria were building their new house, he used this room to store some of their belongings—just during the transition. Most of the stuff had been hauled to the house, but a few stacks of boxes remained. Maria had meticulously labeled everything, so it was easy to see at a glance what he was looking for: two cardboard boxes with a strip of masking tape that said "Chris—college."

Back in his office, Chris opened one of the boxes and removed a couple of old textbooks he must have thought he would need someday but never did. Then he saw them: five spiral notebooks that contained every important thought from the middle of his sophomore year through graduation. He flipped through, page by page, reliving those years when his faith had become real to him, when he'd started to hope and dream that he and Maria could become more than friends, when everything still seemed possible.

Chris came across a series of entries from January of his junior year. He had attended a retreat with his campus ministry, and the words in the notebook—his words—took him back to that weekend:

> *The speaker tonight was amazing! He is so sold out for God. He's been a missionary for almost 20 years. He can't tell us where he's lived. He talked about the legacy we will leave behind. Leaving something behind—I thought everything is just beginning, but I guess it makes sense to think about that now. When I went down to the altar to pray, he got right in my face. "What are you doing with your life that will last for eternity?" I guess I'm not doing anything that important yet. I need to finish college first. My prayer*

this weekend: God, I'm gonna go for it! Help me do something that will last forever. Amen.

Chris closed the notebook, walked down the hall, and knocked on the open door of his office manager, Jane Renfroe.

"Hey, boss," she said. "Need anything?"

"No, I just have to take care of something at home. I'll be out the rest of the day. If anyone calls for me, just take a message."

"You got it."

Before pulling out of the parking lot, Chris whispered a prayer for wisdom. He needed to tell Maria what he was thinking and feeling, and he didn't want to mess it up. *I just hope she doesn't think I've lost my mind.*

4

MARIA BILLINGS KNEW it couldn't be true, but it certainly felt as though her family of five produced more dirty laundry every week than the week before. And while the mound of clothes she battled appeared intimidating, Maria really did not mind the work. Among the thousand tasks required to keep her household running smoothly, laundry day gave her room for spiritual multitasking. While sorting and treating stains, and loading and unloading the washer and dryer, she transformed the laundry room into a sanctuary where she could meet with God. She worshipped. She prayed. She listened for His voice. She looked forward to this time in God's presence — but she was also happy to leave the folding to Chris and the kids.

As she pulled a load of whites from the dryer, Maria heard a vehicle heading up the gravel driveway. Their house sat on a rise surrounded by ten acres of forest, so anyone out here was either lost or coming to see them — and she wasn't expecting visitors this afternoon. She moved quickly to the front door, and there was her husband, parking his Explorer in its usual spot on the side of the garage. He didn't seem to be in much of a hurry.

Maria opened the door just as Chris stepped onto the front porch. "Is everything okay?" she asked, reaching out to embrace him. "You're home early."

Chris held her in his arms a bit longer than normal and kissed the top of her head. "Everything's fine," he said. "Nothing to worry about. Just couldn't keep my mind on work today."

Maria took Chris's lunchbox into the kitchen while he hung up his jacket in the hall closet. She understood that he needed time and space to process his thoughts. If he had something to say, he would eventually say it. He was always open with her, but sometimes she had to wait a bit longer for the conversation to begin than she would prefer.

"Want some coffee?" she called to him in the other room.

"Sounds great," he said as he stepped into the kitchen. "I'd love a cup." He placed his satchel on the table and sat down facing the patio doors that opened onto the deck. Beyond that was their backyard—a small clearing and then trees as far as they could see. The kids had identified varieties of maple, birch, some elm down by the stream. It would take years to get to know this land.

The sunlight streaming into the kitchen caught the side of Chris's head, and for a second it appeared to Maria as though his hair was completely white. Maybe a glimpse of her husband as an old man, she thought. In reality, he had not changed much since they met, at least physically. She recently noticed a few white hairs around his temples, but otherwise he was still tall and wiry and always on the move.

They had met as eighteen-year-olds, freshmen in college who happened to be visiting the same campus ministry on the same

CHAPTER FOUR

night. Maria was there with a teammate, Chris with a guy from his dorm. Chris went back a week later, hoping to see Maria again. And of course, Maria was there — drawn partly by a sense of community within the group, but mostly to run into Chris. Since the end of that school year, they were inseparable.

Maria placed the mugs on the table, and Chris snapped out of his daydream — or whatever was occupying his thoughts. "So, how was work today?" she asked.

He turned in his chair to face her and shrugged as he sipped his coffee. "Not too bad, but I didn't manage to get anything done — except for breaking a cherry column I was working on. I did have a good chat with Sam, though. He's definitely searching."

"How did that come up?"

"Well, you know Sammy. He devours the news, and he was telling me all about the earthquake in China. And then out of nowhere he asked me if I knew what life is all about."

"Now there's a loaded question."

"Yeah, we sat down in my office and talked about what it means to be a follower of Jesus. I think it's kind of a new concept for him, but God's trying to get his attention." He sipped his coffee and inspected his mug for the right words to say next. "And I think God is trying to get my attention too."

"Does this have anything to do with last night?"

He nodded. "Sorry about that. I didn't plan to abandon you and the kids. But —"

"No need to apologize," she said. "And besides, we were the ones who abandoned you. But since we had both vehicles at church, I figured you could find your way home."

"I don't remember an altar time like that since college. Pastor's sermon, the prayer time, my talk with Sammy—it's like God has a message just for me. It's like He wants to take me back to my college days.... So I grabbed some stuff from storage today."

He reached into his satchel, pulled out his old prayer journals, and set them on the table.

"You kept those?" Maria perked up at the memory of their first days together. "Do you remember our retreats? You would write, and I would cry." They laughed at the accuracy of the statement—the analytical business student from Pennsylvania and the emotional soccer player from Argentina.

"Actually, I was just looking at some entries from one of those retreats," he said. He found the page and slid the notebook across the table.

As Maria read, a smile spread across her face.

"I think I remember that one," she said. "Junior year? The one in Cincinnati?... So what do you think God wants to tell you?"

"Okay. This is gonna sound crazy. We've always done our best to live for God. But when Pastor was preaching last night, I felt like God was telling me to step into that story. Instead of talking to the rich young ruler, Jesus was telling me—telling us—to sell everything and follow Him. To go to the mission field."

Chris exhaled slowly and looked into his wife's brown eyes. He wasn't sure what else he could say, so he didn't say anything.

Maria reached across the table and took her husband's hand in hers. "You know how I spend a few days every December reflecting on the past year and looking ahead? I thank God for everything He's done in me and for our family, but I also

CHAPTER FOUR

ask Him to give me a Bible verse or a word or a song for the coming year." Chris nodded, and she continued. "Well, I haven't told you what He showed me last December because I wasn't sure what it means. When I was praying about a verse for this year, or a word or an image, what He said was this: 'There's more.' That was it. 'There's more.' At first I thought He was saying to spend more time with Him in prayer and worship and Bible reading, but I felt it was deeper than that—like He was going to bring about a big change in our lives.... I guess this would qualify."

"So you don't think I'm crazy?"

"I wouldn't say that," she said. "This is the definition of crazy—to think of leaving all this behind and taking our kids to the other side of the world. But if God is in it...."

Maria's eyes welled with tears, and her mind filled with questions. How would they know for sure that this was God's plan? Where would they go? What would they do when they got there? What would it mean for the kids? What about the business? What would Chris's family say?

Chris got up and walked around the table. Maria stood and leaned into him, her arms wrapped around his back. They lingered in the silence of their embrace, and then Chris prayed: "Father, we trust You. We sense that You might be calling us, and we want to obey—no matter what You ask. Please give us confirmation of Your leading, and bring the right people into our lives who can help guide and direct us. Amen."

Maria looked up into Chris's face. "So where is it that you think God is calling us? Please tell me it's Argentina."

"Now that is a good question. I didn't know how you'd react, so I haven't even let myself think much about where we might go."

"Let's see if Pastor has time for lunch soon. I'm sure he'll have some good advice."

5

NYALE SETTLED INTO his favorite bamboo tree overlooking his domain. From this vantage point, he could see most of the village he had ruled for centuries. He thought of this perch as his throne, and from this seat of power his word was the only law that mattered.

After returning from the latest Gathering, Nyale was more determined than ever to keep the Merapu trapped in fear and darkness—if only to avoid the wrath of his master. It should not be a difficult task. This village, Seora, was frozen in time, invisible to the rest of civilization, and a smile crept across Nyale's jagged face as he watched over his handiwork.

The scene below him was nearly identical to one he would have observed a hundred years before—and another one hundred years before that. A woman carrying a bundle of firewood caught his eye. She struggled with the cumbersome load, and the young men nearby ignored her. Another group of men gathered their tools and started off for a day of labor in the fields. Five children surrounded another boy who had fashioned a piece of thin bamboo into a wheel and was pushing it along with a stick.

From his treetop lookout, Nyale monitored the only road leading into or out of the village. Seora was the last stop on a long trail, one of the final hidden regions in the seventeen thousand islands of Indonesia. Nyale had fought construction of the road as long as he could, but the forces of commerce eventually won out. Seora's leaders did not court contact with the outside world, but they needed to get their rice and vegetables to market. The money silenced any objection. Then one day, a man from the provincial government arrived with talk of a well and electricity. Nyale again mobilized his forces to stymie these developments, but it was only a matter of time. When he realized he was fighting a losing battle, he shifted to damage control. So now, the village did have electricity in some buildings and well water, but they were strictly controlled by the village elders—who just happened to be controlled by Nyale.

As he contemplated ways to strengthen his grip on Seora, Nyale spotted a small demon named Fear drifting on the breeze fifty yards away. Nyale summoned this minion, who obeyed at once.

"Let's play a little game," Nyale said.

"Yes, master. As you wish." Fear leaned back slightly, in case this game was to be held at his expense.

Nyale sensed the apprehension in his subject but did nothing to relieve it. Let the little demon swallow a dose of his own medicine.

"Here's the game," Nyale said. "The next person to step outside, that's your target for the day. You will follow them wherever they go. You will whisper your most vile threats into their ears.

CHAPTER FIVE

You will torment them with dread until they settle into bed tonight—and then you will hover in their dreams."

Together they scanned every door in sight. A minute later, Soraya, one of the leading men of the village, one of Nyale's most devoted servants, exited his hut. Fear turned to Nyale to confirm his target. Nyale nodded his head, and Fear cackled at his good fortune.

"Soraya, Soraya," Nyale said. "What fun we will have this day." He gestured toward Fear and bowed in mock formality. "Let the game...begin."

Below them, Soraya marched in the direction of the building where the elders debated village business. His posture and bearing announced his importance, and the other villagers stepped aside as he passed. Fear swooped in behind him, hung above his shoulder, and spoke words that Nyale could not hear but could readily imagine.

Nyale had owned this man since his youth. In those days, Soraya's grandfather was the *dukun* in the village, the healer and link to the spirit world. When he recognized that none of his sons possessed either the aptitude or interest in following him on his chosen path, he quickly identified as his successor one of his grandsons: Soraya. After a year's long apprenticeship, and upon the death of his grandfather, Soraya was initiated as the *dukun* of Seora. In time, this position afforded him the power and wealth to match his vast ambition.

Something about Soraya's determined gait reminded Nyale of a morning much like this one two years earlier. Nyale had been perched in his tree when a fidgety gossip demon interrupted his solitude.

"Master! Master! Your servant, the spell caster, he, his—"

The sudden blow from Nyale's foot had caught the messenger on the side of the head, sending the demon into a nearby cluster of bamboo trees. With a quick shake of the head, the gossip demon gathered himself and approached Nyale with respectful caution.

"Now, little one," Nyale had said, "speak clearly so I might understand. But do not waste my time with gibberish."

"Thank you, master. It-it seems that the spell caster, your servant Soraya, he—his line is being extended through the birth of his son's first child."

"Hmm. How much longer?"

"Master," the demon had said, "there seems to be trouble with the birth. Fear and Death are both in the home, waiting for your orders. Soraya is now calling out to you, master."

"That will be all."

When Nyale had arrived at the hut, he read fear and concern on the face of the father-to-be, Bandu. The young man paced in the small room, wearing a path in the dirt floor, wincing at the cries of pain coming from his wife, Sri, on the other side of the curtain. Bandu once took a step in that direction, but he seemed to remember that fathers are not welcome in that moment.

Across the room, Soraya had sat on a bamboo mat with his legs crossed. In a trance, he called out to Nyale. Beads of sweat appeared on his brow as he heard no response. His pleading sounded to Bandu like a raspy hum, but Nyale understood the words beneath the moan. The demon reveled in the begging and bargaining. Finally, when Nyale heard Soraya's pledge, he whispered in his servant's ear:

CHAPTER FIVE

"I am here."

Nyale dismissed Death from the hut, and immediately the scream of a newborn pierced through the tension in the home. Soraya's first grandchild had arrived, and he was left with an unmistakable impression: It was all because of Nyale. Nyale had come through for him once again.

Before releasing Soraya from the trance, Nyale had given the *dukun* clear instructions. At the appropriate time, he must make Bandu understand what had happened this day. He must overcome his son's resistance to his ways and open his eyes to the unseen realm. He must find a way to convince Bandu to follow in his footsteps.

Soraya had slowly awakened to the physical world. His son sat across from him, relieved yet anxious in the final moments before meeting his own child for the first time. Soraya locked eyes with Bandu and gave a silent, solemn nod that communicated unspeakable truths. Bandu broke eye contact with his father just as the midwife swiped the curtain aside and stepped toward him with a tightly wrapped bundle in a *slendong*.

"It is a girl," she said, beaming with joy.

Soraya fought to hide his disappointment at the news, but Bandu was smitten at the first sight of his daughter.

"Her name," Bandu announced, "will be Fatima."

Soraya leaned in and peered at his grandchild named for the daughter of the prophet. At last he nodded his approval and said, "It is a start." He turned his back on his son and walked out into the heat of the day.

Two years had passed since the birth of Soraya's heir, and Nyale had not yet decided how he would collect payment for his services. He watched the proud *dukun* walk to the center of the village with Fear hovering off his shoulder. Perhaps it was time to remind Soraya of the bargain they had struck.

"That child," Nyale said to no one in particular, "is mine."

6

IN EONS OF SERVICE to God Most High, Sword had witnessed and experienced it all. Wars, natural disasters, treachery—he never knew what challenges he would encounter while carrying out his orders. He had learned to be prepared for anything, and he relished the unexpected. But even armed with this hard-won perspective, the destruction before him now took his breath away.

His latest mission brought him to the northeast corner of Afghanistan, to the forbidding mountain ranges where China and the nations of Central Asia come together. He'd been to this region many times before, of course, but never to this town—or what remained of the town, to be more accurate.

Sword was on protective detail, watching over a small team of the Lord's ambassadors engaged in earthquake relief. They had just reached the edge of the small city after a two-day journey over unreliable roads, and Sword floated upward to get an angel's-eye view.

A green river bisected the ancient town into eastern and western halves, and Sword observed with a mixture of dread and compassion that the section east of the river was completely leveled. Every home and shop and mosque that he could see had been flattened by the earthquake. Making rescue efforts even more difficult, the lone bridge linking the two sides of the town had washed away.

"Looks like we'll be here awhile," he said to himself, just as he spotted a pair of spirit beings flying toward him from the north. He started to drift downward to take cover but soon recognized one of the visitors, even at this great distance. He settled on a ridge overlooking the river valley and awaited their arrival. Sword did not even try to stifle his grin when they landed before him.

"Michael, my friend, welcome," Sword said with a slight bow. "What brings the archangel to this fine corner of creation?"

"It is good to see you, my brother. It has been too long," Michael said. "I come with new orders. The Most High himself has an assignment for you—plans I am not able to divulge."

Sword glanced past Michael to the road a half-kilometer below, where the relief workers were climbing out of their vehicles, stretching sore muscles, and greeting a local official. The archangel recognized Sword's concern and said, "The work in this region is important as well, of course, so I will leave Flame here in your stead." At the mention of his name, Flame stepped forward, greeted Sword with an almost imperceptible nod, and flew off to get a closer look at his new charges.

"Must be a big job," Sword said.

"It is," Michael said, "and you will not be alone. I have already assembled the rest of the team—which you will lead. Light was with prayer walkers in Istanbul. Purity was in Brazil with a healing evangelist. Glory was on guard duty at a revival in London.

CHAPTER SIX

Dew is coming from a family of Bible translators in West Africa. Bravery was in Los Angeles watching over a children's evangelist. And Mercy was with a new disciple in Indonesia. They have all left their posts in capable hands."

"Seven in all," Sword said. "And I couldn't have picked a better team myself."

"It is not my place to tell you what is next. But know this: I have complete confidence in you. Now let us be on our way. The others are waiting."

⌒

He sat high on a glimmering throne, exalted over every being and every object in His presence. His glory cascaded down the foundations of the throne, flowing like a robe fashioned of light rather than fabric. The brilliance of God Most High shone on the armies of heaven, standing to His right and His left, ready to carry out His every command. Seraphim and cherubim filled the throne room with songs of worship.

Michael the archangel suddenly appeared in their midst, bowing low before the awesome presence of his Lord. As he arose, he felt rejuvenated by the power flowing outward from the throne.

"Most High," he said, "I have summoned them from the four corners of the earth, and they are ready to fulfill Your orders."

The seven beings of light—so recently on individual assignments around the globe—appeared in the throne room of heaven as suddenly as Michael had and fell as one in worship before the Most High. All thoughts of their previous and future postings evaporated as they were overcome by the wash of pure light. After being on earth and doing battle with the forces of darkness, it was almost too much to be this close once again to complete holiness, love, and power. The angels could do nothing but listen to the song of the seraphim, who exist to fill the throne room with praise: "Holy, holy, holy is the Lord God almighty," they sang. "Worthy of honor, worthy of adoration, worthy of praise." The seven warrior angels eventually gained the ability to sing themselves, and they joined the seraphim in declaring, "You are worthy, our Lord and God, to receive glory and honor and power, for You created all things, and by Your will they were created and have their being." Each of these angels had been in this presence before, but it was like a new experience every time. If only humanity could understand this would be the greatest reward in heaven—worshipping and basking in the fullness of the most awesome power in the universe.

Finally, they heard the voice they longed to hear, so powerful and yet so sweet and soothing: "Arise, faithful ones."

Michael and the seven warriors stood before the throne, heads still bowed. The Lord issued His instructions: "The time draws near, and I have set you apart for a special task. Michael will guide you to a family for which I have a special mission. Six of you will remain with this family until the appointed hour. Mercy, you will return to your current mission, but your path will intersect with this family in the near future, and your missions will become one."

As they departed the throne room, the angels were amazed that they could receive such strength from just a moment in the presence of the Most High. They longed to be near the throne again, but they were also energized to begin their assignments. The Lord's plans are always good, and they felt honored to be part of this new mission. Through the centuries, they had served as guardians for fishermen, doctors, farmers, teachers, heads of state — men, women, and children from every stage and station of life. It was always a privilege.

Mercy left at once for Indonesia, eager to see firsthand the plans of the Lord become reality. Michael and the others sped off to the other side of the world, to a small town in central Pennsylvania. As they approached the Billings home a few miles outside the town, they covered themselves to avoid detection.

"My friends," Michael said, "be wary of the enemy. Your task is special, and it will soon be clear that this may be our greatest battle ever. We do not yet know if the enemy is aware of this plan, but take every precaution.... I will not be far off."

7

FRITZ AND GLORIA BERNHEIM were already sipping from their coffee mugs at a corner table when Chris and Maria arrived at Tony's Deli. Fritz's coffee order — as hot and as black as you can make it — matched his straightforward, old-school nature. With Fritz, what you saw is what you got, and Chris loved him for it.

Chris had called his pastor the day before to set up a lunch meeting, assuming Fritz would not be available until the following week. Leading a congregation of four hundred souls did not leave many gaps in his calendar. But Fritz's response surprised him.

"How does tomorrow work for you?" the pastor asked. "Gloria and I had a lunch appointment scheduled for noon with a couple in premarital counseling, but they had to postpone. Are you and Maria okay with meeting both of us, or is this something you just need to see me about?"

Chris did not hesitate. "We would love it if Gloria can be there," he said. "The more insight we can get on this, the better."

Just in the past year, Gloria had retired from her position as a vice president for a large health-care company. Chris had often sought her advice concerning his own business, and now she was establishing a counseling ministry through the church.

"Now I'm really curious," Fritz said. "See you tomorrow."

At the deli on Friday, after placing their orders and engaging in an appropriate amount of small talk, Fritz leaned in over the table. "So, what's on your minds?" he asked. "I got the impression that this is more than just a social visit — although we love to spend time with you two."

Chris and Maria glanced at each other. Even though he had tried to rehearse this part, Chris wasn't quite sure where to begin. "Well, Pastor," he said, "I just want you to know that the service Wednesday night was very powerful. It affected me in ways I haven't felt in years." He paused to organize his thoughts.

Fritz said, "I've been at this church ... thirty years? Thirty-one years now? I've never seen anything like this season we're in. It's amazing to see how the Spirit's been moving. I sometimes feel like I could stand up and read the concordance in the back of the Bible and God would still save people."

"I appreciate hearing everyone's testimonies," Chris said, "but I've just felt like an observer — until Wednesday night. I mentioned to you at the altar that I thought the Lord was speaking to me, and I'm almost afraid of what He said."

The waitress arrived with their lunch orders: tuna salad on wheat for Maria, a chef salad for Gloria, pastrami on pumpernickel with lots of mustard for Chris, and a reuben on rye with sauerkraut on the side for Fritz. Tony's had a well-deserved reputation for the best sandwiches in the county, and Chris's mouth watered at the sight of his pastrami. He had to take a quick bite before continuing the conversation.

CHAPTER SEVEN

"So," he said, "as I listened to your message about selling everything you have and following Christ, I thought I understood what that meant. I've heard that passage a thousand times, but this time, for some reason, it hit me like a freight train. It's like I was hearing it for the first time." He paused to take another bite and gather his thoughts.

"Isn't that amazing?" Gloria said. "Ever since I was a little girl, I've tried to read through the whole Bible every year. I've read some parts over fifty times, and every year God shows me something new. It's like, 'Why didn't I see that before?'"

"That's what this was like," Chris said. "I've always read that story through the eyes of the rich young ruler. But this time, it was like Jesus was speaking directly to me: 'Give it all up, and follow Me.' So I went to the altar and thought the Lord would show me something He wanted to remove from my life. Or that we should increase our missions pledge or commit more time to the church. Does any of this make sense so far?"

Fritz and Gloria both smiled and nodded. "It makes perfect sense," Fritz said. "Please go on."

"Well, as I was praying, asking God to show me what He wanted, the strangest feeling came over me. It felt like...like He's calling us to go to another country as missionaries." Chris looked up, focusing first on Fritz, then on Gloria, even glancing again at Maria, perhaps hoping someone would tell him he was out of his mind.

Fritz Bernheim was sixty-two years old. He had served the Lord in full-time ministry for four decades, so this was not the first time he'd heard such a story. Whenever parishioners approached him about a call to missions, he quickly processed their request for guidance through a filter that included a few key questions: Were they currently serving in the church? Were they giving regularly to missions work, above the tithe? Were they praying for missionaries? Were there any obstacles that stood in their way, such as family obligations or major debt?

The pastor had known the Billings family for decades, so he was able to organize his response almost immediately. Yes, Chris and Maria were involved in the ministries of the church. They led a small group together, Chris taught a Sunday school class, and Maria was a prayer warrior who had recently been elected to the deacon board. As far as he knew about church finances, they were consistent givers to the missions fund. And they had both participated in a one-week trip to Mexico two years before.

"Are you thinking this is a short-term trip, or is it a career change?" Fritz asked.

"I think it's a forever change," Chris said.

"Okay, I just needed to clarify what we're talking about. Those are two very different conversations.... I can sense that you realize that we're talking about a significant commitment and life change. Most people doing this kind of thing start the process at a younger age, before they have children.... And yet, I trust you and what God might be saying to you."

"Actually," Chris said, "I was hoping you would tell me I was crazy and to never speak of this again."

Fritz's booming laugh attracted the attention of the deli's other patrons, who glanced over to the corner table but quickly returned to their own meals.

CHAPTER SEVEN

Chris said, "I'm not sure I've ever told you this, but I felt called to missions when I was in college. Until my grandfather had his stroke, I thought that's what I would do with my life. I still have some old journals from those years — man, I was on fire for God. Makes me wonder what happened."

"Chris," Fritz said, "life happened. You served your family in ways no one else could. You saved the business. You might feel like you've ignored God's call, but it seems to me as though He's working out His plans in His perfect time." The pastor turned to Maria. "What are your thoughts about all of this? What are you feeling?"

"I feel nervous and peaceful at the same time," she said. "I know it's going to be a big change, and I'm wondering how it will affect the kids. And I don't even know where we'll end up. But God has given me His peace. When I left Argentina to play college soccer in the U.S., it was a step into the unknown. I didn't know anybody here, but I knew that God was leading me. And when Chris asked me to marry him, it was the same sense of peace. That's what I'm feeling now. I've had an idea that a change was coming, but I had no idea what it would be."

"That makes me feel even more confident that the Lord is in this," the pastor said. "I know you're a woman of prayer — and I also know you'd speak your mind if you thought Chris was off base."

Gloria said, "This is wonderful news. We will definitely miss you, but the greatest joy we have in ministry is seeing people step into complete obedience to the Lord.... What can we do to help you?"

"Well, I have no clue where to begin," Chris said. "This isn't our world. Do you know people? Where do we go from here?"

"The first thing," Fritz said, "is to keep praying. If you're going to do something like this, you have to know that you know that you know God is calling you. That's what will sustain you when times get tough — the knowledge that He has placed you there for His purposes.

"Aside from that, I have someone you can connect with, an old friend of mine from Bible college. He lives in Indonesia, and he's served among the unreached tribes there for years and years. He is a good, godly man, and he can tell you everything you'll need to know. The thing is, I haven't seen him in a decade, and I'm not sure how easy he is to reach. But I'll get you an email address."

"And one more thing, Chris," Gloria said. "I have some homework for you to consider. What would you say about keeping a journal again? What's God saying to you? What are you saying to Him?"

"That's a great idea," Maria said. "He'll start today."

Ω

As the Bernheims and Billingses left the deli, Sword followed them, unseen by human eyes, through the door. Now he understood the priority given his new assignment. *This*, he thought, *is gonna be fun.*

8

SRI EASED HER WAY out of bed, careful not to awaken Bandu so early. She bent over Fatima and was surprised to see two playful brown eyes staring back at her.

"Mama," the toddler said.

"Shh," Sri whispered, turning to check whether the noise had disturbed her husband. She could not leave Fatima in the hut if she wanted to let him sleep, so she reached down and lifted the child out of bed. "Come, little one."

Outside the house, the village was springing to life. Sri and the other women wanted to get as much work done as possible before the sun rose and brought its oppressive heat. Sri's morning routine began with the fire, necessary for boiling water and cooking breakfast. Next, she tossed some feed to the chickens they kept behind the hut. She gathered the two eggs Allah had granted overnight and offered thanks for this gift.

On her way to the village well, Sri greeted neighbors and tried to keep up with her fearless and curious daughter. She was pleased to see Fatima thriving and growing into her personality, but she also wistfully remembered the child's first year of life spent bundled in a *slendong*. The colorful cloth wrap allowed Sri to carry Fatima everywhere attached to her side and, most importantly, to keep working without distraction.

A hard, aged piece of bamboo about a meter and a half in length balanced on Sri's right shoulder. From each end of the stick hung a rope and a bucket used to retrieve water. Arriving at the well, Sri was glad to see she was only fifth in line. Even when the line was longer, she was happy to wait her turn. It was a small price to pay for so great a convenience. The opening of the well just a few years before was cause for celebration. It was hailed by the government officials as a benefit for the entire community, but soon afterward the village elders began to charge a premium so the well could be maintained properly. There was some grumbling among the women about this maintenance fund, but Sri had learned not to ask questions. Bandu's father, Soraya, was one of the elders in charge of the well money, and he made sure she always had access. Still, she felt bad for some friends who could not afford the charge and instead had to walk a kilometer to fetch water from the stream—which everyone knew was not nearly as clean as water from the well.

As Sri waited for her turn at the front of the line, the women filled her in on village gossip while Fatima played with some other children nearby. Sri enjoyed the respect she received from her neighbors because of her father-in-law's stature in the community, but she also suspected his position kept her out of the best conversations. When Sri reached the front of the line, a young man paid by the village secured the rope and dropped her

CHAPTER EIGHT

first bucket to the bottom of the well. Using a pulley, he hauled the container back to the surface—and then did the same with Sri's other bucket. She attached the buckets to the bamboo rod, called for Fatima, and walked past a second man who was there to collect five cents from everyone else.

By the time Bandu awoke, Sri had fetched the water, built the fire, bathed Fatima, and was busy frying the leftover rice, vegetables, and chicken from the previous night's dinner to make their breakfast, *nasi goreng*. As Sri hunched over the stove in the middle of their house, Fatima snuggled next to her. This was out of character for her active little girl, and Sri wondered whether Fatima might be ill. Did the child have a fever, or was this just the heat from the stove? She thought about mentioning this to Bandu when he came back in from his first cigarette of the day, but he had seemed troubled lately. Maybe she would just keep it to herself for now. Surely Allah would be merciful and protect them. And besides, Soraya had the ear of Nyale. That had to count for something.

ω

Sri pulled Fatima even closer. She finished preparing breakfast, making as much noise as possible with her utensils. Unknown to her, in the unseen realm, a demon named Fear lurked next to the stove watching her every move.

"You don't think you can scare me away that easily, do you?" Fear whispered into Sri's ear. "Give in to your feelings. Give in to your doubts. What chance does this child really have? Remember, she almost died at birth. She must be a very unlucky child.... You are going to lose her. You know this, right? What kind of mother are you, to lose a child?"

A second demon, Sickness, stood on the other side of Sri, caressing polio in his hand. "Should we consult with the master of this region?" Sickness asked. "This one is close to the spell caster, the one who often calls his name."

"Ah, the master!" Fear said. "The master thinks too much as of late. How many more opportunities will we have to use polio? It has been a useful tool, but now its spread is almost over."

"If you say so," Sickness said, attaching polio to the child before departing for another village.

Perched in a bamboo tree down the path from Bandu and Sri's hut, Nyale looked over his realm with a protective yet satisfied eye. Nothing happened here without his knowledge and approval. He was the master of this people, and the fact that they worshipped his own name brought a sneer of delight to his face. For centuries he had entrapped the Merapu in a web of deception and fear, and he was prepared to do anything to keep it that way. If only he could make it last for eternity. The Enemy, he knew, was all-powerful and capable of ending this war in a flash. But for some reason the Most High had chosen to work through these weak, pitiful humans, which prolonged the war.

Nyale pondered the contradiction of his situation. He hated these people — all people — but he needed them to remain in darkness to secure his own existence. As long as he kept truth from them, as long as he kept them shrouded in lies, he was safe.

CHAPTER EIGHT

Hiding the Merapu from the rest of the world hadn't been easy. Infecting the people of the light with myths about the Merapu had been even more difficult. But he had succeeded. And he saw no reason to doubt his hold on this village.

Suddenly feeling emboldened, he shouted in a shrill voice, "Come now, if you dare! I am in control here! I am Nyale, god of this people, and this is a fortress no one will take!"

9

"MARIA," CHRIS SAID, "these people are seriously gonna think we're crazy."

"Why do you say that?" They sat side by side at their kitchen table, sipping coffee and poring over the email that would change their lives. With the kids at school, Chris had taken the morning off so he and Maria could make sure the message was perfect before they sent it.

"Think about it," he said. "A couple with three kids decides to move to the mission field. No experience. No real reason except they believe that God said to go. And no idea where He's calling them. If I got a letter like that, I would think it was crazy."

Maria tapped her chin. "You might be right. But we have to start somewhere."

Chris leaned back in his chair and tried to picture the recipient of this message, tried to imagine the reaction it would cause on the other side of the world.

"Okay," he said. "I want to look at it one more time."

They both leaned in again and read the email for what felt like the hundredth time:

Dear Orien and Harriet,

We pray God's blessing on you and your ministry in Indonesia. We are Chris and Maria Billings, members of Lakeside Community Church in Grapevine, Pennsylvania. We received your email address from our pastor, Fritz Bernheim, and he suggested we write to you about some things we have been sensing lately.

A couple of weeks ago, we were surprised that the Lord began to speak with us about going to the mission field. Chris runs a well-established clock and furniture shop, so we weren't sure if this was the Lord giving us a new direction for our lives. We talked with Pastor Bernheim and have continued to pray about this, and we believe it's time to write to you. We both sensed a call to missions while in university, but other things crowded the call out. That is, until now.

Pastor Bernheim said you could possibly give us some advice about where to go from here. We feel very strongly about following the Lord in what He has put on our hearts, but we are open to what you might be able to share with us about going to the mission field.

So you may know us a little better, we are a family of five (our kids are 12, almost 9, and 5) and have been part of Lakeside for almost 15 years. We have served in various ministry capacities here. Chris has a degree in business administration. Maria's degree is in elementary education (although she hasn't taught since our kids were born). We know that serving in the church does not necessarily open the door for ministry in a foreign country, but as we said earlier, we would appreciate any guidance you might have.

Thank you ahead of time for your help.

Sincerely,
Chris and Maria Billings

CHAPTER NINE

"Anything else?" he said. "I'm ready to hit send."

"Wait!" Maria said, grabbing Chris's hand. "Let's pray first."

As they prayed over their email, their family, their journey, and even Orien and Harriet's ministry in Indonesia, Maria and Chris felt comforted by the peace of God and blessed with a sense of His presence. They did not know what would happen next, but the Lord assured them that they were in His hands.

After their prayer, Chris sent the email to Orien Berry's inbox halfway around the world. He wanted to sit there and wait for a reply, but he suspected the Berrys—twelve or thirteen hours ahead of them—were already in bed for the night. And besides, there was work to do at the office. Chris kissed his wife goodbye and headed for the door.

☉

Unseen by Maria and Chris, three others had gathered around the table that morning. Sword, Light, and Purity had looked on intently as this husband and wife joined hands and sent their praise and petitions to the heavens. In the midst of the prayer, the angels felt the love and power of God surging among them.

Even before Chris hit send, Sword had turned to Light. "You must accompany and speed the delivery of this letter," he said. "It is an important part in the plans of the Most High." Light immediately launched toward the home of Orien and Harriet half a world away. The enemy loved to create chaos through technology, and Light was determined not to allow that to happen this time.

In the days since he arrived in this home, Sword had come to a thrilling realization. Each of the angels on this protective detail had extensive experience on the frontier, in those places where the Lord's good news had not yet been proclaimed and where His church had not yet been established. They had accompanied the human messengers of the Most High as they pushed back the darkness with the light of the truth. They had all seen the enemy cede territory to their King. And now, as Sword envisioned the next steps that would inevitably play out, he believed they would see it again.

The presence of angelic warriors in and around the Billings home was also attracting some unwanted attention. In the woods surrounding the house, several local demons had taken it upon themselves to set up surveillance. They had no way of knowing what was happening with this family, but they did not want to be caught off guard. Unwilling to provoke such a powerful retinue of the Most High's host, they were content to sit and watch — for now.

As Chris's truck rolled down the driveway to the county road, a small gossip demon eased toward the house, trying to peer into a window for some useful intelligence. With nothing to report, he returned to his cohort in the forest. "We should warn our master at once that something is not right here," he said. "He needs to know."

"Let's just leave it alone for now," another demon said. "We will know soon enough what their purpose is." The rest of the group nodded in approval of this course of inaction.

"We don't know who these angels are," Gossip said, "but we can all see that they are powerful. And judging from the light they are emitting, they have recently been near the Most High."

Seeing that his advice was unheeded, Gossip began forming a story that would include a bit of truth and a bit of fiction, all to make himself look good to his superiors. He slowly backed away from his tree and headed for the stronghold.

10

SRI SAT ON THE EDGE of the bed and reached a hand toward Fatima's forehead. Still warm. The little girl had never liked to take naps, but in recent days she would lie down without a word of protest. The problem, Sri noticed, was that deep sleep seemed to elude her daughter. Fatima constantly tossed and turned, and the occasional moan hinted at unrelieved pain.

The bamboo door of the small hut creaked open, and Bandu ducked his head as he entered. His colorful prayer rug was draped around his neck, and a black *peci* sat atop his head. He removed his sandals and hat and placed the rug in the corner.

"Hello, *Sayang*," Sri said. She tried to read her husband's mood. It was always a guessing game when he returned from the mosque, depending on his conversation with his father.

"Yeah, hello." Bandu bent over to kiss his daughter's forehead. His brow furrowed as he stood. "Did you know she has a fever?"

"I've noticed it for a few days now," Sri said. "Should we do something about it?" This could have been an easy question to answer. She knew the government operated health clinics throughout the islands, but the village elders had rejected one for Seora. Bandu's father had been the most vocal opponent. Nyale, he had said, did not want those kinds of medicines for our people. Now she was concerned that Bandu would have to involve Soraya, and she was uncomfortable with his incantations and special medicines.

Bandu did not answer immediately. "Let's give it until tomorrow," he said finally. "Then if she isn't better, I will have to go to Father."

Sri slept fitfully that night. Fatima lay between her parents on the bed made of bamboo slats, and Sri awoke often to place a hand on the child's forehead and cheeks. Her little girl seemed to be growing hotter by the hour. In the moments when Sri was able to doze off, dreams of the worst possible outcome tormented her. She resigned herself to the fact that they needed Soraya. Maybe he could save his granddaughter.

Suddenly, in the darkest hour of the night, Sri was awakened by a violent shaking beside her. Fatima's arms and legs flailed, and her head turned from side to side. Then just as suddenly, the child stopped moving but her body was on fire.

"Bandu! Bandu!" Sri cried, leaning over to shake her husband awake. Bandu sat up in a haze of confusion. "Bandu, Fatima had a seizure! She is burning up!" She grabbed his hand and placed it on Fatima's face.

"I will get Father," he said, immediately jumping to his feet. "You stay here."

The jolt of being awakened from deep sleep sharpened Bandu's senses as he raced to his parents' hut. He felt the cool air on his skin. He heard the songs of insects that own the night. He saw the path laid before him under the spotlight of a full moon.

CHAPTER TEN

But the clarity of these stimuli could not dull the questions that pummeled his mind: *Was there still time for Fatima? What would it take to save her? What would he do if he lost her?* It was not uncommon for children to die in the village. They were the weakest of society and most vulnerable to disease. And his little girl faced death now for the second time in her short life. What kind of destiny would this child have?

Bandu reached his parents' hut and found the door to be unlocked. This was not a surprise; no stranger would dare to enter the home of the *dukun* uninvited. He paused to catch his breath and let his eyes adjust to the lack of moonlight. He then quietly pushed back the curtain that concealed the bed from the rest of the hut. His mother, Djum, was asleep on the right, so he tiptoed to the left side of the bed.

"Father," he whispered. "Father."

Soraya grunted as his senses slowly awakened. "What...who is it?"

"It is me, Bandu."

"Why are you calling me in the middle of the night? What has happened?"

Bandu hesitated for reasons he could not understand. Was this a mistake? "It is my daughter.... She is with fever and not conscious. Can you come, Father?"

Soraya sat up in bed, fully realizing what he had to do. "I will consult Nyale," he said. "Wait for me at your hut."

Bandu sprinted home. Inside the candlelit room, he found Sri rocking back and forth, crying. Fatima lay limply in her mother's arms.

"What is it?" Bandu asked, half yelling, expecting the worst.

Sri sobbed, "I don't... I don't want our baby to die!"

"She will not die. My father will not allow such a thing. He will speak to the gods of our ancestors and to Nyale. Now, please, stop this crying, Sri. You have to hold yourself together. Everything will be okay."

A demon named Doubt wrapped an arm around Bandu, and another, Desperation, enveloped Sri and Fatima in a pair of scaly wings. Together, they cackled in delight.

Bandu peered into the eyes of his young wife and tried to convey a sense of confidence he did not possess. Suddenly, the temperature in the hut dropped ten degrees. Desperation and Doubt stopped laughing at once, released their hosts, and disappeared through the walls.

Just seconds later, Nyale himself descended through the roof, settling on a beam in the rafters, and Soraya stormed into the hut and pulled Fatima from Sri's grasp. He lifted the child into the air directly below Nyale and unleashed a shrill cry. Sri desperately wanted to grab Fatima back, but fear kept her paralyzed on the bed. She sensed a near and present danger, just as she had on the day Fatima was born. Bandu sat on the bed and held his wife, saying nothing as they watched Soraya recite the incantations that had been handed down through the generations.

His performance finally complete, Soraya placed his granddaughter on the bed and tied around her neck a small pouch attached to a thin strand of leather. Turning to Bandu and Sri, he said, "This will be the child's protection. Don't ever take it off, not even for bathing. If at any time you need to change it, or if it breaks, tell me at once. Now get some rest. By morning the child will be well enough to eat."

CHAPTER TEN

Soraya, spent from the ordeal, swept out the door. Sri immediately took Fatima in her arms and held her tight, tears flowing freely once again.

From the rafters, Nyale addressed the child: "Have a nice life, little one. You and your parents are mine." Then he turned to Bandu: "You will serve me like your father has served me, and you will learn to come to me for everything." Satisfied, he drifted through the roof to his nest in the bamboo trees.

The temperature in the room returned to normal in an instant. Bandu touched Fatima's face and forehead. He breathed a sigh of relief. Her fever seemed to be subsiding. "Alhamdulillah," he whispered. Thanks be to God.

11

ORIEN BERRY PUSHED his glasses up for the hundredth time that day and studied the screen in front of him. When he became a missionary over four decades earlier, he could never have imagined using a personal computer in his work. Yet here he was, revising the final lesson in a twelve-part series for discipleship among unreached peoples. This document would soon be translated into a dozen languages and distributed to church leaders throughout the archipelago of Indonesia, his home for the full length of his missions career. Even as he clicked away on his keyboard, Orien whispered a prayer that these words would transform lives and yield lasting fruit.

He paused to reread a paragraph that wasn't quite right, then stared out the window in search of the phrase that was eluding him. Tree frogs, geckos, and tokay lizards serenaded him with the songs of the night, the soundtrack of his life. As he turned back to the computer monitor, he felt his glasses begin their gradual descent down the bridge of his nose. The words on the screen blurred momentarily, perhaps a sign that he should call it a night.

Harriet walked into the room as Orien shut down the computer and placed some papers in a file folder. She knew her husband preferred to work in the quiet and relative cool of the evening, but she was relieved that he wouldn't be up too late tonight. While he was still in work mode, however, she did have one subject to address with him.

"Sweetheart," she said, "are you going to answer that email from the couple at Fritz's church? They seem like such nice people."

Orien sighed at the thought of answering another inquiry about going to "the mission field." He had often entertained the idea of ignoring these people until they sent a second or third letter, just to make sure they were serious.

"If it weren't for my relationship with Fritz," he said, "you can guess what I would probably do with their email."

"Orien Berry!" she said, hands on her hips. "Just because most of these don't ever pan out doesn't mean this isn't the Lord sending someone to us." Her voice softened: "We aren't getting any younger, you know. And who knows? Maybe this time this family is the answer to our prayers."

"I know, I know," he said, smiling at his wife's strong spirit. "I'll do it first thing in the morning. And you can read through it so I don't scare off the hot prospects with my gruff ways.... Maybe the internet will be back up and running by then."

Before falling asleep that night, Orien pondered how he could summarize in a single email a lifetime of service among the never-reached. This was not an easy place to live, but he and Harriet had adapted and had long considered Indonesia their home. They never lost sight of the Great Commission, Jesus' expectation that His followers would preach the gospel and

CHAPTER ELEVEN

make disciples to the ends of the earth. And there were many times on these islands when Orien felt like he was standing at the literal end of the world. Oh, the places he had visited—preaching, teaching, baptizing, healing, discipling, training, serving. He and Harriet had traveled to villages with a dozen inhabitants and metropolises with millions of people, and everything in between. They had taken airplanes big and small, boats, canoes, buses, trucks, cars, motorcycles, horses and carts. Through all of their travels, they had never had an accident—testament to the believers back in America who held them up in prayer every day. Orien was as confident as ever in the power of prayer, so maybe, just maybe, this family in Pennsylvania was the Lord's answer to the Berrys' frequent request for more laborers.

The next morning, Orien sat at his computer, asked God for wisdom, and started typing:

Dear Billings family,

Greetings from Indonesia in the name of the Lord Jesus Christ!

I received your email a few days ago; our internet service has been spotty recently, otherwise I would have seen it sooner. Thank you for your interest in missions and for getting in touch with me. I know your pastor very well, and at times here I miss his friendship. You are blessed to have him as your spiritual shepherd.

Harriet and I have been involved in missions almost our whole adult lives. In all of that time, we have served with Every Tribe Mission here in Indonesia. It is a wonderful country filled with wonderful people.

I hope I can answer your questions about going to the mission field. Certainly it is unorthodox for you to begin this work now, especially with the children the ages they are. But I believe that if God has a calling on your lives, He will make a way. As you explore the idea of going to the field, first, understand that this can be a long and complex journey. However, there are some things you can do immediately:

1. Visit our mission's website to learn about our work and the assignments that are available.
2. Continue to pray about this and ask the Lord for guidance.
3. Prepare your family by talking with them about this possible change.
4. At some point, if you are confident of God's leading, you will need to speak with someone at our mission headquarters. The contact information is listed on the website.

If I may be transparent, Harriet and I are approaching the final stage of our missionary service. At our age, we've been praying about someone to come and carry on the work after we are gone. I do not believe it is a coincidence that you have connected with us. Maybe you should prayerfully consider coming to Indonesia to work with us.

In your email, you mentioned your involvement in the furniture business. This country is well known for its teak and mahogany furniture, so perhaps there might be a way to combine your expertise in this field and come here to minister at the same time. Indonesia is the largest Muslim country in the world, so it isn't always easy to get permission to come as a traditional Christian missionary.

You will see that I have copied Bob Hollins on this message. Bob is the director at our mission who oversees this part of the world.

CHAPTER ELEVEN

May the Lord richly bless you as you continue to seek His will for your family.

Sincerely,
Orien and Harriet Berry

Harriet read over the email and gave her stamp of approval. Their internet was still down at the time, but an hour later as he worked at his desk Orien noticed a truck from the telecom company. An imposing angel named Light, unseen in the natural realm, stood by to allow the technician to finish his work without interference from the demons lurking down the street. As the truck pulled away, Orien slid his glasses up his nose and opened his email program. With a quick prayer and a click, he sent his message to the other side of the world.

12

THE NEXT MORNING in Grapevine, Pennsylvania, Christopher Billings took a sip from the coffee mug on his desk. He wondered whether there was enough caffeine in the county to get him through this day. One of the lathes in the shop had broken down, and his engineer just said it would take the rest of the day to get it up and running again—if they had the right part in storage. Sam Tanner was still out with the flu, so that meant someone else, maybe Chris himself, would have to be pulled off his normal job to pick up the slack.

And worst of all, a big order was going to be late and Chris would have to call the customer with the bad news. He didn't think it would be a major problem, but these situations were touchy. Although unlikely, the client could decide to cancel the order on the spot. Chris was rehearsing what he would say during this call when his cellphone rang. It was Maria.

"Hey, honey," Chris said. "How's your day?"

"It's great. How's yours?"

By the tone of her voice, Chris knew Maria had something exciting to tell him so he didn't want to burden her with his business troubles.

"Could be better," he said. "A few mechanical problems, but nothing that can't be ironed out. So what's your news? I could use some cheering up today."

"Well, after I got the kids off to school and had my devotional time, I checked our email. And... the missionaries in Indonesia wrote back."

"Really?" Chris sat up straight in his chair. "What did they say?"

"I just forwarded it to your work email," she said. "You should be able to see it."

Chris woke up his laptop, and there it was. Orien and Harriet Berry's email had arrived just after eleven the previous night, which would have been late morning in Indonesia. He would have to figure out the time difference — another item for his to-do list.

Maria and Chris read through the message together, line by line, filling in their commentary along the way. They had in fact already visited the mission's website to learn about the organization, but none of the assignments jumped out at them. And they had of course been praying about this possibility for weeks. They had not spoken to any of their family members yet, including their children, but in Chris's mind, they were ready to proceed to step four — talking with someone at Every Tribe to get their application started. And as much as the furniture business was annoying him today, he was intrigued by the idea of using his background and experience if it helped them get into a restricted country.

CHAPTER TWELVE

"Indonesia, huh?" Chris said. "I'm not sure that's where we'll end up, but I want to get started on this. I'm gonna give them a call."

"Don't you think we should pray about it first and talk to Pastor Fritz?"

Chris knew Maria was right, but he immediately became defensive. "Well, I thought we had been praying about it—and we did talk to Pastor. We're doing exactly what he told us we should do."

"But are you that sure this is what we're supposed to do? I'm not ready to say we want to go to Indonesia. We really don't know anything about the place. I don't want us to get ahead of ourselves."

Again, Chris saw the wisdom in what his wife was saying, and maybe he was being a bit impatient. The past few weeks had turned his life upside down. He had been content running his business, raising his family, serving in the church. But then God spoke to him about something completely different, and much to his surprise Chris jumped in headfirst. He was ready.

"Okay," he said. "You're right. Here's what I'll do. I'll get on their website, look around, and see if there's a place to request some info. Even if we can just look at the application, that'll help us prepare. And then we can check in with Pastor on Sunday."

Maria concurred with this plan, and they agreed to talk more about it that night. After a few minutes on the Every Tribe site, however, Chris saw that he would have to speak with someone at headquarters. There was no other way even to see an application.

Chris found the number, dialed, and was greeted by a computerized voice. The voice gave him a list of options and numbers to press, but nothing sounded relevant. Finally, something that might work: "If you need to speak to an operator, please press zero now." He complied.

"This is Every Tribe Mission," a polite Southern-sounding voice told him. "How can I direct your call?"

He began to explain his need for an application, but before he knew it the operator cut him off: "Please hold while I forward your call."

With that, he was tossed into the world of upbeat Christian Muzak, instrumental versions of songs he vaguely recognized. As the music played on, he wondered whether anyone knew he was there. *Don't they realize I want to go to the mission field? Or is this a test? Many call, but few are chosen?* He chuckled at his wit, but his patience was wearing thin. Finally:

"Personnel. This is Sally. How can I help you?"

"Hi, Sally. My name is Christopher Billings. I'm calling about an application."

"Is this an application that you've already submitted?"

"No, this would be a new one."

"Thank you, Mr. Billings. Let me ask, do you have a reference for an application?"

"Uhh, reference? I'm not sure what you mean."

"Sorry. I mean, has one of our missionaries requested you to work with them? Or maybe you have a reference from your home church?"

"Oh, of course," Chris said. "I've been in contact with Orien Berry in Indonesia. He's the one who told me to call you."

"Okay, good. Please hold while I check Mr. Berry's request file."

CHAPTER TWELVE

Before Chris could protest or explain his situation further, he was back in the world of Muzak. How hard could it be to get his hands on an application? And why the difficulty? It's not like he's trying to get into the CIA, right?

After a couple of minutes, Sally was back on the line. "Mr. Billings, I'm sorry, but our system does not show that Mr. Berry has filed a request for personnel. If you are interested in working with him, please communicate with him directly. If he wants to invite you, he will have to make an official request with the mission."

"But I have an email from him. I can forward it to you."

"That may be the case, but there has to be an official request in the system before I can send you an application."

Chris felt his frustration level rising, so he politely ended the call before he said something he would regret. Orien Berry had been right: This would be a long and complex journey.

13

SORAYA CLOSED HIS EYES, clasped his hands atop his belly, and leaned back in the large, ornate wooden chair. It was the place of honor in the local mosque, elevated above the main floor by a series of steps and covered by its own canopy. Soraya sat in this seat often, teaching from the Qur'an, giving instruction to the men of the village, presiding over discussions that affected every area of life.

On this day, the conversation had nothing to do with Islam, with the knowledge Soraya gleaned on the *Hajj*, his pilgrimage to Mecca all those years before. Today the topic was much more practical, and Soraya needed to hear from Nyale before weighing in with his decision.

A young man named Slamet stood and cleared his throat. He looked around the room and then, seemingly realizing where he was, turned his gaze to his feet.

"Respected leaders of this village and of this mosque," he began, reciting the expected yet empty formalities. "I know that I am young and inexperienced in many ways. I am aware that my speaking in such a gathering may be offensive to some, so, for that, please forgive me in advance."

He paused to examine some of the faces surrounding him, perhaps seeking a sliver of encouragement. He continued:

"Today we are discussing the use of a modern device called *televisi*. I know there is much fear related to this device, but I have information that may help us in deciding this important issue. As I have walked the trails near our village, I have on occasion met strangers."

This revelation piqued the interest of many of his listeners, as the village's isolation made interaction with outsiders a rare occurrence.

"These men," Slamet said, "were brothers from nearby places, not of the Merapu but of other tribes. They spoke of things in the outside world, things that only the honored Soraya has experienced firsthand."

Slamet glanced toward the influential elder sitting near the mimbar, but Soraya appeared to be in a semiconscious state, oblivious to the discussion taking place below him.

Slamet continued: "These outsiders sometimes talk about *televisi*—a box with a glass front like a window where pictures appear and voices speak. They say this box is very beneficial. It contains educational presentations for children and religious instruction every morning."

The young man read confusion on the faces of his neighbors as they tried to imagine a box that could do such things. But with his reference to education, he sensed an opening. Some of the men began nodding their heads. Others whispered comments to those beside them. Maybe Slamet was winning them over.

CHAPTER THIRTEEN 79

Nyale and his hordes hovering in the room needed no introduction to television. They were well aware of its uses, and many demons cheered the possibility of bringing it to the village. They had heard stories from around the world how television had siphoned off people's time and controlled their minds. One spirit that specialized in violence grabbed and shook another whose focus was lust: "Just imagine what we can accomplish! These people don't have a chance!"

In the rafters, Nyale quietly observed his minions celebrating this potential breakthrough. But he was not pleased. He clearly remembered the last Gathering, when the Prince of Darkness had banished Sheol specifically because he had allowed this corruption device to infiltrate the tribe he had ruled. With a nod of his hideous head, Nyale positioned four large fear demons in the corners of the room.

Small conversations had broken out in the mosque around the idea of *televisi* in their village. In general, it seemed the young men were open to exploring the device while the elders hesitated. As the arguments for both sides grew in fervor and volume, Soraya broke out of his trance and his voice boomed throughout the room:

"Silence!"

All conversation ceased, and the temperature dropped immediately. Without rising, Soraya addressed the men of the village.

"Respected fathers and sons, as you know I have traveled widely in this world. I have made pilgrimage to the cradle of Islam and birthplace of the prophet. I have visited the islands of our vast nation and beyond. I have witnessed the decadence of many peoples and the destruction this decadence has caused everywhere. Is it a coincidence that wherever I have seen decadence and corruption, *televisi* is there as well?"

He paused to examine the face of each man present.

"Is this something we want to give to our people?" He dared his opponents to speak. "I say no! The few benefits of this device would soon be wiped out by the evil philosophy it spreads. I say, let us remain loyal to our ancestors and the jinn that call our village home. Even as we have committed to Allah, Nyale must be appeased."

Several men shuddered at the mention of the village's ancient spirit. They knew Soraya was powerful and in direct contact with forces they did not understand.

Soraya stepped down from his elevated seat and slowly made his way to the door. Everyone knew the issue of *televisi* was now closed. No one had the power or influence to bring up the topic again — let alone to challenge Soraya's authority.

As the crowd dispersed, many of the younger men surrounded Bandu. Slamet asked, "Isn't there anything you can do to change your father's mind?"

Bandu knew better than anyone that no one short of Nyale himself would be able to convince Soraya to change his decision. But he also did not want to disappoint his friends.

"Please, my friends, give me time," Bandu said. "You know my father is a stubborn man. But I will talk with him about the benefits of modern things. We must be patient. Our generation will be different, but its not yet our time."

Bandu took in the hopeful faces of his friends and, for the first time, felt as though he could be a leader. These young men were

CHAPTER THIRTEEN

looking to him, counting on him. Adrenaline surged through his body at this realization. *They are really listening to me.*

Nyale recognized the pride all over Bandu. *I must watch this one closely*, he thought. *He is the future. Soraya's power will end soon enough, and I will need another to lead these people.*

The god of the village then called to an underling: "Pride!"

Pride arrived at once and bowed low before Nyale. "Yes, my master?"

Nyale gestured toward Bandu. "Make sure our young friend here stays intoxicated by his newfound influence," he said. "He will be useful to us in the future."

"Yes, master. I will not leave his side."

14

AFTER A STRESSFUL WEEK at work and a disappointing first contact with the mission agency, Chris was really looking forward to church that Sunday morning. More than most weeks, he needed the encouragement that comes from gathering with God's family. And once again, the Lord blessed them with a tangible sense of His presence. The people weren't just singing songs; they were truly worshipping. They weren't simply saying their prayers; they were communicating with their Creator. They weren't just listening to a sermon; they were receiving a message from God specifically for them and for this moment.

In the lobby after the service, Chris and Maria hung back to allow Pastor Fritz Bernheim to greet congregants and visitors on their way out the door. When the line thinned out, they stepped in for their own handshakes.

"Great service today, Pastor," Chris said. "That message really spoke to me."

"Thanks, Chris. I really felt the Lord here as well. Can't wait till tonight."

"Pastor, we received an email this week from your friend Orien in Indonesia."

"Wow, that's pretty fast. Sure beats the old days when we had to use air mail. I would send a letter and not get a response for two months. So how's my old friend?"

"It sounds like he's doing well," Chris said. "He gave us some good advice. He said to get in touch with the mission and let them know about our interest—and he also mentioned that he and his wife need some help there. He asked us to pray about joining them."

"That's great!" Bernheim said, turning to Maria. "So what do you two think about that? Is it something you'd consider?"

Maria said, "Absolutely, we are praying about it. But when Chris called the mission, they didn't really have any answers for him."

"Truthfully," Chris said, "I was pretty disappointed. It felt like they were giving me the runaround. I kept being put on hold, and they said they needed Orien's approval before they would even send me an application. I thought they were trying to get people to go to the mission field—not keep them away."

They all laughed, but Chris wondered whether there was some truth to his remark.

"It might feel that way sometimes," Bernheim said, "but keep in mind that they get hundreds of calls every month from well-intentioned people who think they want to be missionaries but have no clue what it's about. I feel part of the application process is finding out who's tenacious enough to stick with it. If these people get so discouraged right away, maybe their calling isn't

CHAPTER FOURTEEN

that serious. So if you two decide to continue in this direction, get used to hearing 'no'—and be ready to politely give them a 'but.'"

The Billings children gathered around their parents in the lobby, inching toward the exit, and Bernheim asked, "Are you planning on coming tonight?"

"Of course," Maria said. "We wouldn't miss it."

"That's what I figured," the pastor said. "I've been thinking about your plans, and I have a proposal I want to run by you. Are you able to come early tonight? Say, five-thirty? We can talk in my office."

"Sounds good," Chris said.

Sunday was always a family day for the Billingses. They ate a big breakfast together, hustled to make it to church on time, then spent the afternoon playing games, running around the yard, hiking in the woods—doing whatever the weather and their interests suggested.

On this sunny day, they decided on a little soccer in the front yard—with Mom dominating as always—and then headed down the hill into the forest with tool belts and scrap lumber. Chris had agreed to help the kids build a treehouse within view of their back deck, and the plans grew more elaborate by the week. At this rate, it wouldn't be so much a house as a fortress.

Chris usually did a good job compartmentalizing. When he was at work, he worked. When he was on the softball field, he focused on each at-bat. And when he was at home, he tried to be totally present for his family. But this afternoon, he couldn't keep his mind from wandering a bit to his pastor's proposal. What could he have in mind?

After dinner at a Greek restaurant near the church, they showed up a few minutes early for their meeting with Fritz. The kids sprinted to the youth room where the foosball table sat waiting just for them, and Maria and Chris found Pastor Fritz and Gloria in his office.

"Thanks for coming a little early," Fritz said as they settled in. "Ever since you told me the Lord might be calling you overseas, I've had this idea rattling around in my head. First of all, I'm not surprised He has called you, only that it's taken this long. You're the kind of family every pastor dreams about; I would trust you with any aspect of ministry in this church."

"And you know," Gloria said, "that he wouldn't say that unless he meant it completely."

Chris and Maria simply nodded, unsure how to respond.

"I believe there's some special purpose in this," Fritz said. "Here's what I'm getting at: I would like you to consider being sent out from our local church rather than going through the mission agency. I've been sensing that the Lord wants to do something different through our church, and it seems that with your desire to go, this might be it."

"Wow," Maria said. "First of all, your words are too kind. We appreciate the level of trust you have in us. But could we really do that? Just bypass the application and paperwork and just go?"

"Yeah," Chris said, "what would that even look like?"

"Well, it wouldn't happen immediately," Fritz said. "The church board and missions committee would have to discuss the idea—and as you know we have a few people who would want to examine every detail—but I'm confident they would approve. Rather than going out as missionaries with Every Tribe

CHAPTER FOURTEEN

Mission or some other organization, we would be able to send you out as missionaries from Lakeside Community Church."

"I didn't even know churches did that," Chris said.

"It is rare," the pastor said, "mainly because the financial commitment is so great. Most churches don't have the means to fully support one couple or family."

"That's an area where we're a little unusual," Chris said. "I crunched some numbers, and I think we can make it without raising money from donors. I can hire someone to run the business, and the company's profits would still allow us to live modestly in a place like Indonesia."

Fritz folded his arms over his chest and held his chin in his right hand. "I'd wondered about that," he said. "Yes, your circumstances are certainly unique — and it actually makes my idea more feasible. We could still contribute to your work financially, but maybe some of that money could go to support local pastors and to plant churches."

"Can I ask why you're interested in doing it this way?" Chris asked.

"That's a good question," Fritz said. "I see several benefits along with a few disadvantages. Do you remember how you got the runaround when you called the mission?"

"Do I ever," Chris said.

"Well, at this point, you're just a name to them. They don't know who Chris and Maria Billings are. They don't know what makes you tick, what your gifts are, how you operate in a ministry setting, how you respond to stress. There's no relationship there. If you join the mission, you start from zero, and relationships take a long time to develop. But this whole church already knows you and loves you and trusts you. We share the same spiritual DNA. You never know how you'll connect with team members who don't have that DNA. And one of the things I love most about this is the prayer support. If our people see you as *our missionaries*, I guarantee they will pray for you every single day. And not just a 'bless the Billings family' prayer. They'll be invested in knowing how to pray for each one of you."

"This sounds interesting," Maria said, "but what about the negatives?"

"The big one is that a larger organization can give more on-the-ground support. We will support you however we can, but keep in mind that Indonesia—if you end up there—is a long way from Grapevine, PA. I've always had a burden for missions, and the churches I've pastored have always supported missions. But I've never been a missionary. I can give you pastoral care, even from a distance, but we will not be able to effectively mentor you in your work. You'll need someone on the ground for that. Someone like Orien and Harriet. And these agencies also have an infrastructure in place for things like visas, housing, banking, and probably a dozen other areas I'm not aware of. The pioneers in these groups worked through these processes years ago."

"Pastor," Chris said, "let's think of ourselves as pioneers. I've been an entrepreneur my whole life. With God's help, I know we can set up shop in Indonesia. If others have done it, we can do it. Besides, the idea of freedom and accountability to you and this local body sounds really good to me. And I'd be happy never to have to call a mission agency again."

Bernheim turned to Maria. "I realize I just dropped this on you, but what are your initial thoughts?"

CHAPTER FOURTEEN

"Well, it is a lot to process," she said. "But I've always preferred relationships over organizations. And just like you said that you trust us, we trust you too."

The pastor then looked to his wife. "Are we missing anything?"

"Not that I can see," she said, "but I would love to hear what Orien and Harriet have to say about this."

"That's exactly what I was thinking," Fritz said. "After the service tonight, I'll give him a call. I think they're about twelve or thirteen hours ahead of us. He shouldn't be too tough to reach on a Monday morning."

As the four of them prayed for wisdom and for the service that was about to begin, Sword, sitting on the pastor's desk, couldn't suppress his grin.

"What's with you?" Light asked.

"Indonesia," Sword said. "The front lines. It's gonna be amazing."

15

ORIEN AND HARRIET BERRY'S breakfast table was colored by the bounty of the tropics. Along with coffee and toast, the couple always started their day with fresh fruit grown on the islands of their adopted homeland, sometimes within miles of their table. On this day, their spread included papaya, mini sweet bananas, and honey mangoes.

The Berrys had been partners in ministry for over forty years, sometimes working side by side on the same projects and at other times taking on tasks better suited to their individual gifts and interests. Early on in their shared life, they designated breakfast as the time to go over each day's activities and coordinate their calendars.

Harriet said, "I'm meeting with the leaders of the ladies' discipleship groups at one this afternoon, so let's plan for lunch at noon."

"Works for me," Orien said. "I'll be on campus most of the day. I meet this afternoon with the church planters who are going out in the fall."

"Did you see that Pastor Purwono called?"

Orien nodded as he chewed a chunk of papaya. "He's been calling every month. He wants us to put together another trip into the remote villages around Makassar. I'll try to call him today. Maybe I'll suggest the church planters go out there next month. They could use some more experience, and Purwono could certainly use the laborers."

He grew quiet as he speared another piece of mango. Harriet detected sadness in her husband's body language. "What is it, dear?" she asked.

"Oh, I was just remembering the days when I would go along with those teams. Riding horses, hiking through the rainforest, looking for a man of peace in each village. I don't think I have the strength anymore. I'd just slow everyone down."

Harriet saw an opening to bring up a sensitive topic: "What about the young couple from Fritz's church? We could use someone to come and help us."

Orien had been disappointed so often through the years by prospective reinforcements that failed to pan out. It was easier not to get his hopes up.

"Harriet, we have all the help we need," he said, thinking of the army of Spirit-filled workers they had discipled through the Bible school. Their former students were serving as pastors and church planters and leaders throughout Indonesia.

"I know we do," she said. "But what about the call? You weren't the last person God ever called into missions, you know. Shouldn't we try to help someone else fulfill their call and obey the voice of God?"

CHAPTER FIFTEEN

"We'll see," Orien said. "Let's wait to hear back from them. If it's meant to be, the Lord will make a way in His time."

"Time!" she said with a mischievous look. "You talk like you have all the time in the world!"

"Look who's talking," he said. "Don't tell me you've forgotten that you're a year older than me."

Later, in his office, Orien returned a call to Pastor Purwono, one of his former students. Purwono wanted a team from the Bible school to join him on a short-term trip to the province of Southern Celebes, where they would minister among the Bugis and Makassar peoples. They discussed details, and Orien prayed with Purwono before hanging up.

Just after ten o'clock, Orien's phone rang. "Hello?" he said. The soft buzzing on the line and the delay in response told him the call might be from overseas.

"Hello, Orien? Is that you?"

"It sure is. Who's calling?"

"Man, you sound like you're a million miles away. This is Fritz Bernheim in Pennsylvania."

"Fritz—it's great to hear your voice. And it's only about ten thousand miles, not quite a million. How are you and Gloria?"

"We're doing great," Fritz said. "And Harriet?"

"She's great, too. Keeping me in line as usual. How goes the war by you?"

"We're in the middle of an amazing season. God's been doing some incredible things in our community. And we regularly pray for you and keep up with your newsletters."

"Glad to hear someone's reading them. And thanks for the generous support each month. Be sure to pass along our gratitude to the congregation."

"Absolutely," Fritz said. "We're glad to be a small part of what you're doing."

"So what time is it there, around ten? Don't tell me—you were in your evening service just now and God called you to Indonesia?"

They both laughed. "Can you imagine?" Fritz said. "I think Indonesia has enough old guys as it is.... Orien, I called to talk with you about the young couple in my church who wrote to you last month."

"Of course," Orien said. "Harriet and I were just talking about them this morning."

"Well, I just want you to know they are top-drawer people. Every pastor's dream.... Orien, I wouldn't be calling if I didn't think they were high-quality people. And they're serious about this. The call is strong in their lives."

"Fritz, hearing that from you means a lot. As you can imagine, this isn't the first time we've heard this song.... So what do you have in mind? I gave them some contact information for the mission."

"That's one of the things I want to talk about," Fritz said. "When they called headquarters, they felt like they got the runaround a bit. And considering their circumstances, I'm not sure that's the best way for them to go. Chris owns a very profitable business, so they wouldn't need to raise support. I think that opens up some other possibilities for them. I'm thinking we could send them out of our church rather than through the

CHAPTER FIFTEEN

mission. If you're up for it, you and Harriet could mentor them and they could work with you as you see fit."

Over the years, Orien had learned to recognize the voice of the Spirit. As he sat at his desk with the phone to his ear, he felt as though this was one of those moments.

"Well, as I said, Harriet and I were just discussing this matter today," Orien said. "But give us a few days to pray and talk about it some more. How soon would they be looking to come?"

"It's hard to say," Fritz said. "We haven't even discussed that yet. I'll talk with them as well and then call you again in a week or so."

They settled on a time for their next conversation and exchanged goodbyes. Orien hung up and shook his head at God's sense of timing. He thought, *Harriet is going to love this.*

16

FROM HIS NEST in the bamboo trees overlooking Seora, Nyale grew agitated as two small boys playing a game drifted in his direction. *How dare they approach!* In their pursuit of fun, the boys had lost their bearings and wandered too close to the forbidden grove. Their laughter sickened Nyale, and he would make them pay.

When they were almost directly beneath him, Nyale started to shake the trees violently—an unmistakable sign to the children that they had strayed too close to his perch. They screamed and sprinted back toward the center of the village, leaving their makeshift toys behind.

Nyale had many tricks at his disposal to keep the people of Seora in the grip of fear. This one, one of his favorites, was also one of the simplest. A rustling of the trees—especially on a pleasant and calm day—reminded everyone that they were not alone, that there were unseen forces watching their every move.

As the children ran away, Nyale and several of his minions erupted in laughter at the mischief they had witnessed. In the midst of their mirth, they did not see a sentry flying toward them, and the sentry did not realize that his master had descended from his perch. In his blind haste, the sentry crashed into the midsection of the much larger Nyale, bouncing off his master's armor-like scales and nearly being slashed by the swipe of Nyale's talons.

"You fool!" Nyale screamed after he realized he was not under assault from opposing forces. He burst forward for an attack on the smaller demon.

"No, master! Please, I beg you!" The sentry covered himself and prepared to receive blows from Nyale. "I have important information!"

Nyale restrained himself. He knew he needed to learn to control his temper. "Speak," he said. "And your news had better be important."

"Master, I only flew with such haste because strangers are approaching our village."

The sentry's words went off like a bomb among the assembled demons.

Nyale shouted, "I want all of the spirits within the sound of my voice to follow this sentry at once!"

The group was frozen by the urgency and decisiveness of the master's command.

"Now!" Nyale screamed. "At your greatest possible speed! I will pass through the village to gather the rest of our horde and warn Soraya. Then I will proceed down the road to meet you and the strangers. Do nothing until I arrive."

With the sentry leading the way, the assembly of demons left for the road. Nyale flew through the center of the village,

CHAPTER SIXTEEN

gathering most of his subordinates but leaving a few behind to tend to the people. He found Soraya and hovered over the *dukun* for an instant. Soraya fell into a trance almost immediately.

Nyale flew with all haste down the path that met the road that led to this place at the end of the earth. A million thoughts battered his mind like ocean waves in a storm. Who were these people? Why had they come? What if they were bringing the news of the Most High? He always knew it would come to this eventually, and he had a plan to stop it.

Nyale found a cluster of his demons huddled in the woods next to a fork in the road. Through the trees, they could see a group of humans below them standing around a vehicle. A map was spread out on its hood. One of the men pointed up the road to the left, but another shook his head and stabbed the map with a finger. Nyale caught the eye of the sentry demon and summoned him to his side with a nod of his head.

"Yes, my master," the sentry said as he approached. Nyale's glare forced him to look away.

"You will redeem yourself for colliding with me," Nyale said. "Approach the vehicle carefully—if it's within your ability to do so. Gather all of the information you can. Who are these people? What are their intentions?... But do not allow yourself to be detected. I sense the presence nearby of warriors of the Most High."

The small demon's eyes widened, and some of the others leaned closer to hear if Nyale had any more intelligence to divulge. "I will move with all care, master," the sentry said.

Nyale was pleased with his plan so far—right down to the detail of which demon would gather this vital information. This insignificant little sentry had been faithfully guarding this pass for the last three decades. No one knew the layout and terrain better.

Suddenly, without warning, Nyale felt an unwelcome presence behind him. He turned over his right shoulder and was greeted by the messenger of Lucifer himself. He did not look happy, though he never did. Spending most of one's time in the presence of the greatest force of evil in the universe has a way of affecting one's mood. The messenger was tall and looked almost human except for the large, black, bat-like wings.

"You have come at a most inopportune time," Nyale said with a slight bow.

"Yes, I can see that you are facing some difficulty. What is the situation here?"

Nyale considered the ramifications of his answer. The messenger held a lower rank than his own, but anything he said, and the manner in which it was stated, would be reported directly to the master.

"Our sentries are still out gathering intelligence on who these strangers might be," Nyale said. "I must attend to this work, then I will be able to receive your message. Please stand aside."

Nyale called four of his most trusted and capable guards to execute the next stage of his plan.

"Before the beringin tree is a sharp curve with a cliff rising on the left side," he said. "At the top of the cliff, there are boulders already prepared. If these humans continue their journey in this

CHAPTER SIXTEEN

vehicle, we must stop them by closing off the road before the sacred tree. Be on your way—and do not fail me."

As the four headed up the road, the sentry returned from his scouting mission. He stood before Nyale but averted his gaze.

"Master," he said, "these strangers are most assuredly servants of the Most High. I could not overhear everything they said, but I was able to see into the back of their vehicle. They are carrying copies of the Most High's holy book and other materials marked with His symbol. I counted five humans—four male and one female. They are all outside the vehicle looking at a map of this region.... And I also saw two warriors of light on protective detail, but they did not see me. Master, they did not appear very...impressive."

So, Nyale thought, *it comes to this. And yet the group seems weak. Only two guards for a team of five. Could there be others in hiding?*

On the road below them, the visitors got back in the vehicle. Before initiating the next step of his plan, Nyale waited to see whether they would turn around. Instead, they drove forward, choosing the left fork in the road, which would lead them directly to Seora. Nyale grabbed the sentry.

"Go with all haste to your brothers up the road," he said. "Give them my order to spring the roadblock. I will engage the Most High's contingent."

He called to his side two of the largest demons in his squad.

"Quickly," he said, "you two engage the first warrior that reveals himself, and I will take on the second. We must distract them from their charges in the car. But do not attempt to defeat them. We must disguise the size of our force. Attack and withdraw, and I will do the same."

To another demon, Nyale said, "During the attack, I want you to destroy one of the tires on the vehicle—but only one."

In a matter of seconds, Nyale and his forces carried out the three-pronged attack to perfection. Up the road, out of sight of the strangers, the landslide closed off vehicle access to the village. It would now take days to clear the boulders from the roadway.

At the same moment, Nyale's two lieutenants shocked the first of the angels with a surprise attack. Seasoned warriors, they knew precisely how and when to strike and back away without sustaining any damage themselves. Just as the second angel realized what was happening to his partner, Nyale landed on him with a flurry of blows. Nyale was by far the largest and most powerful of the dark spirits in this region, but he was an even match for this angel of no reputation. Nyale was impressed by the light, beauty, and strength of the angel, but he also glimpsed a look of concern on his adversary's face—perhaps surprise that so large a demon was present on such a remote jungle track.

Engaged in combat with the demons, the two angels were unable to protect the vehicle as it rolled up the road. The spirit assigned the third part of the offensive glided in untouched and punctured the rear passenger-side tire before disappearing into the trees. Just as suddenly, Nyale and the two other warriors broke off their attacks and scurried into the underbrush. The angels let them go and returned to the vehicle, which was slowing to a stop.

CHAPTER SIXTEEN

"Pastor," one of the men in the vehicle asked, "what was that?"

"I'm not sure," the driver said. "It felt like a tire exploded." All five humans got out to inspect the damage. It didn't take them long to see what was wrong, but no one could guess how it had happened.

As the humans started to replace the tire with a spare, Nyale gathered his entire contingent in a nearby thicket, hidden from the suddenly watchful eyes of the two angels.

"I am not pleased that these visitors are here," he said, "but the first phase of the plan has been successful. Now we must complete the strategy and force them out."

He ordered one-third of his horde to fly over the area in an effort to distract the angels.

"Do not get too close, or you will be obliterated," he said. "Some of you will need to engage the enemy, but be wary. They are more powerful than they appear."

Lucifer's messenger, who had been observing events from a comfortable distance, now stepped forward. He said, "Why only a third, if I may ask?"

Nyale suddenly rose to the full height of his stature, and his words nearly spat in the face of the visitor. "Because I am trying to keep the significance of this place a secret, especially from the humans," he said. "I also do not want the heavenly host, such as it is at present, to discover our strength." He continued his performance, directed as much at his subordinates as the messenger. "I have been ruling this domain for millennia. I will defend it as I see fit. Now if you please, stay out of the way and keep your comments to yourself. We may yet be successful."

The visitor did not respond, nor did he back down. He was, after all, the messenger of Lucifer himself. He had vital information, but it could wait.

Nyale then summoned five smaller demons with the power to instill fear.

"You have the most dangerous of missions," he told them. "You must get close enough that the humans feel your presence. The diversion overhead should give you time and space to attack. Now... let's begin!"

As before, Nyale's plan unfolded flawlessly. The flyovers drew the angels' attention away from the people at the car. And when the fear demons saw their opening, they swooped in. The effect was immediate, and the lone woman in the group gave voice to what all of the humans were thinking.

"Pastor Sutanto, did you feel that?" she asked. "All of a sudden, I have a sense of dread about this place. It felt like a cloud settling over me."

The pastor, who was changing the tire with one of the other men, stood to stretch his muscles and consider her question.

"Hmm," he said, nodding. "What are your thoughts?"

Another man answered: "It is pretty late in the day, and we don't even know how far we are from the village. This map doesn't appear to be accurate. With all of the adversity we've faced, what about going back to Haria for the night and trying this again first thing in the morning?"

"Okay," the pastor said. "Let's finish changing the tire, head back to the hotel, get some food and a good night's sleep, and head out at first light. We go home in two days, and I want to lay eyes on this village before we leave."

CHAPTER SIXTEEN

Unmolested by Nyale's forces, the humans quickly replaced the tire, found a spot to turn the car around, and headed back down the mountain. A cheer mixed with hatred and curses echoed through the jungle as the vehicle disappeared around a corner.

Nyale summoned a small, hideous, bat-like creature from the fringe of the crowd and gave his instructions: "Follow this group into Haria. Find where they are staying. Then report to the prince of Haria. Tell him to sicken this group in their evening meal tonight. They cannot be allowed to return tomorrow — even with the road blocked."

He then assigned three additional demons to sentry duty along the road with orders to report any developments to him at once.

When he was satisfied his directions were being followed to the letter, Nyale invited Lucifer's messenger up to his nest overlooking Seora.

"Now," Nyale said, "speak your message from our master."

"I have come to report that five humans plan to bring the message of the Most High to your village," he said.

"Oh, really?" Nyale said as his insides began to boil with anger. "Please, do tell."

"Of course, you have dealt with them as our master had hoped, and I will deliver an accurate report of your success. This group came from a church on a neighboring island, and our master wants you to be prepared for others to follow. You will have also noted that this group came with very light protective detail. They had no one in the presence of the Most High stating their names."

Nyale considered the events of the day and the fact that only two angels accompanied five humans on such a crucial mission. Now it made sense.

"Continue," Nyale said.

"The master wants you to remain on alert. Your number is down to fifteen. We have lost three more nations in recent weeks, and the master believes the Enemy and His people are building momentum. More groups are coming. Be prepared for the worst."

Later Nyale tried to enjoy his personal victory on this day, but he knew the war would eventually be out of his control. He just had to hold on. Deep in thought, he noticed the son of Soraya pass by. *Yes. He will be the key.*

17

CHRIS LIFTED THE Yankees cap from his head, wiped the sweat from his brow, and replaced the hat in one smooth motion. This was serious business, and he could not afford to lose focus. The meat sat on the grill before him like paint on an artist's palette, and it was his responsibility to produce a masterpiece.

It was a Saturday afternoon in June, Hannah's ninth birthday. In the Billings family, birthdays meant parties, parties meant barbecue, and barbecue meant Chris was at the controls. He wielded his tongs like a pro, flipping burgers, adjusting foot-long hotdogs, moving pieces of chicken into and out of the flames. Maria handled the rest of the birthday spread, but Chris was in charge of the meat. He would have it no other way.

Hannah and six friends zigzagged across the backyard, giggling and squealing as Timmy gave chase with his neon yellow water cannon. Bethany led her cousins Abigail and Joshua a short distance into the woods to show them the progress on the treehouse. And the deck, at least for the moment, was adults only: Chris and Maria were joined by his mother, Laura, his younger brother Will, and Will's wife, Sally.

As Chris checked the temperature of the chicken, Will handed him a cold Dr. Pepper and filled him in on the present whereabouts of their other brothers. The eldest, Dave, was based in Florida but was rarely home; he drove semis across the country for an auto-parts company. The youngest, Nate, lived in Colorado, where he hiked and skied and paid the bills by working security at night.

Among his brothers, Chris had always been closest to Will, partly because of age, partly because of life circumstances, and, now, partly because of geography. When Chris was ten and Will eight, their dad ran off one night without warning. At last word, he was in Montana, maybe Wyoming. The boys had worshipped their father and had tried to compensate for his absence by being together as much as possible. In time, they were the ones who stayed in Grapevine, where Will now taught history at the high school.

"I think this chicken is about perfect," Chris said. At the moment he started to transfer the chicken to a platter, Timmy and his squirt gun broke the peace, drilling his uncle in the back with a stream of cold water.

"Hey, Timmy!" Chris called before his five-year-old got too far away. "Come back here and apologize to Uncle Will."

Timmy sprinted back to the deck.

"Sorry, Uncle Will."

And just like that, he was gone again, around the corner in hot pursuit of one of Hannah's friends. Will laughed and shook his head.

"Sorry about that," Chris said. "That one has more energy than the rest of us combined."

CHAPTER SEVENTEEN

"I know what you mean," Will said. "If I could bottle up and sell whatever it is that makes Josh so energetic, I'd be a millionaire tomorrow."

Right on cue, Josh burst out of the woods into the clearing, well ahead of his sister and cousin.

"So how's work these days?" Chris asked. "Teaching summer school again?"

"Yeah, you know. Same old, same old. It's mostly kids who failed a class or two during the school year. Trying to make up some credits. It's better than seeing them drop out, that's for sure. How about you? Anything new?"

Chris and Maria had talked about the timing of their big announcement but decided to wait a bit, until the details were more solid.

"It's about the same," Chris said. "Business is good. Just got a big order for some Eli Terrys. Should keep us busy for a while."

With the meat ready, Maria called everyone together and they stood around the buffet table. Timmy and Josh started jostling each other for positioning. Maria stepped between them and said, "Okay, your father will say a *quick* prayer for Hannah."

Chris cleared his throat and began: "Lord, thanks for a beautiful afternoon. Thanks for family and friends and good food. We thank You for giving Hannah to our family nine years ago today and pray that her tenth year will be full of happiness, health, and adventure. In Jesus' name we pray...and everyone shouted..."

Their "amen!" rang out, echoing off the trees.

As the kids started to go through the line, Hannah walked over and hugged Chris.

"Thanks, Daddy," she said. "Do you think my next birthday will be in Indonesia?"

Will, Sally, and Laura all heard Hannah's question, but the looks on their faces showed nothing but confusion. They waited for the kids to fill their plates and head out into the yard before saying anything.

"What was that all about?" Will asked. "What's with Indonesia?"

Chris caught Maria's eye and merely shrugged. He hadn't wanted to bring this up now, but he saw no other option.

"Well," he said, "I was planning on telling you later, but I guess the cat's out of the bag. Maria and I are praying about going to Indonesia as missionaries."

"With the children?" Laura asked.

"Yes, we plan to take the kids," Chris said. "This isn't just a two-week trip, like when we went to Mexico with our church group a few years ago. We're thinking about a career change."

"And you didn't want to tell us before the kids?" Laura said. "I don't like feeling I'm being kept in the dark."

"Mom, we didn't plan to tell the kids before you," Chris said. "We were talking about it the other night, and the girls overheard. We didn't go into detail with them, but we did say this is something we're praying about."

Will plopped a scoopful of potato salad onto his plate. "Yeah, right," he said, smirking and shaking his head.

Sally didn't know how to respond. She turned to Maria, who just shrugged her shoulders.

"Will," Chris said, "we're serious. We—"

CHAPTER SEVENTEEN

"You mean to tell me you're gonna leave all of this to go to some place in the middle of nowhere? For what? To get killed and endanger your family?"

"Where is Indonesia, anyway?" Sally asked. "I want to say Africa, but I don't think that's right."

Maria corrected her. "No, it's in Southeast Asia."

"Either way," Will said, "you're out of your mind to even consider something like that. Why don't you take some vacation time and go over there and get it out of your system. You can leave the kids with us."

Chris and Maria knew that many people would not understand their calling, but they had hoped their family members—who considered themselves Christians—would show some support. Will took a bite of his burger and glared at his potato salad.

Chris said, "You know it's always been on my heart to do something like this, ever since I was small. We've talked about this, and you never said anything before. So why am I out of my mind now all of a sudden?"

"It's different now," Will said. He finished chewing his burger, and the teacher in him came out. "Okay, first of all, you have a great life here. I mean, look at all this: a house in the woods on ten acres. SUVs in the driveway. A great income. The ability to buy whatever you need. Go on vacation wherever you want. Secondly, you're talking about going to a place where they hate Americans and Christians. And knowing you, everyone there will know you're a Christian because you advertise it wherever you go. Thirdly, what about the kids? You have to take their education, health, and wellbeing into consideration. Lastly, why don't you stay here? America is in such bad shape itself. Why are you going overseas when we need help here? I hear that a lot of these countries are sending missionaries here now."

Will sat back and folded his arms over his chest. He felt good about his arguments. On some level, Chris understood that Will didn't want anyone to go because he didn't have the courage to go himself. But he also thought, *My brother is brilliant, and his points are logical — except for one thing.*

"Will," he said, "everything you just said to me makes perfect sense, except that the whole reason we're praying about it is because we feel like God is calling us to go."

Will threw up his hands.

"Oh, come on, big brother. Don't give me that 'God told me to' thing. That line just shuts down the conversation. How can I argue with that?... But I'll just say this: You'd better be careful about it. Better men than you and I have made mistakes following a voice they thought was God's."

And with that, the subject was closed. The kids played games. Hannah opened gifts. Everyone enjoyed cake and ice cream. But no one mentioned missions again — until it was time for goodbyes.

At the door, Chris's mother hugged her son and daughter-in-law with tears in her eyes. "Pray for me," she said. "If the Lord is calling you, I want to be happy for you."

Will, however, was entrenched in his position: "Think about what I said. I wouldn't want you to make a bad decision. You know I just want the best for you."

18

PASTOR BERNHEIM probably preached another great message the next morning, but Chris missed it. His body was seated right there where it was every Sunday, but his thoughts were elsewhere, flitting from his backyard barbecue to the islands of Indonesia to his shop to the schools his kids attended. The conversation with Will had highjacked his mind and robbed him of much-needed rest. He'd tossed and turned through the night, replaying Will's arguments in his head, coming up with impeccable responses, just eight hours too late. But was there a pinch of wisdom in his brother's warning? Was he being irresponsible? He didn't think so, but he needed the reassurance of God's peace.

After the service, Maria and Chris rounded up the children quickly and shepherded them toward the door. Three hours' sleep and a pot of morning coffee would carry him only so far on a day like this; he was looking forward to a Sunday afternoon nap. Pastor Bernheim was positioned at his customary post near the exit, shaking hands and giving hugs as his congregation streamed out. When the Billings family reached him, Bernheim grabbed Chris by the arm. "Can you hang around for a minute?" the pastor asked. "I want to tell you something. Just let me finish shaking hands first."

Chris and Maria moved off to the side and greeted some friends from their small group, making plans for lunch later in the week. When their conversation broke up, Bernheim stepped in. "I spoke with Orien Berry this past week," he said. "He seems enthusiastic about the plans we've discussed. And I get the sense they really are in need of help." He scanned the lobby for eavesdroppers, leaned in a little closer, and lowered his voice. "Actually, Gloria called Harriet a couple days after Orien and I talked. Harriet confided in her that his health isn't what it used to be. He's still sharp mentally and, of course, spiritually, but he's slowing down. Which, when you think about it, is natural—he's a few years older than I am."

"Thanks for helping us through this, Pastor," Chris said. "We'd be lost without your advice. And keep us in your prayers, especially as we start to tell people what we're doing. At Hannah's birthday party yesterday, the news kind of slipped out that we're praying about going to Indonesia."

"Oh, and how did that go?"

"Mom was kind of quiet. She'll eventually come around. But Will basically called me crazy. Gave me a list of reasons why it's not a good idea. I didn't think of this until later, but I bet he's feeling abandoned. First, Dad disappeared. Then our brothers ran off to find themselves. Now I'm talking about leaving—and it didn't come out in the way I wanted it to."

"That's a good insight, Chris. That can happen in divorce. Even though you're only a little older than Will, you've taken on some of your father's responsibility. I will certainly pray for your mom and the rest of the family. Sometimes in missions, it's easier to go than to be the family left behind.... In the meantime, why don't you try to connect with the Berrys by phone? When I talked with Orien, I mentioned sending you out from our church instead of going through the agency's hoops. He said he'd pray about it, so feel free to bring that up with him. And remember, they're twelve hours ahead of us, so plan your call accordingly."

Their handshake morphed into an awkward handshake-hug combo — right hands clasped together and left arms draped around each other's back — and Chris reflected on the fact, not for the first time, that this man was more a father to him than his own dad ever was.

"Oh, one more thing, Chris. We have a new attendee. Just moved into the area. Name is Jim Tucker. He's from somewhere near Pittsburgh originally. You should meet him. He said he has some experience running a furniture business. I'm not sure where you are in your process of getting your company in order, but he might be someone to talk to. I have his number if you want it."

"That sounds great. I'd love to meet him."

That night, after the kids had fallen asleep, Chris and Maria sat at their kitchen table. Chris picked up the phone, and Maria arranged the pen and notepad to record any important information.

"Ready?" he asked. "How sure are you about this?"

She gazed through the window at her moonlit backyard and the forest beyond. "I knew it was God's will to come to America," she said. "I knew it was God's will to marry you. And I know it's

God's will that we follow this path. If they say no, they say no. But we have to move ahead."

"Then let's do it."

Chris began punching in all of the numbers required to get a call overseas. It took several seconds before the phone began to ring on the other end. After about four rings, someone picked up the phone. Before Chris could say anything, he heard a strange voice say, "*Selamat pagi.*"

Chris was not expecting this. "Uhh, yes," he said, "could I speak with Orien or Harriet Berry, please?"

"*Aduh orang Inggris ya,*" the other voice said.

Chris repeated his earlier request, only more slowly and more loudly. "I'm looking for the Berrys!" he finally yelled.

"*Bapak ibu* no here!" The line went dead.

Chris shrugged and set the phone down. He noticed that Maria was doing everything she could to stifle her laughter.

"Yes?" he asked. "What's so funny?"

"Oh, I don't know. But I assume yelling in English did the trick?"

Chris suddenly realized what he had done and began to laugh at his technique. "That poor woman!" he said.

When Maria had first moved to Pennsylvania from Argentina for college, her English grammar and vocabulary were solid, but she sometimes had trouble understanding accents. And when she encountered these problems, occasionally people would try to overcome them by shouting. "I don't understand you," she would say, "but I can hear you!"

"Well, that was the number Pastor gave me," Chris said. "Guess I'll try tomorrow."

CHAPTER EIGHTEEN

Early the next morning, Chris dialed the fourteen digits he'd tried on Sunday night. After several rings, a rasping voice answered: "Hello?"

"Hello, Mr. Berry?"

"Yes?"

"This is Chris Billings from Pennsylvania.... I'm from Fritz Bernheim's church."

"Oh, yes. Yes. It's good to hear from you. Sorry, I'm a bit out of breath. I just ran in from the backyard when I heard the phone. We were watching the bats in the mango tree. Now what can I do for you, young man?"

"Well, since we sent you our initial email, we have continued to pray about it, and we feel more confident than ever that this is the Lord's plan for us. In fact, we've taken your advice to heart and prayed specifically about going to Indonesia to learn from you and work alongside you. And we believe this is where God is leading us."

"That's wonderful news, Chris, and a real answer to prayer. Your pastor filled me in on some of your conversations."

"Yes, and that's one of the reasons I'm calling. As he might have mentioned, we are in an unusual situation in that we won't have to raise financial support. I own a business that will be able to generate adequate income for us while we live overseas. That gives us the freedom to operate outside of normal structures. Once we get my company organized, we could be on our way very shortly. And it would also allow us to be sponsored by our local church here instead of jumping through the hoops of a mission agency."

"Yes, yes, Fritz did bring that up when we spoke," Orien said. "My wife and I have prayed about that idea, and I even made some inquiries within our organization concerning how that would work on our end. At this point, I think you should reconsider your plan and look into coming with our mission. I can sense your entrepreneurial spirit — and that will serve you well on the ground. There are some independent operators here, and they're good people, but they tend to not be as fruitful as those who come with a mission. We have built-in fellowship with our team here, not to mention all of the infrastructure that supports us. Things like visas, banking, housing, orientation to the country, vehicles and culture. With the systems and resources we have in place, we can focus on ministry. The independent missionaries end up working on problems we solved years ago. I imagine that's not the answer you were hoping for."

"No, not really, but of course we'll reconsider," Chris said. "But honestly my first interaction with the mission left a bad taste in my mouth. It seemed like they were intentionally giving us the runaround."

Orien laughed. "It can feel that way sometimes," he said. "But if you give it time, you'll see that it's just one big family. Yes, there are structures in place that can seem rigid, and yes, there are times when you'll catch people stressed out, but it's a great mission to be part of.... Here's what I'll do. I'll contact headquarters and make sure they know I'm inviting you here. That will open doors you didn't even know were closed. And I'll also have Bob Hollins get in touch with you. He's my boss — a veteran missionary who leads the workers in this part of the world. He can get things done."

CHAPTER EIGHTEEN

"Okay, I'll wait for his call."

"One other thing," Orien said. "How long do you expect to stay once you're here?"

"Honestly, I hadn't even thought of that yet. But I guess we'll look at two or three years to start with."

The line started to break up, so they said their goodbyes and made plans to talk again. Chris set his phone down and prayed for wisdom. He saw the benefits of an established agency, and he trusted Orien, but he had to find a way in.

19

"JIM, GOOD MORNING," Chris said. "Come on in." He walked around his desk and shook hands with the man stepping into his office.

It was Tuesday, the day after he had phoned Orien Berry. After their call, Chris updated Maria and then Fritz on Orien's suggestion that they apply for placement through the mission. Chris couldn't hide his disappointment, but Fritz encouraged him not to make any decisions before hearing from Orien's director from the organization.

Fritz said, "Even though I'm the one who proposed the idea of sending you out from Lakeside, Orien brings up some good points. He *is* the expert. And even if you go through the mission, we can still adopt you as *our* missionaries."

Then just this morning, Chris received a call from Jim Tucker, the man Fritz had told him about at church on Sunday. Chris had planned to get in touch later in the week, but Jim contacted him instead. Chris thought, *Now that's a good sign.* And when Jim offered to stop by today, Chris agreed.

"Jim, thanks for coming in on such short notice. Can I get you a cup of coffee?"

"No thanks. Never touch the stuff."

Chris shrugged and grabbed a bottled water from the small fridge in the corner. He poured himself a cup of coffee. He was still drinking regular but would switch to decaf after lunch. He handed the water to his guest and sat behind his desk.

"So," Chris said, "Pastor Bernheim tells me you're from the Pittsburgh area?"

"Yeah, that's where I grew up. Still have some family there. But I haven't lived there in years. I've spent most of my time in North Jersey. I managed a successful furniture store on Route 46." He slid a resume across the desk. "I have references if you want them."

"Thanks, but this is fine for now," Chris said. "We're a family business and have always done things through relationships and getting a feel for people. I can't remember the last time we hired someone we didn't know previously…. So, what did you do for"—he found the name on the resume—"was it Mavis Furniture?"

"Yeah, I was the nighttime store manager," Jim said. "I was there from two p.m. to nine p.m., closing time six days a week. Not to toot my own horn, but we broke national sales records each year."

"Wow, that's great." Chris inspected his guest over the top edge of the paper. Jim was a bit overweight, and his pants were too tight. His tie was too short and didn't seem to match anything else he was wearing. But then again, Chris knew he wasn't supposed to judge by outward appearances. "So why did you leave Mavis? Pastor said you're semi-retired?"

CHAPTER NINETEEN

"After a while, the challenge was gone and I just didn't have the excitement anymore. Plus, the bosses were getting pretty demanding—the overtime, the lack of appreciation. I had some money saved up from an inheritance, so I just decided it was time for a change of scenery."

Chris nodded and took a sip from his coffee mug. "You know, I wouldn't ask this in a normal interview, but since you come recommended by Pastor Bernheim, what about your faith? What church did you attend in Jersey?"

"Oh, I don't mind your asking. I've been a believer for many years—since I was a kid, really. Me and the missus went to a small Bible church over in Little Ferry. You wouldn't have ever heard of it. I was a deacon there for many years. When Elaine and I packed up and left, it was a sad day. We're hoping we'll find a home at Lakeside Community. Pastor Bernheim seems like a good man, but we'll just wait and see."

Before Chris could respond, Jim got up and walked over to the clock mounted on the wall. "That's an Eli Terry, isn't it?" He leaned in for a better view. "Looks like an antique. Boy, you don't find clocks like that anymore. It's gorgeous. How long have you had it?"

Now Chris was impressed. "It certainly is an Eli Terry. It was my grandfather's and his grandfather's before that, if I have the story straight. This is the clock that inspired my granddad to start this business years ago. I think it's been in the family over a hundred years. We do good business making replicas of this very model."

As they stood appreciating the ageless timepiece, Jim turned to face Chris. "I'll put it to you straight," he said. "I have the utmost respect for what you and your family are about to do, goin' to another country and all to help those people. Chris, you can trust me to do my best for you while you're there. I believe the Lord has sent me here so you can do what He's calling you to do."

"Well, Jim, I really appreciate that. I have a lot to think about. I'm gonna talk this over with Maria and get back to you. I've got to make a decision fairly soon, but I don't want to rush anything."

"I understand completely, Chris. And I realize that selling furniture isn't the same as managing an operation like this, so if you decide to bring me on, I'm up for any training you think I might need."

Throughout the rest of the day, Chris found his mind wandering back to his conversation with Jim Tucker. The sudden appearance of this experienced salesman seemed like an answer to prayer. But on the other hand, he couldn't shake one of Granddad's well-worn sayings: "If it seems too good to be true, well, son, it's too good to be true."

20

THE SMOKE FROM the cooking fire shot back into Sri's eyes, and she could no longer tell whether her tears were caused by the smoke or the frustrations of life. She turned her head and blinked and continued to feed the thin logs into the front of the oven, a small, simple cement box built directly onto the floor of her hut. She picked up her biggest pot and placed it on the grill that made up the stove's top. The water from the village well had to be boiled before it would be safe to drink. This pot would keep the family supplied for a couple of days.

Sri heard Fatima drag herself across the floor and then felt her brush against her leg. The little girl, still unable to walk since her seizure and her grandfather's intervention weeks before, had not lost her sense of joy and wonder. Even now, as Sri turned to look at her, Fatima met her gaze with a smile that spread across her round face. Sri was amazed that her little one would not stop moving and had learned so quickly to use her upper body to propel herself.

The heels of Fatima's hands had developed thick calluses through constant contact with dirt floors and rocky footpaths.

Sri noticed that the muscles in her daughter's legs were shrinking from lack of use. Yet, when Sri permitted it, Fatima happily joined the other children at play, even in the rare times when they laughed and ran away, leaving her alone. Her body had been transformed, but so far her attitude was as positive as ever. *This one*, Sri thought, *is different. She is a survivor.*

Fatima looked up with hopeful eyes, and Sri followed her gaze to the shelf. "So," Sri said, "you are wanting something before dinner, are you?"

"*Iya, ma*," the child said. Yes, mom. She pointed to the lone mango that Sri had been saving for later.

"Okay, just don't tell your father."

Fatima bounced on the floor to show her excitement. Sri grabbed the fruit and began to peel its skin.

As she worked on the mango, Sri felt a breeze at her back and heard the soft rustle of the curtain. "Hi, Bandu," she said. "How was your day?" Bandu supervised several farmers who worked on land owned by his father. It was a privileged position, watching over other men breaking their backs on the outskirts of the village.

"It was okay," he said. "We're close to taking in the cabbage harvest." Each year, if they got lucky with the weather, they could harvest three times. Seora's location was perfect for growing cabbage, carrots, ubi, and other vegetables.

"Do you think your father will let you take the harvest to market this year?" Sri asked.

"Maybe. He hasn't said anything. He will let me know in his time." Bandu washed up for dinner and crouched next to his daughter. He caressed her cheek and watched her eat the mango.

CHAPTER TWENTY

He placed her on his lap, content to relax before the meal, hold Fatima close, and forget the troubles of his day.

Sri, however, was ready to talk. Her day was spent working and thinking, thinking and working, and she needed adult conversation. "I was really hoping your father would let you go with the harvest this year," she said. "I wonder if there isn't a shaman or doctor of some kind in the city that can give medicine for Fatima."

Fatima looked up at the mention of her name, and Sri patted her head and urged her to keep eating. Bandu sat silent, pulling his daughter closer to his chest.

Sri continued, "I just don't understand why he won't let you go. I'm afraid that unless we get some help, she may never walk again."

"Come now, dear," Bandu said. "My father always has the best intentions for me and you."

"You may think that, but I've seen the way he treats people around here. He walks around this village like he's a god."

"Really, dear, I've got to trust him. He's my father, and I know that family is everything to him."

"Well, he is your father, but when he looks at me through those evil eyes of his, it scares me. He hates Fatima because of her deformity and doesn't want to do anything—or can't do anything—to help."

Bandu tried to concentrate, but this was a conversation they'd had many times. His wife could not grasp that his options were limited. There were some things he simply could not bring up to his father, and it had always been that way. Bandu pledged to himself that he would be a different kind of father to Fatima. He loved his precious little girl as much as life itself and would do anything for her—despite her disease, despite how society viewed her, despite the questions about a curse or a sin of his that caused all of this.

Other men his age would simply ignore this child and try again with a second or third. But Bandu was afraid of what might happen if he brought another child into the world—and besides, he could never neglect Fatima. Even as a boy, he was guided by compassion for the hurting. Holding his frail daughter in his arms, he drifted back to the day all those years ago when he'd found a small kitten that had been abandoned by its mother in a shrub in his neighbor's yard. Bandu had gently wrapped it in a banana leaf and carried it home in the hope that he could nurse it back to health. He hid the kitten in the room he shared with some of his siblings, but that night it began to bawl for its mother. No matter what he tried, the animal would not stop crying. The commotion woke his father, who flew into a rage, picked up the kitten still wrapped in the banana leaf, carried it to the door, and flung it into the field that bordered their hut. "Never bring sick things like that into my home," Soraya had said, "or next time it will be you thrown out into the field." In the morning, after the longest night of his life, Bandu ran into the field to look for the kitten. The longer he searched, the more his hope drained away—and the more his resentment of his father grew. He found the animal cold and dead with a broken neck. Bandu in that moment decided he would never forgive his father. He would stand up to him, someday. Yet here he was, seventeen years later, still helpless in the shadow of this powerful man.

"Aren't you listening to me?" Sri asked.

"What? I'm sorry. I was just thinking."

"Well, if your father was here, I'd tell him—"

CHAPTER TWENTY

Before Sri could finish the sentence, a noise at the door drew their attention. Standing in the doorway with his hands on his hips was Soraya.

"I'm here, daughter-in-law. Please do not let me interrupt what you were saying."

21

THE WARRIORS OF LIGHT assigned to the Billings family had settled into a comfortable routine, but they sensed that the battle would soon escalate. Although opposition forces had so far avoided face-to-face confrontation, Sword detected a growing amount of demonic activity on the periphery.

It was Thursday morning, and Chris Billings was in his happy place. His laptop was closed, his cell phone sat on his desk, and the door to his dark and empty office was locked. This was the one day during the week when Chris rewarded himself with a full eight-hour shift in the shop. At the moment, he was bent over his favorite lathe, fashioning a table leg that would eventually end up with a repeat customer in New York.

Sword could read the joy on Chris's face as he worked. Most of this, he knew, was a result of the fact that the Spirit of the living God resided within him. But the angelic warrior also understood this man's pleasure in a job well done. It was a gift from God, really—meaningful work that one enjoys. Sword inspected Chris's uniform: hardhat, safety glasses, earplugs, long-sleeved flannel shirt, jeans, steel-toed boots. It was a world apart from what he would end up wearing in Indonesia, and Sword wondered how Chris would handle the transition. He had seen it before: accomplished men and women accustomed to success in their home cultures struggling with the adjustment to ministry in a new land where results are sometimes measured in decades. Those who survived and thrived, Sword had noticed, were the ones backed by an army of intercessors at home.

Sword glided across the floor of the shop, pausing at times to watch the craftsmanship of Chris's employees. He passed through the loading dock and into the back parking lot. His mission on these days was not necessarily to see but to be seen. He wanted the enemy to know he was there. Maybe his presence would draw some out from the shadows, and then Light, stationed and hidden up the road a bit, could spot them. Sword slowly circled the building and made his way to the front entrance. He caught a glimpse of a dark figure scurrying behind the hardware store across the road. He considered pursuing but decided to continue on his rounds. Knowing was enough for now.

Later that night, the members of the Billingses' detail gathered for their regular debriefing. With the family all in bed, the house was dark and quiet. Sword sat at the head of the kitchen table and first turned to Light. He asked, "See anything unusual at the shop today?"

"Seems like there's a little more attention directed that way," Light said. "I haven't noticed anyone new, but surveillance seems to be getting more intense. It started earlier this week. They have more eyeballs on the place."

"That's what it feels like to me as well," Sword said. "They're still keeping watch on the house, but it looks like their center

CHAPTER TWENTY-ONE

of attention has shifted. Something to keep an eye on.... What else is new?"

Glory, Bethany's guardian, spoke up: "Man, middle school is awful. I'd forgotten how hard this time is on people. Bethany is a sweet girl with a pure heart, but this whole stage of life is full of landmines."

"What this family needs more than anything is prayer cover," Purity said. "Of course they will need it even more when they get to Indonesia, where the enemy feels like he owns the place, but they're in a precarious situation right here. I've sensed discouragement, even in Maria."

"By now," Sword said, "I think we have a clear picture of our mission. The Most High has identified and called this family to serve Him, likely in Indonesia. And we know what that means. They will be in close proximity to tribes that have never been reached by our Master's good news. So the enemy, when he and his forces become aware of this plan, will do everything in their power to thwart it."

"How much do you think the enemy knows?" Bravery asked.

"At this point," Sword said, "it's hard to say. If they knew the full picture, we would be under constant attack. Our presence here has no doubt raised an alarm in their camp, but I don't believe any of them has been able to get close enough to overhear sensitive conversations and prayers. We will do what we can to keep it that way. Eventually, their news will go public and we will not be able to contain its spread. For now let's be vigilant and watchful, but I see no need to alter our assignments. Glory, stay with Bethany. Dew and Bravery, you're still with Hannah and Timothy. I will remain with Chris, and Purity with Maria. Light, we'll keep you as a rover. Let's check in each morning, and you'll double-team whoever has the most taxing day. Sound good?"

The warriors around the table nodded in agreement with their leader's plan. "Now," Purity said, "we just need to build up prayer support for the battles that are coming."

22

THE DRIVE FROM GRAPEVINE to State College always reminded Chris of Granddad. Even on this Friday morning nearly three decades later, that first trip was as vivid in his memory as the scrambled eggs he'd eaten for breakfast yesterday.

It had been a Saturday morning in early autumn. Chris and his older brother, Dave, were still in bed in the room they shared. Will and Nate were asleep in their room across the hall. Dad had been gone for two months. Chris remembered waking up to the gentle nudging of his grandfather: "David. Christopher. It's Granddad. Time to get up." When that information failed to elicit a proper response, Arthur played his best card: "I have a surprise for you."

The four Billings boys bolted out of bed, dressed, and swallowed their Cocoa Puffs whole. When they were unable to coax the secret from Granddad himself, they turned their attention to their mother, who merely smiled back at them. She didn't speak a word all morning, afraid that if she opened her mouth the whole plot would come tumbling out.

They piled into Arthur's Cherokee and headed for the interstate. The boys eventually realized Granddad was not going to answer their pleas for information, so they sat back and took in the roads they had never before traveled. About two hours into the trip, they started to see signs for Penn State, and then Beaver Stadium, but even those clues were not enough. Not until Arthur turned into the parking lot near the stadium did the boys realize he was taking them to a Nittany Lions football game. They floated from the vehicle to their seats high above the northwest end zone, grins plastered on their faces.

The day was magical. The Lions destroyed Temple, the rains held off, the hotdogs had never tasted better. Chris decided right then and there that if he ever went to college, he would go to Penn State.

He often wondered how his life would have turned out if Granddad had not taken him to that football game when he was ten. Would he have still fallen in love with the school? Would he have applied for admission? Would Granddad have thought to take the boys if Dad hadn't disappeared? And if he had gone to some other college, what about Maria? He didn't want to imagine a life different from the one he now lived, so he simply thanked God for directing his steps.

On this summer Friday, Chris had two appointments in State College. The first was with a longtime customer named Richard, a furniture wholesaler whose father used to buy tables and chairs and bookcases from Granddad. Richard was ready to place a new order that would keep the company busy for a few months, and Chris wanted to close the deal in person. A discussion like this could be conducted over phone or video, but Chris preferred the personal touch, especially with longtime clients. And it would also give him a good excuse for his second appointment — a meeting with one of his favorite people at his favorite pizza place.

The sales visit went better than expected. Without any urging from Chris, Richard increased his order by ten percent and said he would be keeping some of the pieces for his daughter and son-in-law. After the meeting, Chris drove slowly through the Penn State campus just like all of the nostalgic alumni he once laughed at. He spotted the building where his campus ministry met — the building where he first laid eyes on Maria — and then drove past his freshman dorm. He went out of his way to catch a glimpse of Jeffrey Field, where Maria had played midfield for one of the best soccer teams in the country.

Just off East Beaver Avenue, Gino's Pizza had not changed much in the past fifteen years. It still offered New York style pizza by the slice or the whole pie. It still majored in takeout but had a handful of small tables off to the left side. It was still staffed by college students who would rather be anywhere else. The pizza itself wasn't the best he'd eaten, but Chris's memories drew him here whenever he was in town.

He stepped through the door and saw that his lunch companion had already claimed a table. Aaron Patterson jumped to his feet and engulfed Chris in a bear hug, just like the old days. He motioned for Chris to take a seat.

"I already ordered for us," Aaron said. "You still eat meat?"

"Yup."

"Good. You'd be scandalized otherwise."

Chris grinned and inspected his old roommate, all barrel chest and thick, red beard. "You're lookin' pretty decent," he said. "You lose half a pound?"

"Oh, stop. You're too kind.... It's been too long, man."

"Agreed," Chris said. "Twice a year isn't enough."

A waiter placed a large pizza on the table between them. Sausage, pepperoni, bacon, ham. Chris nodded his approval. Aaron prayed, thanking God for food and friends, "but not necessarily in that order."

They each grabbed a slice and got to work. Between bites, Chris asked, "So how was the school year?" Aaron had just completed his tenth year as director of Penn State Christian Fellowship, the same campus ministry Chris was part of when he met Maria—and Aaron.

"It really was a good one," Aaron said. "We had a solid core of student-leaders who love Jesus and love each other. Can't ask for much more than that. A bunch of students gave their lives to Christ, including four or five frat boys. We haven't seen that before. One of 'em just graduated and will be joining our staff for a year."

"That's incredible. I don't imagine it's easy to break into the Greek world."

"Not at all. Sometimes I wonder if it's even worth directing any resources there, but God's doing His thing. So what's new with you?"

"Well," Chris said, "God's doing His thing. That's one of the reasons I called." He paused to collect his thoughts. He opted for the straightforward approach. "We're praying about going to Indonesia as missionaries."

CHAPTER TWENTY-TWO

"Wow," Aaron said, setting the slice on his plate. "That's huge. What's the story?"

Chris filled in the details as they ate.

"You know," Aaron said, "I was beginning to wonder if this would ever happen. I remember talking about the call with you, maybe even right at this table. We sure ate here enough. But when you had to go back home after graduation, I thought maybe that was the end of it."

"You're not the only one. I'm as surprised as you."

"But I have to say, I'm *not* surprised. In my prayer times over the past year or so, I've had a sense that we're living in the last days, that more people will be answering the call to go. We might be the generation that gets to see Jesus come back. And before that, there's gonna be a great harvest of souls."

"You think so?"

"Absolutely. And you can count on us for whatever you need. When do you start raising support?"

"Actually," Chris said, "the business is doing so well that we'll be able to live off the profits, even when we're there. And don't worry—we'll be able to keep supporting you and Amy."

"We appreciate your generosity, that's for sure. One of the cool things about raising support is that we have so many alumni who've decided to give back."

"That's the way it should be. That ministry changed my life."

"You might not need money right now," Aaron said, "but you definitely need prayer covering. You're heading right into the lions' den. Whenever you're ready to go public, let me know. I'll help mobilize the prayer warriors."

23

BEFORE HEADING BACK to Grapevine, Chris had one last stop to make in State College. The Syllabus Bookshop was a narrow, two-story brick building on McAllister with used books stacked floor to ceiling. The lower level was a maze, but the upper floor was the birthplace of Chris's love affair with coffee. He'd discovered the shop — and the life-sustaining beverage — at the end of his sophomore year, and the Syllabus soon became his default study spot. And on this day, near the end of his conversation with Aaron Patterson, he knew he needed to go back for a purchase he'd been putting off.

"Did I ever tell you," Aaron had asked, "that I use you as an example in one of my messages every year?"

"Oh, no. I'm not sure I want to know."

"No, it's all good. I do a series of sermons every spring on spiritual disciplines — prayer, Bible reading, fasting, stuff like that. And when I talk about spiritual journaling, I mention you. When we lived together, I don't remember you ever missing a day. Do you still journal?"

The question reminded Chris of his promise to Gloria Bernheim—actually Maria's promise to Gloria—that he would start journaling again. He'd been avoiding incorporating this new habit while upending the rest of his life, but sitting in Gino's he resolved to start today. If nothing else, he could keep track of his prayer requests and be able to see how and when the Lord answered.

So after lunch he walked over to the Syllabus, and the scent of old books and fresh coffee transported him back in time. An hour later, he walked out with two purchases: a cup of coffee for the road and a leather-bound journal with two hundred blank pages.

That night, after getting the kids into bed, Chris sat down on the back deck and pulled his new journal from his satchel. He set a timer for ten minutes and started writing:

> *As I was saying before I was so rudely interrupted.... Not sure why I ever stopped journaling. This practice kept me sane through college, kept me focused on the most important things. I'm so thankful for those years. For Maria. For friends like Aaron and Pastor Greg who showed me what it looked like to follow Jesus. I was ready to go anywhere. Do anything. The call to missions was so strong in those days, so clear. It was like God sent me a postcard that said, "You will serve Me among the nations." There was no doubt.*
>
> *And then we all know what happened. Granddad had a stroke. The business he'd spent a lifetime building started to slip away. I didn't really know what I was doing, but I said I'd step in to help. Apparently I did know what I was doing, because we started to*

CHAPTER TWENTY-THREE

make a lot of money. I remember Maria asking in those early years what I thought about missions, but the timing was never right. When we got married, she thought she was marrying a missionary, and now here she was with just another Pennsylvania guy making clocks. The amazing thing? She never complained about it. Never held it against me. Just kept loving me. Kept loving Jesus every day and serving Him.

What happened to me? Did I fall in love with the money, with the idea of being a successful business owner? I admit that I loved it on those days when Granddad was feeling good enough to stop by the shop for a few minutes to chat with the boys, to inspect the product. I could see on his face how proud he was, even if he didn't always have the words to express it.

My story is that life happened. But is this the truth, or just another fiction that people write around their selfish choices? Honestly, I'm not sure. I always thought I was doing the right thing for my family—first for Granddad and Grandma and Mom, and then for Maria and the kids. I don't remember ever deliberately telling God no. Pastor Bernheim likes to say that God is more powerful than our bad decisions. Even if we head down the wrong path, He is able to reroute us. I receive that word.

However we ended up in this place, I dedicate the rest of my days to serving God wholeheartedly. My hope is to wake up every day and tell Him, "I'm open for business. Use me however You want."

So here's the big news: I think He's telling us to pack up and move to the other side of the world. A couple months ago, I don't think I could have even found Indonesia on a map. But sitting here tonight, I realize that God has transformed my heart. He's given me a new heart for the people of Indonesia. I'm ready to lay down my life.

I'm sure that every new missionary has thoughts like this when they're just starting out. We're so inexperienced that we don't even know what we don't know. But here's what I do know. God is great, and God is good. What a concept.

My number one prayer request right now: I'm nervous about going to Indonesia with the mission. I don't know them, and they don't know me. So Father, as You have so many times before, change my heart. Help me to see things as You see them. Speak, for Your servant is listening.

24

THE FOLLOWING WEDNESDAY morning, after ending a tense phone conversation with a wood supplier, Chris was wondering whether he would ever be able to hand off the company to Jim Tucker—or anyone else, for that matter. The business was complex, and he did not relish the idea of teaching a new manager everything that a transition would require. He whispered a prayer for wisdom and pulled Tucker's resume from the top drawer of his desk. He needed to learn more about this guy.

Suddenly, Chris's cell phone chirped to life. It was Maria.

"Hey," she said. "Is this a good time?"

"It's great. What's up?"

"How do you feel about a road trip this Sunday?"

"I'm game," he said. "What do you have in mind?"

"I'm forwarding you an email. Bob Hollins from the mission wrote this morning. He's the Berrys' boss. He wants to meet."

"Bob Hollins," Chris said. "I've been meaning to call him. He probably thinks we're deadbeats for not getting in touch."

He opened the email and started scanning the message.

> Chris and Maria,
>
>   My name is Bob Hollins, and I am the regional director for Asia with Every Tribe Mission. I have been in communication with Orien and Harriet Berry, and they tell me that you are praying about applying for a missions assignment. The Berrys mentioned that you live in Pennsylvania, but your specific location escapes me at the moment. I am writing because I will be speaking at a church in Wilkes-Barre this Sunday. I'm not sure how far that is from you, but if it's feasible I would like to meet you for lunch after the service. If the drive is too far, do not feel bad about telling me so. Please advise.
>
>   In Christ,
>   Bob

The drive would not be too far—just under two hours—and Chris and Maria immediately wrote back to exchange details and confirm the plan.

That Sunday, they walked into the lobby of Cornerstone Church in Wilkes-Barre and spotted Hollins at once. He was posted near a banner for Every Tribe, listening intently to a white-haired woman who had attended the first service that morning. After a few minutes, she walked away and Bob turned to face Chris and Maria.

"Good morning," he said, extending a hand. "I'm Bob Hollins."

"Chris Billings. This is my wife, Maria."

"I thought you might be the Billingses. Great to meet you." His eyes followed the older woman as she passed through the doors into the parking lot.

"That's one of the saddest things I experience in my job," he said, nodding toward her. "I hear the same story at least twice a month.

CHAPTER TWENTY-FOUR

She felt called to missions as a young woman, but ended up marrying a guy who had no interest. Now she's a widow, the kids and grandkids live out of the area, and she's left with a twinge of regret every time a missionary comes through. I'm still not sure how to respond—except to say that God has enough grace for all of us."

During the service, Hollins told the congregation part of his story. He and his wife and children had spent twenty-four years in Cambodia and Thailand before he was appointed to his director role. They had helped to start several churches as well as a gospel magazine and a Bible college. In his sermon that morning, he sounded to Chris like a combination of a revivalist preacher and a college professor. He was logical and linear in his presentation, but there was fire in his words.

"I'm sure you've heard of the unreached," he said. "There are people groups out there that have just a handful of believers in Jesus—a dozen among thousands. But I want to tell you about the *never-reached*. Jesus told His followers to take His good news to the ends of the earth, but two thousand years later there are still tribes and ethnic groups on His planet that have never in all of human history even heard His name. I wish I could stand up here and tell you great stories about how our mission and others have broken through those barriers and introduced Jesus to some of these never-reached tribes. But I can't. Jesus said go, but we've stayed."

At lunch, Hollins was just as blunt. Even before the waitress stopped by to take their orders, he started in on his unofficial interview.

"So, what are you thinking?" he asked Chris. "Are you planning to get an application started?"

"Well," Chris said, "we're getting to the point where we're confident this is the time and Indonesia is the place. But I'm not totally certain that we're supposed to go through the mission. Hearing you today definitely helps, though."

"What's your issue with the agency? And be honest. I don't take this stuff personally."

"A couple of things. I'm an entrepreneur. I prefer to be self-directed, and it's been a long time since I had someone looking over my shoulder. And then the first time I called the mission, it felt like they thought I was a nuisance—like they were just trying to pass me off to someone else. I don't want to be just another number."

Hollins set his coffee mug on the table.

"You don't strike me as the kind of guy who gets thrown off by a little bureaucratic inefficiency," he said. "If you're called, you're called. And the truth is that it really is a family, after you get over the first hump.

"And to your first point, about working independently... I hope you don't take this the wrong way, but you don't have the experience to be on your own. You'll need a veteran missionary to learn from and lean on."

"I agree," Chris said, "and I thought the Berrys could mentor us."

"The Berrys would be ideal mentors, but I'm not going to sign off on that arrangement unless you go through our process. We have housing available, a vehicle, training. We will do everything we can to set you up for success, but I can't commit our resources unless you commit to us as well."

"That makes sense," Maria said. "What would the process look like for us?"

CHAPTER TWENTY-FOUR

"First, we'd have you complete an application," Hollins said. "It's pretty extensive. We'll look at your background, references, finances. If everything looks good at that point, we'll invite you down to our headquarters in Memphis for a week-long training. And because you haven't served in full-time ministry, we'll place you in our apprenticeship program. It's a two-year assignment designed to give you the training, mentoring, and spiritual formation you'll need for a career appointment, if that's what you eventually decide to do. Two-thirds of our career missionaries start this way, so it's something we take seriously. Our apprentices are not afterthoughts."

On the drive home, Chris and Maria rehashed their conversation with Bob. Chris appreciated the missionary's straightforward nature. They definitely didn't have to wonder where he stood.

"I can follow that guy," Chris said. "There are unknowns whatever we decide, but I feel good about moving ahead with an application."

"I'm glad you feel that way," Maria said. "I've already started."

25

IN THE WEEKS THAT followed, Chris and Maria tackled their task lists like people on a mission—which, they knew in the deepest part of their beings, they were.

God had called them. This truly was the time, and Indonesia was the place. But before their vision could become reality, there was work to do. They had to complete their application, which involved tracking down references and transcripts, compiling a personal history, filling out a stack of forms, getting medical and psychological exams, sitting for an interview, and filling out even more forms. They had to prepare their home for rental—the home they had designed and built and grown to love. They had to start learning about the country of their calling. And they had to find and train someone to run the business that Chris had saved and grown to profitability.

In the middle of this forward-looking activity, Chris found comfort in looking back. Since his visit to State College, he had reintegrated journaling into his daily routine. Some nights, he would write for only a minute or two. On others, he would set a timer for ten or twelve minutes and let his thoughts flow, uninterrupted by his internal critic. He didn't evaluate. He didn't edit. He just wrote.

One Wednesday night, as the kids were winding down after church, he grabbed his journal and fell into his favorite chair on the deck. A full moon illuminated the backyard, and millions of insects sang to him from the trees. He opened his journal, read his entry from the previous night, and started writing:

> *I know Pastor Bernheim isn't preaching directly to me—or only to me—but he's been on a roll lately. It seems that every sermon, every single sermon, has my name on it. Maybe he should just place a chair on the platform and we can have a conversation for everyone to listen in on. Tonight was no different.*
>
> *It's no secret that I've had some concerns about joining Every Tribe. I guess part of it is pride. I've always had a healthy belief in my own ability. Maybe too healthy. But it's foolish to think I can take my family to Indonesia and start working with Orien and Harriet and pick up all the skills and knowledge I'll need without anyone else. I can see that, and the Lord has been changing my heart. He's been showing me that I can't do it alone. And even more than that, He's giving me the desire to be part of something bigger than myself or my family. In my interactions with the workers at ETM headquarters, He is giving me a love for them and a love for our future teammates in Indonesia, whoever they might be.*
>
> *Where was I? How did I get here? Oh, yes. Pastor Bernheim. So tonight, his message was from 1 Corinthians 12. Many parts, one body. Okay, God, I think I get the hint. For our bodies to be healthy, we need a diversity of parts and we need all of these parts to be functioning properly. The same is true in the body of Christ.*

CHAPTER TWENTY-FIVE

Pastor laid out three points from this chapter, and they each spoke to me right where I am. I know I won't be able to remember the exact wording he used—he likes alliteration—but this is close enough. First, God is the one who determines our position. In His sovereignty and wisdom, He decides what part we'll be, what role we'll play. He's given us different gifts and abilities. Our place is to be obedient and serve joyfully wherever He's called us.

The second point was that we all need each other, or something like that. If I'm a hand, I need the fingers and thumbs to be functioning well or I won't be able to accomplish my mission. And I also need the legs to work properly and get the whole body into the right position. We all benefit from the contributions of others.

And the last part is that we're all connected to each other. A disconnected kneecap or disconnected eyeball on their own won't accomplish much. They are incredible, amazing, and complex body parts, but they're useless apart from the rest of the body.

So this is something I'll have to pray and think about over the coming days and weeks. What is my place in the body of Christ? What is my place in Every Tribe Mission? When it comes to my company, I know exactly what I need to be and do in order for the team to be successful—and part of my role is also to know what everyone else's job is. I can do that job with my eyes closed and one hand tied behind my back (unless I'm in the shop working on a lathe). But this new life that God is calling us into? No clue. I can't even envision it. My prayer is that the Prince of Peace will bless me with His peace as we step out into the unknown.

An update: As of today, our part of the application process is complete. We've given them everything they've asked for. I think they might still be waiting on some of our references, but there's nothing more for us to do but wait. Bob H. said there's a committee that reviews applications. If we get a thumbs-up from that committee, they'll invite us to headquarters for some training and interviews next month. Bob said since he's already met us, that shouldn't be a big deal — unless our references and psych evaluations turn up any red flags. He said there's a sweet spot on the psych tests. They want to know that we're not too crazy, but just crazy enough. Love that guy.

My prayer for tonight: Father, You know all about the to-do list that's staring us in the face. It sure feels like a ton of work. It really is a ton of work. Help us to not be overwhelmed when we think about everything we still have to do. Help us not to feel anxious. Give us Your peace. Give us Your assurance that You're right here, walking beside us through this process. We know in our heads that You're in this. But sometimes our hearts need a little more convincing. Help us to have great God-honoring attitudes about this process. Give us joy in the journey.

26

EVERY TRIBE MISSION occupies the top three floors of a six-story office building in the heart of Memphis, Tennessee. Several times each year, the agency's home office is overrun by dozens of missionary candidates in the final stages of their application process. Behind closed doors, mission staff members refer to this orientation as The Gauntlet—a full week of training, appointments, prayer gatherings, and interviews.

Maria and Chris Billings flew in on a Saturday afternoon and immediately jumped into their packed schedule. On the first night, they had dinner at a raucous barbecue place with all of the other applicants hoping to serve in Asia. Back in their hotel room that evening, they collapsed on the bed.

"We found our people," Maria said. "It's amazing. We just met them, but it feels like we've known each other our whole lives."

"It's really incredible," Chris said. "I guess when people talk about the missionary family, they're not exaggerating. It felt like a family reunion. Now we just have to learn their names."

As Maria pulled up the next day's schedule on her phone, a pair of unseen warriors huddled around the small table in the corner.

"I'm excited for them," Purity said. "This is a big moment. I love that spark of recognition when brothers and sisters meet for the first time. It's like their spirits are speaking to each other: 'Oh, you belong to the Father? Me too.'... And I think the Father is going to expand their heart for the nations."

"So true," Sword said. "And that's why this is a big job for us. We can't allow anything to hinder what He wants to accomplish here. I visited mission headquarters during dinner. It's a very secure perimeter. It's clear that many of the Most High's followers remember this place in their prayers. Our colleagues appear to be numerous and vigilant—but I did notice signs of the enemy's presence in the neighborhood."

ω

Lunch on Tuesday was a taco bar in the fifth-floor conference room. Chris and Maria got their food and sat with new friends from Seattle, Joe and Heidi, who were headed to Mongolia.

"Tired of drinking from the fire hose yet?" Heidi asked.

"Yeah, talk about information overload," Chris said. "It's all great stuff, but I need more space to process everything."

"Just imagine what our brains will be like at the end of the week," Joe said.

A few minutes later, a young woman approached the table. "Chris and Maria? My name is Chloe. I'm the budget coordinator.

CHAPTER TWENTY-SIX

We were scheduled to meet tomorrow afternoon, but I have to move your appointment up to today. Can you stop by my office at one? Bob said it's okay if you're late for the next session."

When they found Chloe's office, she invited them to sit at a small table in the corner. She opened her laptop and turned it so they could read the document on the screen.

"I will be emailing this to you," she said, "but it can be confusing for people seeing it for the first time. That's why I like to meet everyone in person. I can explain all of the pieces of the puzzle, and you can ask any questions you might have."

The first pages of the document explained the components of the budget—salary, housing, insurance, language school, and what seemed like a hundred other line items. Then Chloe turned to Chris and Maria's individualized budget, which took into account their country of service, family size, and other needs.

She then turned to the final page and pointed out two numbers. "This one here is the monthly commitments you will raise," she said, "and this one is the cash you will need on hand before you receive final clearance."

"I think there's been a misunderstanding," Chris said. "We're planning to be self-funded. We own a business, and the profits will be able to provide for us on the field."

Chloe looked at him as though he were speaking Latin. She turned the laptop toward herself and typed a series of commands.

"I don't see anything here about that," she said. "And honestly, I'm not sure that's something we can do. I've been here three years, and I've never seen that. There were a handful of cases where someone applied part of a military pension toward their budget, but that was guaranteed income."

"The business has a proven track record," Chris said.

"I'm not saying it's not possible, it's just that I don't know what to tell you. Any kind of exception like this starts with the regional director and needs the approval of the leadership team.... When is your interview with Bob Hollins?"

"Thursday morning," Chris said.

"You'll have to bring it up with him at that time," Chloe said. "And you might want to send him an email today with the relevant details and specifically what you're asking. Until I hear from him, I'll just set your budget aside and hold off on the approvals."

When they stepped out of Chloe's office, Maria grabbed Chris's hand and looked him in the eyes. "This is just a miscommunication," she said. "It's going to be all right."

Ω

At nine o'clock on Thursday morning, Bob Hollins's administrative assistant welcomed Chris and Maria into Bob's office.

"Make yourselves comfortable," she said, gesturing to a pair of upholstered armchairs. "Bob was called into an emergency meeting this morning and is running a few minutes late. He shouldn't be long."

Maria settled into one of the chairs, but Chris made his way to a bookcase on the opposite wall. Mixed in with the volumes on theology, missiology, and history were the artifacts of a career spent in Asia. At least a dozen photos showed Bob and his wife alongside people Chris assumed were other missionaries or national church leaders. Chris examined a hat whose name

CHAPTER TWENTY-SIX

he could not begin to guess, a delicate teacup and saucer that he associated with Sri Lanka, and even an ornate yet lethal dagger.

"Sorry I'm late," Bob said as he pulled his door shut. "There's a coup brewing in one of our countries, so we're making sure our logistics are lined up. The fun part of the job."

Chris took his seat next to Maria, and Bob asked him to begin their meeting with prayer. Then after a rundown of the week so far, Bob brought up the big issue on the Billingses' minds: the budget.

"I did have time to read your email yesterday," he said. "First, allow me to apologize. I remember Orien mentioning the possibility that you could be self-funded, but I forgot to follow up with Chloe.... So how much are you capable of contributing each month?"

They discussed the numbers, and Bob leaned back in his chair, crossed his arms over his chest, and stared out the window. After about ten seconds of silence, he nodded and said, "It shouldn't be a problem. We've had similar scenarios with workers in the past — not the same exactly, but similar enough."

Chris and Maria exhaled in relief.

"However," Bob said, "I'm not gonna let you off that easily. I'm gonna have you raise a chunk of your cash budget from other sources — churches, friends, family. I want you to be able to cast vision for what God is calling you to do, and I want you to give people the opportunity to partner with you — and eventually get some of the eternal reward.

"And one other thing," he continued. "Our support-raising process is focused on finances and getting that budget raised, but prayer support is also crucial. I don't want you to miss out on the opportunity to recruit an army of prayer warriors to stand with you. Before I clear you to go to the field, I want to see a list of two hundred fifty people who will commit to praying for your family at least once a week. Raise some cash, show me that list, and we'll let you buy your plane tickets."

27

CHRIS BILLINGS guided his Explorer to the curb, shifted into park, and cut the engine. He took a slow, deep breath and turned to Maria, who was holding a crock-pot full of meatballs.

"We ready to do this?" he asked.

She smiled, nodded, and closed her eyes. "Dear Jesus," she said, "thank You for being with us. Help us to communicate clearly what You want to say to our friends."

"Amen," Chris said. "So be it."

As they made their way up the sidewalk to the house, Chris paused to take in the scene off to his right. Snowshoe Lake glistened in the sunlight of early evening, inviting him to its celebration of summer. Four speedboats churned its surface, muffling the joyful shouts of their passengers.

"I'm gonna miss this," he said.

Maria looked at her husband and waited a beat. "From what I hear," she said, "they do have water in Indonesia."

"Very funny."

As usual, Chris and Maria were the first to arrive, and they immediately began helping their hosts, Andy and Megan, with last-minute preparations. Within ten minutes, six couples filled the kitchen and living room, the usual five plus a new pair, Jim and Elaine Tucker.

About five years earlier, Pastor Fritz Bernheim recognized that his town—and therefore his church—was changing. It was becoming more transient, with many new families moving into the area, some only for the summers. In an effort to build a stronger sense of community within the church, Bernheim canceled the first Sunday-evening service of each month and replaced it with fellowship meals in members' homes. There was no agenda other than food, conversation, and prayer.

Chris and Maria committed to a group at once and made their monthly gathering a priority. Over time, the pastor's vision had become reality. These people were the Billingses' closest friends in the congregation, and tonight they would be the first to hear of their move to Indonesia.

After the meal, as they settled in the living room for prayer, Chris took charge. "Before we get started," he said, "we have some exciting news to share." He and Maria took the next five minutes to explain what God was calling them to—followed by another fifteen minutes answering a barrage of questions.

"All I can say is 'wow,'" Andy said. "Not that you need my permission, but I sense in my spirit that this is God's calling and God's timing for you. I'm sure you still have a lot of questions, but God is in this."

The others nodded in agreement. Megan asked, "So what can we do to help? I imagine you need to raise some money."

CHAPTER TWENTY-SEVEN

"Thankfully, our monthly expenses will be covered by our business," Maria said, "but the mission is asking us to raise a portion of our startup cash."

"How much do you need?"

Maria cleared her throat. "Ten thousand dollars," she said.

Brett, a dentist who had moved his family to Grapevine a few years earlier, leaned forward. "Well," he said, "I don't want to speak for everyone else, but I will anyway. I think this group can take care of a big chunk of that, if not all of it. If we really believe God is calling you—and we do—then I think God is calling us to send you."

"And of course you can count on us to keep you in our prayers," said Liz, Brett's wife. "It sounds like you're going to the front lines."

"We'll definitely need your prayers," Chris said. "The agency doesn't normally make new missionaries report on prayer partners, but our boss said they won't let us go until we have a list of two hundred fifty people who'll pray for us each week."

"Well," Liz said, "you can put us on the *daily* prayer list, if you have one."

"We don't have a daily list," Chris said, "but we'll take anything we can get. The closer we get to leaving, the more I'm seeing the need for prayer warriors."

"If you don't mind my asking," Andy said, "what are you planning to do with your business? Do you have someone lined up to run it for you?"

"That's a great question," Chris said. He glanced at Jim Tucker, who sat with his hands folded in his lap, a thin smile on his face.

"I'm still processing the details, but I believe the Lord is working in that area. He's always provided the right people in the past, and we're sure He'll keep providing in the future."

"It sounds like there's only one thing left to do," Andy said. "Let's gather around Chris and Maria and take their needs to the Lord."

As the humans opened up their communication line to the heavens, the leader of the angelic force, posted on the deck overlooking Snowshoe Lake, scanned the horizon. Sword turned to face Purity, who was completing a circuit of the house.

"There's something we're missing here, but I'm not sure what it is," Sword said. "We must remain vigilant."

28

IN HIS OFFICE later that week, Chris had to force himself to concentrate on his to-do list. It wasn't that he was bored with the work. He still enjoyed his job and the variety it brought to his day. But the simple truth was that he was drawn to something else, something bigger, more urgent. Whenever he had a free moment, he gravitated toward the books at the corner of his desk that were revealing to him the mysteries of life in Indonesia. Guidebooks, history, biography—bit by bit, they were introducing him to the land of his calling. And when the books raised a question they could not answer, the internet's bottomless pit awaited just a few keystrokes away.

Focus, he told himself. *There'll be time for this later.*

Chris used a project-management app on his phone to keep himself on task. Everything he had to do before leaving for Indonesia was on that list. But it seemed as though every item he finished was replaced by two more that he or Maria just thought of. It felt like their departure date was slipping deeper and deeper into the future.

But Chris understood that one task loomed over all of the others. He needed to find someone to manage his company. The shop was not the issue. His foreman, Tom Hansen, could handle everything back there. But he still wasn't sure about the business side. Could Jim Tucker do the job? His sales experience would certainly be useful. But could he handle marketing? Supply chains? Accounting? Payroll? Before even thinking about buying plane tickets, Chris had to replace himself here and make sure the new manager had the training to be successful. The last thing he wanted was to have to put out fires from the other side of the world.

He opened a drawer and pulled out Tucker's resume. No time like the present. Jim had listed three previous employers going back about fifteen years — business names, locations, but no phone numbers.

A quick internet search gave him the number for Tucker's most recent employer, a furniture store in New Jersey. He jotted a few questions on a piece of scrap paper, refilled his coffee mug, and placed the call. Someone on the other end picked up right away.

"Mavis Furniture. This is Alan."

"Hello, Alan. My name is Christopher Billings. I own a furniture manufacturing company in Pennsylvania. I'm calling about a former employee of yours who's applied for a job with us. Is there a manager there I can speak with?"

"That would be me," Alan said. "Who are we talkin' about?"

"Jim Tucker. He says he was a nighttime sales manager there for about seven years."

"Yeah, Jim worked here. I guess it probably was around seven years. And he was a manager for a couple years, but definitely

CHAPTER TWENTY-EIGHT

not the whole time. New owners came in around a year ago, and I don't think they saw eye to eye. They didn't fire him or anything, but they gave the impression they wouldn't be sorry to see him go."

"Huh. So what can you tell me about him?" Chris asked.

"There's not much I'm allowed to say. The new owners said all we can do is confirm that someone worked here. Can't give a reference or anything like that. I've probably said too much already."

"Got it. But I understand your sales history has been pretty strong there?"

"I wouldn't go that far," Alan said. "Before the sale of the company, it was touch and go just about every quarter. Much more stable now."

"All right. Thanks for your time."

"No problem. But make sure you find someone who worked with Jim and is free to talk. If you know what I mean."

"Understood," Chris said. "Thanks again."

Chris was confused. The details he just heard did not line up with the impression Jim had given the first time they met, right here in this office. Or had Chris simply heard what he'd wanted to hear in that first meeting? Either way, he now had more questions about Tucker than answers.

The next business on Jim's resume was a car-rental shop near the Philadelphia airport. Chris typed the name into a search engine and was informed the business was permanently closed. He tried the phone number anyway. An automated voice told him what he already suspected: The line was out of service.

Chris needed some insight into Jim Tucker's prior life, but the trail was going cold. One business remained on the resume — a furniture and appliance outlet Jim worked at a full decade ago. Chris was not hopeful.

Against all odds, however, he managed to get through to the manager, a woman named Juliette.

"Oh, sure, I remember Jim," she said. "He left just after I started here. I think he was upset that my dad, who owns the place, hadn't made him manager."

"What can you tell me about him?"

"He was a friendly enough guy. Most people liked him. His sales numbers were pretty good, from what I remember. But there was one incident that he got caught up in. I'm not sure how much I should tell you."

"Well," Chris said, "I'm thinking of bringing him in and giving him a lot of responsibility and authority. If you know anything that would affect my decision, I would appreciate hearing it."

"Okay," Juliette said. "I want to make it clear that none of this was proven. But we had a major burglary one night. Someone hit us hard. TVs, stereos, DVD players, we even sold computers at the time. Tens of thousands worth of inventory walked out the back door. And it just so happened that our security system malfunctioned that night. The police thought it was an inside job, but they couldn't make a case. And you know who had lock-up duties that night? Jim Tucker. My dad thought Jim was involved somehow. But he was very apologetic afterward. He even broke down in my office the next day, just weeping."

"So what do you make of it?"

"At a minimum, I think he knows more than he ever said."

"Thanks for your candor," Chris said. "I appreciate it."

CHAPTER TWENTY-EIGHT

"My pleasure. And if you see Jim, tell him I have something that belongs to him."

"Yeah? What's that?"

"His final paycheck. About three weeks after the burglary, he disappeared. Didn't show up for his shift, and never said a word to anyone. I still have the check tacked to my bulletin board. This one's expired, of course, but if he has the guts to show his face here again, I'll cut him a new one."

29

AT NINE O'CLOCK the next morning, Chris met in his office with Jane Renfroe, his office manager, and Tom Hansen, his shop foreman. Jane immediately spotted the box of pastries from Snowshoe Lake Bakery.

"Check it out, Hansen," she said. "The boss has something important to tell us. He splurged on the good stuff."

"Am I that obvious?" Chris asked.

"Well…" Tom said.

"So what's up?" Jane asked. "The company's not in trouble, is it?"

"No, we're doing great," Chris said. "Which you know better than anyone. You're in the books every day."

"True," she said. "But I get the impression this is more than a social visit."

"You're right," Chris said. "And I don't know how to say this except to say it. You two are the backbone of this company. You've been here even longer than I have. You worked hard for my granddad, and you've worked hard for me. I appreciate that, and I wanted to tell you this before anyone else.… Maria and the kids and I are moving to Indonesia as missionaries."

Chris stopped talking and allowed them to process the news.

"Are you selling the business?" Jane finally asked.

"No, I couldn't do that," Chris said. "My plan is to bring someone in to help pick up the slack, but I'll be counting on both of you. If you're game, I want to give each of you a bigger role—with a raise, of course."

"I'll help out wherever I can, Chris," Tom said. "You know that.... What's your timeline?"

"We hope to leave sometime this fall," he said. "A lot depends on how quickly I can bring someone else on board. I have a guy in mind, but I'm not confident he can just come in and take on my full portfolio. I think the best solution is to divide the work among the three of you—you two plus the new guy."

"Whatever you think is best," Jane said. "Do we know this mystery man?"

"No, he's new to the area. And I want you to know I'm not gonna force anyone on you. If you don't think he's a good fit, I'll trust you. In the meantime, I want you to think about which aspects of the operation you'd be comfortable overseeing. Then we'll hash things out over the coming weeks. I have some ideas, but I value your input as well."

"I'll do whatever you ask, Chris, but I don't wanna be stuck in no office," Tom said. "No offense."

"No need to worry about that. I wouldn't think of doing that to you. Your domain is the back shop."

Tom nodded. "Sounds good to me."

"Speaking of the shop," Chris said, "I'm planning to head back there right now and let the guys know what's happening. Anything in particular I need to bring up?"

CHAPTER TWENTY-NINE

"Just let 'em know the show'll go on," Tom said. "I don't want anyone to start thinking about finding a new job."

☼

Thirty minutes later, Chris was back at his desk. He ran through his conversations with Jane and Tom and the guys in the back. Overall, he was happy with how things had gone. The men were especially pleased that Tom would have a larger role in the operation. And Chris felt good to finally have everything out in the open. Now he could focus on getting to know Jim Tucker.

Chris refilled his coffee mug, grabbed a pastry from the box, and opened an atlas of Asia he had checked out of the library. He lost track of time as he studied the islands of Indonesia. He read the names of cities and villages and wondered how many followers of Jesus lived in them—if any. He prayed that the Father would send the light of His good news, and he gave thanks to God that he would someday become the answer to his own prayer.

A familiar voice at the door snapped Chris out of his thoughts. "How's my favorite clock maker?" Aaron Patterson asked as he stepped into the room.

"And how's my favorite campus minister?" Chris said, rising from his chair to greet his old college roommate. "What's this all about?"

"We had a support-raising appointment an hour away and thought we'd surprise you," Aaron said. "We did text Maria to make sure you'd be here."

Aaron enveloped Chris in one of the bearhugs he was known for.

"Well, I'm glad you did," Chris said. "You said 'we.' Does that mean Amy's with you?"

"Yup. She just dropped me off and is headed to your place. Maria invited us to stick around for dinner."

Aaron helped himself to some coffee and a danish and settled into a chair. "Anything new to report on the missions front?" he asked.

"We are officially approved and ready to go public," Chris said. "Our pastor's interviewing us on stage during the service this Sunday, so word will spread pretty quickly."

They discussed the Billingses' projected timeline and finances — and their need to recruit a specific number of prayer partners.

"Two fifty?" Aaron said. "Not a problem. You'll get most of that from your church, and the campus ministry can cover the gap with our alumni and students." He paused to take a sip from his mug. "Our semester starts in a few weeks. If someone can get a video of your interview this Sunday, we can play it during one of our large-group meetings. Or better yet, if you're still around, you and Maria can come up to campus and do it in person."

"Seriously? I'd love to do that. Especially if we can grab some pizza at Gino's."

"It's a deal. Vegetarian, right?" Aaron almost fell out of his chair laughing at his own wit.

Sword glided into the hall for a sweep of the building's perimeter. "Two hundred fifty prayer warriors," he said. "It's a start."

30

THE WORSHIP BAND played its final chords, and Pastor Fritz Bernheim moved into position behind the music stand he used as a pulpit.

"Thank you, musicians, for leading us in worship this morning," he said. "Scripture tells us that our God inhabits the praises of His people, and we have had the privilege of His presence today.... Before I get into the Lord's message to us this morning, I want to take a few minutes to address a topic that is near and dear to my heart: global missions. It's appropriate that missions — God's great mission in the world and our role in that mission — is part of a worship service like this one. An author and pastor named John Piper wrote that missions exists because worship doesn't. I take that to mean that missions is still necessary because there are places in the world where worship of the One True God is not yet taking place. Worship is the fuel and goal of missions.

"Friends," he continued, "we have a rare privilege this morning. While Lakeside has financially supported dozens of missionaries serving around the world, we have never sent missionaries out directly from our church family. Well, that is about to change. I would like to invite Maria and Chris Billings to join me up here."

A murmur rippled across the congregation as Chris and Maria mounted the steps and self-consciously crossed the platform.

"So, Chris," Bernheim asked, "anything new with your family?"

Chris waited for the chuckles to die down before officially breaking the news: "We have been approved as missionaries with Every Tribe Mission and plan to leave for Indonesia sometime this fall."

The congregation erupted in applause, catching Chris by surprise. But the smiles on the faces of his church family told him their reaction was genuine — even though the clapping lasted a bit longer than he would have preferred.

"That's wonderful news, wonderful news," the pastor said. "We will certainly miss you around here, but we're thrilled to send you to a nation that so dearly needs the message and love of Jesus. Now Maria, can you tell us about the focus of your family's work in Indonesia?"

"Our first term will be two years, and that time is really all about learning," she said. "We'll be studying language and culture, adapting to a new way of life, and serving our mentors in whatever ways we can. They are veteran missionaries who have been involved in church planting, discipleship, and a Bible college. We've been told to be flexible."

"That's good advice," Bernheim said. "And I'm thrilled that your mentors are people I have known for about four decades — Orien and Harriet Berry. Some of you might remember the

CHAPTER THIRTY

Berrys. Our church has supported them for years.... Chris, what does this move mean for your children and their schooling?"

"First of all, they are very excited about being missionaries. Of course, they'll miss their friends here, but they view this as a great adventure with Jesus. As for education, they'll start out in an online school that's affiliated with our mission. And at the same time, they'll begin Indonesian language lessons."

"What about living arrangements?" Bernheim asked. "Do you know what that will look like?"

Maria said, "When we first arrive, we'll live in a house right on the Bible college property. The Berrys live nearby, and they said we can reevaluate the situation after a few months. The utilities aren't always reliable, but we've been told it's a nice place."

"Okay, Chris," Bernheim said. "Now the big question: How can we support you? What are your needs right now?"

"Two things," Chris said. "We do need some startup cash for airfare and other upfront expenses. But the big thing is prayer support. Oswald Chambers said that prayer doesn't prepare us for the greater work; prayer *is* the greater work. So we need prayer partners. In fact, our mission is requiring us to recruit two hundred fifty people who will pray for us at least once a week. So if you can commit to that, we have prayer cards and a sign-up sheet out in the lobby. We need your prayers."

"Two fifty seems a tad low to me," Bernheim said. "We have at least three hundred in the room today." He turned his gaze toward his congregation. "Friends, can I give you some blunt pastoral counsel right now? If you already pray regularly, you can add the Billings family to your list. I believe it's our responsibility as their church family. And if you haven't developed a discipline of prayer, now is the time. Grab one of their prayer cards, write your name on their sign-up sheet, and pick a time to pray for them every week. Sound good?"

Bernheim then invited the Billings children to the platform, along with the church's deacons and missions board. "Let's gather around this family and commission them in the name of the Lord Jesus," he said. "And let's dedicate ourselves to support them in every way possible. They might be going out under the banner of Every Tribe Mission, but they are *our* missionaries."

31

CHRIS COLLAPSED into his chair on the deck, exhausted yet energized by the day he'd just experienced. It all began with their big announcement in church that morning. After the service, it seemed as though he and Maria hugged every person in the congregation. The outpouring of love was overwhelming, and more than two hundred people signed up to pray for them regularly. They shook hands, received hugs, and chatted in the lobby for a full hour as the kids played foosball in the youth room. And just before they headed out the door, Pastor Bernheim pulled them aside and told them the offering to support their work was almost seven thousand dollars.

Then after the evening service, a couple in their mid-twenties invited the Billings family to join them for dessert at a restaurant near the church. They said they sensed God was calling them into missions as well, and they had a lot of questions. Did they have time tonight?

"Of course," Maria had said at once. "We'd love to join you."

Now they were back at home, the kids were in bed, Maria was taking a well-deserved bath, and Chris opened his journal to a fresh page.

> *What a week! It's amazing how quickly life can change. Seven and a half days ago, only Pastor and Gloria knew about our plans. Then we told our fellowship group. Great response. Then I told my employees. Good response. Then today we announced it to the whole church. Overwhelming response. Seems like people really want to get rid of us!*
>
> *I don't feel any different, but I can see how some people are starting to look at us in a new way. Like we're special or something. I guess when some people hear the word "missionary," they have preconceived ideas about what that means. To me, it simply means that we're being obedient to what God has asked us to do. I don't want to be placed on a pedestal by anyone, and I know we definitely don't deserve to be placed on a pedestal. We're just normal Jesus followers who said yes to Him.*
>
> *In the business world, a "yes man" is seen as a negative. With good reason. I don't want to employ anyone who simply agrees with everything I say. If we have two people in the company who agree about everything, then one of us is unnecessary. As a leader and manager, I need people around me who will ask critical, thoughtful questions about my plans and ideas.*
>
> *But in the Kingdom of God, may we all be "yes men" and "yes women." May we all respond with a "yes" even before we think of what the consequences might be. Even before we consider what anyone might think of us. Because God's ideas are always flawless. As a business owner, I have to recognize that I have blind*

spots. There are perspectives that I cannot see. That's why I need others to challenge me and process ideas with me. But because God's plans are perfect, there's nothing we can contribute to the process by questioning them.

Am I rambling? Yes. Here's the takeaway: Human leaders need other voices in the room. But God does not. All He wants from us is "yes."

I'm not going to name names, but I talked with a guy after the service this morning who left me speechless. He said, "I think it's great that God has called you into missions. But I'm glad He's never called me. I'm not sure I could do it. I love sports too much." This guy is hoping and praying that Jesus never calls him because he cares too much about the Eagles, Phillies, Sixers, and Flyers. He can't imagine a life where his teams' schedules aren't dictating his calendar. I really didn't know what to say. I had a few thoughts run through my head, but I don't think they would have been received well.

What a contrast to Logan and Courtney, the young couple we met with tonight. They seem so eager to serve Jesus. And they had great questions about missions. It's clear that they've been thinking about this for a while. How did we know God was calling us? How did we know Indonesia was the place? How did we navigate the application process? What are we doing about financial support? I hope our answers were helpful. All we can do is share our own experience and pray with them.

As I ate my pie — cherry a la mode, which was incredible — I had the sense that this is part of our calling. Yes, we will represent Jesus among the never-reached in Indonesia. But we also represent our church and our agency. Part of our role now is helping people *to see that God wants us to be "yes men" and "yes women." Part of what we do is listen, ask questions, answer questions, and help people process what it means to be called. May the Spirit equip us to do it well.*

My big prayer focus for the week concerns the business. Specifically: Is Jim Tucker the right guy to add to the team? I have some questions, and I plan to meet with him this week. It seems as though the Lord has brought him here for this time and purpose, but I don't want to assume anything. I need wisdom.

32

ON TUESDAY MORNING, five minutes before ten, Chris pushed open the glass door of The Daily Grind, his favorite coffee shop in downtown Grapevine. A ringing bell over the door announced his arrival, and he scanned the room for an empty table. Instead of finding a seat, however, he spotted Jim Tucker waving at him.

Chris slalomed through the disorderly crowd, and Jim rose to shake his hand.

"You're early," Chris said, glancing at the clock on the wall. "Didn't expect you here already."

"Yeah, that's one thing about me. Can't stand being late for anything."

"You too? When I was a kid, it seemed like we were always running behind. I swore to myself that I wouldn't live like that. Too stressful."

"Yup," Jim said. "If I'm honest with you, I can get pretty judgmental when people are consistently late. It affects how I view their character."

"I hear ya.... Hey, why don't you save our table, and I'll order our drinks. What are you having? It's on me."

"Green tea would be perfect."

When Chris returned to the table, he pulled Jim's resume out of the monogrammed leather portfolio his grandparents gave him when he graduated from Penn State. "So, Jim, thanks for meeting with me on short notice."

"Not a problem," he said. "It's my pleasure."

"As you know, our news is public and we're barreling toward a big change. It's looking like we could head overseas within a couple of months. The major hurdle right now, in my mind, is my company. I have some highly qualified, dependable people there, but no one is capable of sliding in and taking on all of my responsibilities. I'm beginning to see that my duties will have to be spread out among a number of different people."

Jim nodded slowly. "Makes complete sense," he said. "It sounds like you're involved in every aspect of the company."

"That's accurate. And the biggest gap I see is in sales. I have someone who does a great job with payroll and bookkeeping. I have an excellent manager in the back shop. The guys love him. But I don't have anyone with experience in sales and marketing, the public-facing roles. And I can see how your experience could help us out in those areas."

"I appreciate that," Jim said. "I'm a people person, and that's been my professional focus."

"I do have a few, uh, concerns, however," Chris said. "I know I didn't ask you for references when we first met, but I placed a few calls recently. I got through to a couple of the businesses you listed on your resume, and their comments have raised some questions."

CHAPTER THIRTY-TWO

"Oh, really? I have to say, that's surprising. I'm proud of my work at each of those places.... But I guess it depends on who you talked to."

"What do you mean by that?"

"Well," Jim said, "let me put it like this. Those are sales environments, and sales is competitive. If you have five sales reps selling the same product, the boss can look at the numbers and see who's doing the work. The guys at the top of the list are gonna get the love, and the others might feel slighted. We're all working for the same company, but not everyone views it as a team sport."

"Was it like that at Mavis Furniture?"

"As a matter of fact, it was. It was a pretty collegial place for a while, but then a new owner came in. It became much more cutthroat. My numbers were still strong, but the company was encouraging some practices that were borderline unethical. I didn't need the job, so I walked away.... I had some tough conversations with the new managers on my way out, but I can get you in touch with the previous owners. They can give you a pretty accurate picture of my time there."

"I would appreciate that.... And there was one other call — Madison Furniture and Appliance in New Jersey. Sounds like you had a tough situation there right before you left."

"Yeah, the end was rough," he said. "There was a major burglary one night after I closed. I know I locked everything up according to procedure, but the security cameras in the alley out back weren't working that night. The manager thought that was suspicious, but the fact was the cameras had been malfunctioning for months at that point. Some nights they would be fine, and then they would go out. I felt terrible about that.

"I got along great with the owner, a guy named Julius Butler. Great sense of humor. But he started slipping at the end. Early dementia. He ended up hiring his daughter as manager. Juliette was her name. She was kinda paranoid. Thought all the employees were trying to steal from her dad. Which couldn't have been further from the truth. We had several churchgoers on that staff, but Juliette didn't like that one bit. She was an atheist—and a vocal one at that."

"She said you left without giving notice. She still has your last paycheck."

He laughed. "After ten years? No, I didn't run off. Well, I guess I did run off, but I had a good conversation with Julius before I left. My son was in trouble at the time, up in Boston, and I had to get up there to help him out. I was already planning on giving two weeks' notice, but Julius sent me off with his blessing. Said he'd take care of everything with Juliette. Guess it slipped his mind.

"Chris, I appreciate you giving me the chance to clear the air. I can see how you'd have questions after talking with Juliette and whoever you talked to at Mavis—Jerry or Alan or whoever it could've been. I'd have concerns too. But that's not who I am. I'm happy to get you some names and numbers to put your mind at ease."

"That sounds good to me," Chris said. "Shoot me an email with two or three names and numbers, and we'll reconnect in the next week or so."

"You got it. If I were in your shoes, I'd do the same thing. You can't be too careful."

33

WILL BILLINGS placed his ball on the tee and turned it ever so slightly so that the logo pointed toward the hole four hundred yards downrange. He settled into his stance, grasped his driver a little too tightly, took a deep breath, balanced his weight evenly on both legs—and then swung as hard as he could.

The ball immediately started slicing away from Will's intended target, heading for the trees that marked the course's eastern boundary.

"Do you see it?" he asked. "I lost it right away."

"I think I have it," Chris said. "Just past that big oak."

Will picked up the broken tee, cursed under his breath, and slammed the club into his bag. He plopped down behind the steering wheel of the cart and watched as Chris drilled his shot down the left side of the fairway.

The Billings brothers had played a monthly round of golf together for the past ten years, except for a few months each winter when the course was closed. They'd started when Will came back home to teach at the high school, and he realized the tradition would soon end now that Chris was moving to the other side of the world. Will had hoped the idea would pass, but that was looking more and more unlikely. They would have to squeeze in a few extra rounds this year.

On this Saturday morning, they had the course to themselves. They were the first customers of the day, alone with the squirrels and rabbits and the birds that favored the water hazards. A thin blanket of dew on the greens glistened in the rising sun.

It was a perfect day for golf. If only they possessed an aptitude for the game.

"You know," Will said as he drove the cart in the general direction of his wayward ball, "I think I've figured out my problem."

"Yeah? Your club face is too open?"

"No. That might be the case, but my problem is that I take this way too seriously. I play one round a month. I never spend any time on the driving range. I've never taken lessons. So why should I expect to be any good at this? Of course I'm gonna be in the trees and water all day."

"That," Chris said, "might be the wisest thing you've ever said."

At the end of the round, the brothers initiated the second phase of their tradition: They made their way to the clubhouse dining room, where the loser treated the winner to the weekend brunch buffet. From their vantage point on the top floor of the clubhouse, they watched the action on the ninth and eighteenth greens below them. "Tell me you won't miss this," Will said, gesturing toward the course.

"Of course I'll miss it. I'll miss a lot of things about living here. But honestly, I don't play golf for the golf. This is just a way to spend a little time with you. That's what I'll miss the most—just the two of us out there looking for our golf balls in the woods."

CHAPTER THIRTY-THREE

Will ate a forkful of hash browns and watched a guy miss a four-foot putt on the final hole. "I want you to know something," he said. "I'm not happy—"

"Big surprise," Chris said.

"Let me finish.... I'm not happy that you're leaving. I can't fake happiness, so I won't bother trying. For my own reasons, I wish you were staying. But I'm happy *for you*. If that makes any sense. You get to do the one thing you really wanted to do when you finished college. And for years, it looked like it would never happen. So I'm trying to see this from your perspective. And if you say God is telling you to do it, who am I to say He's not? You know I believe in God, but I don't think He's ever told me anything—at least that I can hear. But that doesn't mean He's not talking to you and Maria in a way that you can hear. I know you. I trust you. And if you say this is what you're supposed to do, then I'll believe you and support you."

He took a sip of coffee and turned his attention back to the activity on the greens.

Chris cleared his throat. "Wow," he said. "I can't imagine that was easy to say, and it really means a lot to me."

"Yeah, I know you don't need my blessing, but I wanted you to know that I'm not mad at you or anything like that. Hearing the news the way I did, well, it was just a shock.... And don't worry about Mom. We'll take good care of her."

"Can I ask you something else?" Chris said.

"Sure. Whatever you need."

"If anything happens to me and Maria in Indonesia—"

"Stop right there. You know I'll do everything I can for those kids. But we don't need to think about that."

34

"Hello, friends," Bob Hollins said. "Can everyone hear me?"

The miracle of technology had shrunk the world, allowing the mission executive to hold a meeting with his oldest missionaries on one side of the world and two of his newest on the other.

"You sound great," Maria said as she leaned toward her laptop. "Can you see and hear us?"

"It's like you're in the room next door," Bob said. "Orien and Harriet, how are things in Indonesia?"

Harriet Berry started speaking, but the others heard nothing.

"Harriet," Bob said, "I think you're muted."

Harriet glanced at Orien, and they inspected their screen together. They found the proper icon and clicked it, activating their microphone.

"Sorry about that," Orien said, sliding his glasses up his nose. "I guess we've become a cliche—the old people who can't keep up with technology."

"Old has nothing to do with it," Bob said. "Even the young people I meet with need to be reminded about the mute button."

"It really is amazing to see your faces," Harriet said. "Our boys years ago used to watch *Star Trek* or *Star Wars*, one of those, and the characters had phones with little TV screens on them. And here we are looking at your smiling faces.... One of the grandkids had a birthday last week, and we were able to watch him blow out his candles and open his gifts."

"So where are you now, Bob?" Orien asked.

"Tokyo. Just flew in yesterday for a few days of meetings. Then off to Bangkok to see the team there, then back to Memphis. On one of these trips I'll have to swing by your place."

"We would love it," Harriet said. "You're welcome anytime. The guest room awaits."

"Let's plan on it," Bob said. "Maybe after the Billings crew is on the field for a few months. And speaking of that: Chris and Maria, I have some great news for you. I just approved you for departure. The office will send details on booking your flights, but from our end of things, you're good to go."

"That's great news," Chris said. "We're so excited to get there."

"So what are your plans at this point?" Bob asked. "Do you have a departure date in mind?"

"I think we can be ready to go in a couple of weeks," Chris said. "I've hired a guy to help run the company, and his training is going well. And we still have a few things to do around the house, but it's not much."

"Harriet and Orien, how does that sound to you?" Bob asked. "Would you be able to receive them in two weeks?"

"I would feel better about three weeks," Harriet said. "I know how much work they have in front of them, and I'd hate to have them arrive here totally exhausted."

CHAPTER THIRTY-FOUR

"That's what I was thinking as well," Bob said.

"And it'll give us a little more time to get the house ready," Orien said. "I went over there a few days ago. No one has lived there since the Australian family left. When was that? Two years ago now? Nothing major, but the guys at the Bible school will have to take care of a few repairs."

"Chris and Maria, how does that sound?" Bob asked. "If it's okay with you, let's look at a departure in three weeks."

"Works for us," Maria said. "I won't argue with more time to pack."

"One of the reasons I wanted to schedule this call is to give you a chance to ask me or the Berrys any questions you might have," Bob said. "So what's on your mind?"

Over the next thirty minutes, Chris and Maria worked through their list and asked their leaders about everything from luggage requirements to language study to grocery shopping to what a typical day would look like.

Before signing off, Bob left the Billingses with a final set of instructions: "Chris and Maria, I can't think of better mentors in our entire organization than the Berrys. You don't know how fortunate you are to have them.... We'll talk again before you leave, but I want to pass on what our regional director told us at the beginning of our first term a thousand years ago. From my point of view, this is what a successful first term looks like: Learn the language, make some local friends, and be excited about going back. That's what a win looks like."

35

SWORD AND LIGHT rounded the back corner of the garage just in time to catch a glimpse of movement at the tree line.

"You saw that, right?" Sword asked.

"Not one of ours," Light said.

"Position yourself in the middle of the backyard, and I will alert the others. Make yourself obvious."

Sword shot ahead toward the deck at the back of the house. On his way there, he scanned the bedroom windows. All was quiet and dark on this side except for Chris and Maria's room upstairs, from which a dim light shone. At the moment Sword reached the deck, Purity and Bravery exited the house side by side, having completed their scheduled sweep of the interior. Glory and Dew arrived from their surveillance on the opposite side of the house.

"What's up, boss?" Purity asked.

"Some activity at the edge of the yard," Sword said. "They're getting bolder by the day." He sent Glory around to the front door, instructed Dew to remain on the back deck, and quickly organized a sortie into the forest. "Defend yourselves if necessary," he said, "but do not initiate. We want to let them know that we know what they're up to."

Sword, Light, Purity, and Bravery fanned out across the backyard and penetrated the dark woods. They were methodical in their inspection but took no measures to conceal themselves. Sword once sensed a presence behind an ancient maple, but by the time he got there the scene was clear. He wondered whether the enemy was attempting to lure a contingent away from the house in order to stage an attack—although that would have been out of character for the demons posted in the vicinity. Up to this point, they had seemed content simply to monitor the comings and goings around the home. Maybe they were getting bored.

When he was convinced there was no credible threat for the moment, Sword looped around to the south and inched his way back to the house. When he stepped into the yard, he saw that Purity and Light had already arrived. Only Bravery was still in the woods.

After ten minutes of silent observation, Light sidled up to Sword. "Any cause for concern, chief?" he asked. "I can head back out."

"Not yet. If he was in danger, he would have raised an alarm."

"Unless he was taken by surprise."

"Yes, I suppose there's a first time for everything.... For now, we'll wait."

Ten more minutes passed, and Sword seriously began to consider dispatching a search party. Just then, Bravery entered the yard near the garage. Sword met him, and the two talked privately for a couple of minutes.

CHAPTER THIRTY-FIVE

"Everyone," Sword called to his team, "let's gather in the kitchen."

When they settled around the table, Sword addressed Bravery: "Tell them what you told me."

"Based on what I've observed, I do not believe they were intentionally showing themselves. Therefore, I do not believe this was an attempt to draw us out from the house. My opinion is this was an isolated incident of either boredom or carelessness or a combination of the two. However, my line into the forest carried me in the direction of the children's treehouse. As I approached the structure, still some distance away, I saw two distinct beings flee in the opposite direction. One of them could have been the scout you saw at the tree line, but there is no way to be sure. Either way, it's clear the enemy has been using the treehouse as a staging point. So those of us assigned to the children must be aware of this and never leave them unattended outside the house. In addition, if these demons are claiming the treehouse, at least temporarily, this is their closest staging base thus far.... One other thing. And perhaps this is most important. As the two beings took flight from the treehouse, I decided to pursue with all due haste. I calculated that they would not engage and that, if they did, I could hold my own against them. So I followed them across the brook, hoping they would make a mistake. They did. They led me right to the clearing just beyond the S-curve in the brook. As I approached, at least six or seven others scurried into the brush. As we know, this means there are more out there than we had previously counted. The good news is that all of these demons appear to be small. They're watchers, not necessarily brawlers."

"Thank you," Sword said, "for that thorough assessment of the situation. It seems clear to me that the enemy has become aware of this family's plans. They are allocating more resources in this direction. But based on past experience, I would be shocked if there were an outright attack on this side."

"Agreed," Purity said. "The enemy will most likely wait until the humans arrive at their destination. The attack will come when they are tired, possibly ill, and not as vigilant."

"Still, we must not let our guard down now," Sword said. "Let us remain watchful. I have received word that reinforcements are on the way. The prayer band supporting this family is growing in number, consistency, and fervency. Their pleas for protection are reaching the Most High every day. And when the new forces arrive, we will work to set an impenetrable hedge around the family until the day of departure. When that day comes, the six of us will accompany them to Indonesia. And maybe others. As we know, our numbers are not as great in that land. But, on the strength of the prayers of the saints, that will soon change."

"May it be so," Light said.

36

AT THE PRECISE MOMENT when Sword wrapped up his team meeting in the kitchen, Chris Billings opened his journal in the study upstairs. Most of the family's books, along with other belongings, had been boxed up and moved to a storage unit in the back corner of the Custom Clock and Furniture property. The bookcases and desk and chairs in the study would remain for the renters who were scheduled to move in two weeks later—one week after Chris, Maria, and the kids would board a jet for Asia.

The previous weeks had been a whirl of activity for Chris, both at home and the office. He typically started his day before sunrise and returned to the house in the gathering dark. By the time he found his way to the bedroom, he was often too exhausted mentally and physically to compose more than a few lines. The night before, in fact, he'd fallen asleep in his chair while thinking about what he wanted to write. But on this night, he would do whatever it took to summarize his thoughts for posterity. He tried to picture himself as an old man rediscovering this very journal in a dusty cardboard box and reliving the emotions and memories of these days. It was much easier, however, imagining someone else reading them — maybe Bethany or Hannah, maybe his far-off grandchildren. For himself, and for his future audience, he wrote:

T-minus seven days and counting until our departure. It still doesn't seem real. When exactly will it feel like more than a dream? When we're on the way to the airport? When we're on the plane? When we finally land in Indonesia? I'm actually looking forward to the flight, especially the first one, the long one. Although I usually don't sleep well on planes, I'm hopeful this is the time that changes. Being exhausted should help, right?

It's been a busy few weeks, to say the least. I finally pulled the trigger and hired Jim Tucker. I've had questions about him. Is he a good fit? Am I getting the full story? If I wasn't desperate, and if I wasn't going anywhere, would I even consider hiring the guy and letting him represent Granddad's company? Can I afford to bring him in? Can I afford not to?

I finally tracked down a couple people he used to work with. They said pretty good things about him. One guy told me Jim always had good numbers but never came across as pushy. That's what I'm looking for. I think our product is good enough that I don't need to talk anyone into buying anything. Either they want to buy or they don't. But I need someone to at least make the calls and follow up on those who are interested.

Jim's references set my mind at ease, but I needed to see that he could get along with Jane and Tom. So I brought him in to the shop one day and let them interview him — ask him whatever they wanted. I went home to help with the packing and then went

CHAPTER THIRTY-SIX

back to the office later. They both said they liked him and thought he would be a good fit. They got the impression he was a man of integrity. If they'd said they didn't want him, I'm not sure what I would have done.

Then Aaron P. invited us to speak at the campus ministry meeting earlier this week. I can't describe how meaningful that was. We probably should have said no. It took up most of the day, and we really don't have time at this point to do that kind of thing. And Aaron wouldn't have minded if we said we couldn't swing it. But we went anyway. Maria and I don't get back to Penn State that often, so we made sure we left enough time to walk around campus and reminisce.

And the gathering was amazing! Such a joy to be around students who love Jesus and want to share His love with the world. We didn't preach a sermon or anything—just told our story going back to our student days. I think it helped some of them see a path to missions. We didn't give an altar call, but Aaron came up at the end and did a great job tying in what we shared with a call to obey Jesus no matter what He asks and no matter where He sends us. And part of that is Jesus's invitation to follow Him. He said four students raised their hands and said they wanted to become followers of Jesus. I know the leaders will help form these students into disciples, which is what it's all about.

And Maria got to meet a couple players on the women's soccer team. One of them even wears her old number seven. Not saying that has any meaning or anything, but it was still cool.

I've felt a burden for the kids recently. They're all still excited, but they're also beginning to see what they'll be giving up by living on the other side of the world. They're seeing some of their friends *for the last time in what could end up being years. And when they come back, some of these friendships will pick up right where they left off, but most of these kids will just move on without them. So I pray for their emotional and spiritual health. I pray that heavenly warriors will watch over them and keep them safe from harm no matter where they set foot. I pray that the Spirit of God will guard their hearts and minds. It's not an easy time to be a kid. I know that God loves my kids even more than I ever could. Not sure how that's possible, but I believe it's true. I place Bethany, Hannah, and Timmy into Your hands, Lord. I know You can do a better job of protecting them than I can. I trust Your plans for their lives. Give them eyes to see the world as You see it. Let nothing stand in the way of them becoming the people You have created them to be.*

37

THE LAST OF the worshippers left the mosque in a cheerful mood, happy to spend a few minutes together before continuing the duties of the day. The prayer gathering on Friday, *Jumaat*, was the best-attended of the week, and the larger crowd made for a celebratory atmosphere. Soraya, always the last to leave, confirmed he and Bandu were alone and locked the door from the inside.

"Follow me," the shaman said, leading his son to the front corner of the mosque. "Sit."

Soraya and Bandu faced each other and sat crosslegged next to the mimbar, rather than in the direction of Mecca, as was customary during prayers.

Soraya said, "Nyale wishes for me to teach you a new way to pray. When the others join us at the appointed times, we pray to Allah in the prescribed manner, according to the book. But when we are alone, we will seek Nyale. He will give us power and insight to lead and protect this people."

"Just tell me what to do, father," Bandu said. "I desire the power to heal my daughter. Your granddaughter."

"I know you do, my son. But for now, you will sit and I will conjure the presence. If Nyale chooses to meet us, we will know."

An unseen spirit hovering over the mimbar summoned a messenger that was loitering near the door. "Tell the master that the spell caster has called for him. He is with his son."

The messenger flew off at once to Nyale's nest in the trees above the village. Upon arrival, it bowed slightly and relayed the news. Nyale turned to a trio of demons nearby. "Follow me," he said. "Let's have some fun with the humans."

In the mosque, Nyale was pleased to hear Soraya reciting an incantation he had taught the shaman's grandfather decades earlier. For minutes, the demon did nothing but listen. He then grabbed the spirit named Fear, whispered instructions in its ear, and released it to torment Bandu. The shaman's son visibly reacted to whatever Fear was telling him. Nyale wished he could read minds, but sometimes it was more entertaining to imagine what his subjects were thinking.

Nyale sent Deception and then Pride with more messages for Bandu. Finally Nyale said, "Clear the room. I have some things to teach this *dukun*." The master of the village drifted to the floor of the mosque and enveloped his loyal servant.

An hour later, Nyale floated through the roof just as Bandu and Soraya opened the door. Soraya, bent over and drenched in sweat, clutched his son's arm as he shuffled home.

A messenger approached Nyale. "Master, you have a visitor," the spirit said. "It appears to be your regular territorial report."

Nyale made himself comfortable in his perch and called for the visitor. A small spirit with beady eyes and pointed ears bowed before him. "Nyale," it said in a buttery voice that did not

CHAPTER THIRTY-SEVEN

match its appearance, "I bring greetings from the prince of Asia. He has received reliable intelligence that many followers of the Most High are making plans to come to this group of islands in order to disseminate the story of the Son of the Most High."

"As is the case every month, no?"

"That is true," the visitor said. "I delivered a very similar message to you just four weeks ago."

"Very similar? I believe it was the same message as last month. And the month before that. And the month before that. And every month for the past forty years."

"That may be the case. However, the prince has received intelligence that some of these visitors are intent on infiltrating the last nations that still have no subjects calling on the name of the Most High."

"Again, this is the same report I hear every month. And you will go on to the next tribe and tell them the same thing. And the same to the next."

"Yes, but the prince has heard rumors that your island has been identified."

Nyale shuddered ever so slightly. "Rumors?" he asked.

"At this point, unconfirmed rumors. The prince reminds you to remain watchful."

"As always, my friend. As always."

"Our master has lofty expectations for the Merapu, Nyale. He does not deal well with disappointment."

"I am well aware, my friend. I will see you next month. Give the prince my greetings and report that all is well."

Jumaat was normally a day for Nyale to celebrate his hold over this tribe. He took pride in the way he had blurred the lines between their Islamic practices and worship of himself. But the visitor's report left him in a foul mood.

Rather than being praised for creating a stronghold around the Merapu, I receive nothing but scrutiny and criticism. Where is my reward? Where is my recognition? The servants of the Most High have known about this island for years. And what has come of it? Nothing. This lackey speaks of rumors. You want to talk about rumors? Well, this entire tribe is a rumor. It's totally cut off from the outside world. And why is that? It's because I am here remaining watchful. For hundreds of years!

Nyale called Sickness to his side and gave his orders: "Before sunrise tomorrow, you are to pay a visit to everyone in this village. Do not take any lives, but leave no doubt that I am in charge and I am not pleased."

38

"Okay, kids," Chris called from the doorway of the study. "Family meeting."

It was five days before departure, and he needed to get a handle on the packing situation. He wanted to call it a fiasco, but he restrained himself.

When the children entered the room, they saw ten suitcases spread out on the floor. In front of one was a piece of paper with Bethany's name written on it. Four others identified the suitcases assigned to Hannah, Timothy, Mom, and Dad.

"What's this?" Bethany asked.

"The airline says that, as a family, we get a total of ten pieces of luggage," Chris said. "So each of us will have one suitcase that is just yours — clothes and any personal stuff you want to take."

"Are you kidding?" Bethany said. "There is like no way I'm going to pack twelve years worth of birthdays, Christmases, and all my stuff in one suitcase. That's impossible."

"Mister Berry told me that we can find everything we'll need in Indonesia."

The kids looked at each other, unconvinced.

"But there are ten suitcases here," Bethany said. "We should get two each—but that's still probably not enough."

"The other five are for household stuff for the whole family," Chris said. "Towels, utensils, books, stuff that we'll all use."

"Dad," Bethany said, "we all want to be missionaries, but this isn't going to work." She spotted Maria leaning against the doorframe. "Mom, you have to help us out."

"Well," she said to Chris, "maybe it makes sense to pay for excess baggage. If we have to."

Chris pictured himself wrangling a mountain of luggage through foreign airports and fought back a twinge of dread. He recognized he was fighting a losing battle. "Just remember," he protested weakly, "we each get a carry-on as well."

Timmy asked, "Can I bring my ninja action figures? I don't need clothes."

Maria and Chris noticed that Hannah wasn't saying anything—which was unusual. Normally she would be right in the middle of the conversation, backing up whatever her big sister had to say. They exchanged a knowing glance—the special skill of parents—that said they would have to follow up later.

Chris said, "Why don't we all start out by making a pile of everything we want to take with us? From that pile, we can think about what's most important and then put that stuff in the suitcase. Whatever we don't have room for can go into storage, and it'll still be here when we come back in two years."

Bethany immediately turned to Maria in protest—"Mom, are you hearing this?"—and Chris knew the meeting was over.

CHAPTER THIRTY-EIGHT

As summer had yielded to early autumn and their departure for Indonesia neared, Chris and Maria had relaxed the kids' bedtime routine. Within reason, they allowed the children to stay up as late as they wanted, which in reality was never very late. That night, Maria and Chris knew that one of them needed to talk with Hannah and figure out why she'd seemed distant. While Chris was in Timmy's room reading a tale from a land called Narnia, Hannah stuck her head in her parents' room and told Maria she was going to bed. Maria gave her a few minutes to get ready, then went in to pray with her.

"Hey, baby, are you feeling all right?" Maria asked.

"Yeah, I guess."

"You didn't seem like yourself earlier today. Is something bothering you?"

"No," she said, burying her head in her pillow. "I just want to go to sleep."

"Okay." Maria knew not to push too hard. Hannah would open up, but it might take some time. She was like her father that way. "Why don't we pray? Is there anything you want to pray about?"

"No."

"Okay."

As Maria placed her hand on Hannah's back and began to pray, she could feel her nine-year-old crying softly. "What's wrong, baby girl?"

Hannah's reply was spoken into the pillow: "I don't want to go to Indonesia."

"Why not?" Maria asked as gently as she could.

"I like it here.... I have my friends here."

"I hear that. It's not easy to leave a place you like and people you know. But I have a feeling you'll like this new country too. And you know what? I have a feeling you'll make new friends there. You're a great friend, and people there will want to be your friend. Then you'll have friends in two different countries.... What else are you thinking about?"

After a pause, Hannah finally said, "I'm scared. Emma told me her dad said they kill Americans over there. Will they kill us if we go there?"

"Hannah, that's simply not true," Maria said as confidently as possible. "Plus, Emma's father doesn't know that your dad and I have been reading the news about Indonesia every day. It is a very safe place to live. Think about it. The Berrys have lived there for years, and they're fine."

Hannah rolled over, sat up, and leaned back against the headboard. Maria reached out and engulfed her daughter in a long hug. Hannah's breathing seemed to settle into a normal rhythm.

"It's okay to be scared, sweetie," Maria said. "I'm scared too sometimes. Whenever you go to a new place, you get scared. Remember when I told you that I grew up in another country, Argentina?"

Hannah nodded.

"Moving to America was very scary," Maria said. "My English wasn't perfect, and I was all alone. I prayed, 'Jesus, help me to be safe and make some friends here and help me make it through college so I can go back home.' God will always be with us."

"But then your mommy and daddy died."

CHAPTER THIRTY-EIGHT

"Yes, they were in a car crash in Argentina when you were one. You don't remember them, but they loved you very much. That was very hard and scary too. But even then, I knew God was with me. He is always with us—when good things happen and when hard things happen."

39

CHRIS AND MARIA collapsed into bed on the wrong side of midnight. Maria was asleep within three minutes, but Chris's brain would not allow him to join her. Their flight was scheduled to take off in about fourteen hours, and the checklist kept running through his head.

That day, they had finished a sweep of the house, packing what they absolutely needed and sending everything else to the storage unit. Chris took a short phone call from Bob Hollins, who wanted to pray with him and see if the plans were still on schedule.

In the late afternoon, Chris and Will picked up the church's fifteen-passenger van and filled it with the family's luggage. In the end, Chris had given in to the wishes of his wife and children and agreed to splurge on excess baggage. They would be making their international move with fifteen pieces of luggage, a combination of suitcases and trunks, in addition to carry-ons. The five extra pieces would cost at least a hundred bucks each, and Chris reminded himself it was just money. It was worth it to put an end to the whining and lobbying.

They then moved the operation to Will's house, and Chris and Will's mother joined them for dinner. She savored every minute and would be back in the morning for the final sendoff.

The church van now sat fully loaded in Will's driveway, guarded by Sword and team, maybe thirty feet from the sleeper sofa Chris and Maria now occupied.

Let's see. What else? What was he forgetting? Jim Tucker was helping to run the business. Maria's car was already sold. Chris's Explorer would go on the market tomorrow. Renters would move into the house in a week. They had given Will power of attorney for financial matters. Passports and plane tickets sat on the table. Orien's phone number was in his wallet. He drifted off to sleep wishing he had just one more day.

Ω

The alarm that morning gave a rude awakening, but Chris immediately popped out of bed with the to-do list running through his head and adrenaline coursing through his body. He and Will had planned this day with military precision. Newark International was just over two hours away, and they wanted to arrive at least three and a half hours before the scheduled flight time. With fifteen pieces of checked luggage, they didn't want to take any chances.

After breakfast, Chris's mom and Fritz and Gloria Bernheim stopped by to say goodbye and pray with the family. Then right on schedule, Will jumped into the driver's seat, signaling to Chris, Maria, and the kids that the time had come. They

CHAPTER THIRTY-NINE

squeezed into the van and held back tears as Will maneuvered the vehicle out of the driveway and headed east.

By the time they reached the interstate, Chris saw that his wife and kids were already asleep. He wasn't surprised. Maria could sleep anywhere, and they had all been working so hard over the past couple of weeks. Chris knew he would be unable to rest until the luggage was out of his hands and all five of them were settled in their assigned seats on the plane.

A few miles after merging onto the interstate, Chris spotted a van much like their own pulled off the road with a flat tire. He and Will exchanged a glance, and Chris prayed a very specific prayer about several specific parts of the vehicle.

"Think the Eagles are gonna be any good this year?" Will asked.

"Hard to say. They've looked decent so far. Their division is putrid again, so they might be able to make a run."

"Yeah. Too bad you'll miss it."

"Hey," Chris said, "they've won it all once already in my lifetime. As a fan, that's all I can really ask for."

"I guess I'm more greedy than that. I want 'em to win it every year."

After a minute of silence, Will spoke again: "Hard to believe you're actually doing this. When you first told us, I thought you were crazy. Still do a little bit. I thought you'd eventually come to your senses. But as I said, I'm trying to be happy for you. That said, if this doesn't work out and you end up coming back home, no one will think any less of you."

"Thanks, Will. I know you're trying hard to understand this whole thing—and it is pretty crazy when you think about it. Even last night when I finally got to bed, I thought, am I out of my mind? And I realized this has been the path all along. Ever since college. I'd say the American dream became a distraction for me. But now, I have no doubts. This is it."

"Okay, big brother. Just be careful over there. We'll miss you."

ω

They pulled up to the congested drop-off area for Trans-Pacific Airways, and Chris grabbed two skycaps to help with the luggage. Will stuck around until everything was loaded onto the carts. He hugged Maria, then the kids, and finally Chris. "Love you, brother," he said. "Be careful." He jumped into the van and darted into the stream of traffic.

As they approached the ticket counter inside the terminal, Chris gave Maria all of their documents and let her go to work. She was made for this. Her demeanor seemed to put people at ease in situations that could turn tense.

"Hello," the agent said, eyeing the mound of luggage behind Maria. "What is your final destination today?"

"We are going to Indonesia," Maria said as she slid the passports and tickets across the counter.

"Hmm, paper tickets. Don't see these very often."

Chris had booked their flights through a travel agent, who said the local carrier in Indonesia was still using paper tickets. So that's what he printed, for every leg of the trip.

"How many pieces of luggage are you checking today?" the counter agent asked.

"Fifteen."

CHAPTER THIRTY-NINE

"Okay, fifteen." She caught the eye of the skycap. "Your tickets entitle you to two bags each. So you will be charged a fee for excess baggage."

"Yes, we are aware of that," Maria said. "But it's okay. We're moving there."

As the airline employees started to process the luggage, Chris took Timmy for a short walk to keep him occupied. This would be his first flight, and he was growing fidgety with anticipation. "Can I sit in the driver's seat?" he asked. "Just for a little while?"

"No, I don't think so," Chris said. "The pilots are going to be very busy. They have their seats in the cockpit, and we have ours behind them."

It took thirty minutes to check all fifteen pieces of luggage, and Maria was still smiling at the end of the process. She handed the documents to Chris for safekeeping. "Good news," she said. "They only charged us for three extra bags since some of the others were light."

"That's great," he said. "I wasn't aware they did that."

"I don't think it's normal. I think they felt sorry for us."

Chris was happy with the discount, but he was mostly relieved that the luggage was out of his hands. After making their way through the security line, he called for a family huddle. "Well, since we still have over two hours until our flight, and since mommy saved us so much money, let's blow it on snacks!"

The eruption of cheers from the Billings children startled some of the other passengers, who apparently had confused the terminal for a library. Chris and Maria herded the kids toward the last American junk food they would taste for some time.

40

THE ECONOMY SECTION in a Boeing 777 is nine seats across: three seats, an aisle, three more seats, another aisle, and three more seats. On their flight out of Newark, Chris and the girls sat on the left side, with Maria and Timmy across the aisle in the center section. For Timmy, the takeoff and first forty-five minutes of the voyage were thrilling. But once the plane leveled off and routine set it, he turned to his mother and asked the age-old question: "How much longer?"

Maria was not sure how open to be with her five-year-old. Tokyo was still thirteen hours away, followed by seven more to Singapore and then, after a long layover, another two hours to Indonesia. She opted for complete honesty: "We're going to be on airplanes for an entire day. Wanna play a game on your Switch?"

After beverage service and dinner, the cabin lights dimmed and the jet screamed toward the International Date Line. Nearly seven miles above the surface of the earth, surrounded by the drone of two turbofan engines, it was not difficult for Maria and the children to fall asleep. Chris, on the other hand, was having trouble finding a comfortable position for his six-foot-one frame. Business class was out of his budget, but a man could dream.

As he observed the sleeping passengers around him, Chris wondered whether it was possible that time progressed more slowly in a jetliner. He wouldn't swear to it, but it certainly felt that way. The flight stretched toward Asia and eventually, finally, reached Japan at the advertised time. After navigating an efficient security check, the Billingses were happy to be on the ground for a couple of hours, if only to be able to spread out and walk through the terminal.

Chris thought Narita Airport was unlike anything he had experienced before. But he soon realized he was mistaken. He had seen this all many times — at every mall in America. Restaurants, clothing stores, book shops, and electronics retailers lined the corridors of the terminal, beckoning customers with neon and the promise of a great deal. The family ducked into a convenience store for some snacks and recognized at once that they were in fact in Asia. Instead of American potato chips and pretzels on the shelves, they saw seaweed strips and shrimp-flavored peanuts.

The next leg of their journey — Tokyo to Singapore — would be seven hours. That's a long time to be on a plane, but after their first flight it didn't sound like much. Once onboard, they immediately noticed a shift: Most of the members of the cabin crew were Asian. But they also noticed another change: These attendants were much friendlier than those who had flown out of Newark. After the plane reached cruising altitude, many

CHAPTER FORTY

of the crew members went out of their way to check on these American children, paying special attention to Timmy. An attendant gave each of the kids a certificate and plastic flight wings commemorating their first experience in the air. Timmy immediately pinned the wings to his shirt and asked Maria if he could go sit with the pilots now. As she began to explain that was unlikely, Chris gave in to exhaustion and did not awaken until the wheels touched down in Singapore.

It was midnight when they landed, but the Billings family had lost all sense of time and place. Their bodies disagreed with the clocks displayed on the walls of the terminal, which told them it was now time to sleep. They did know, however, that their final flight was not scheduled until the following morning, so they had booked a room in the hotel inside the airport. Walking to the hotel, Chris was in awe. "This is the most impressive airport I've ever seen," he told Maria. "I'm not sure what I was expecting, but it wasn't this." The airport was spotless, efficient, orderly, and had even more shopping and dining possibilities than they had seen in Tokyo.

When they reached their room, no one was interested in sleep. Their body clocks told them it was noon — the current time in Grapevine, Pennsylvania. But after nearly thirty hours of travel, they were all ready for the same thing: a shower. Even Timmy cleaned up without his usual protests.

After everyone was showered and refreshed, they headed back out to explore the terminal. Maria and the girls found a bookstore, and Hannah seemed to be embracing the adventure. Chris and Timmy settled into an all-night coffee shop with internet access and a TV displaying Cartoon Network of all things. Chris logged in to his email account and sent a message to Orien Berry: "We're in Singapore, right on schedule. What an amazing airport! Very smooth trip so far. Long, but uneventful. We'll see you in the morning with our smiling faces and twenty pieces of luggage."

41

ONE MORE FLIGHT. In a matter of hours, the Billings family would arrive in the land of their calling. Chris tried to picture what lay ahead, but the urgency of the morning crowded out any thoughts except the immediate.

In their final hours in the Singapore airport, each member of the family luxuriated in another hot shower and relaxed in their room. Chris and Maria kept running through the remaining steps on the journey. Passports and tickets? Check. Confirm the current time and status of their flight? Check. Pray that Orien would be at the airport in Indonesia to meet them? Check.

Before leaving the hotel and heading to the gate, the family enjoyed a breakfast buffet fit for royalty, which was included in the price of the room. Their table sat next to a soundproof floor-to-ceiling window that offered a view of the airport's arrivals and departures. Chris spotted a small tractor pulling a string of trailers, each overloaded with suitcases and trunks. What would they do if any of their luggage was missing? He couldn't assume that anyone at the airport would be able to speak English. Just another reminder of how helpless they would be until their language skills were up to speed.

After breakfast, they navigated one final check-in process without incident, boarded the Boeing 737, and settled into their seats. From what Chris could see, they were the only Westerners onboard. But like before, it seemed as though this fact brought out the best hospitality in the cabin crew and other passengers. Their reception was even friendlier than on the previous flight, and again, Bethany, Hannah, and Timothy were the center of attention. What a contrast to American flights, where travelers hope to avoid children like they're carriers of a dread disease.

Twenty minutes after takeoff, the flight attendants began distributing a meal. When the trays were placed in front of them, none of the Billingses could identify what they were looking at. When Maria inquired, an attendant said something about chicken. Maria nodded, unconvinced. She leaned toward Chris and whispered, "Looks like the days of burgers and pizza have come to an end." Maria, Chris, and Bethany politely picked at their trays while Hannah and Timmy ignored theirs entirely. They were all grateful for the satisfying meal they'd shared back at the hotel.

The pilot made an announcement on the intercom, first in Bahasa and then in English, but it all sounded the same to the Billings family. As the plane began its descent, they figured that's what the briefing had been about. Maria and Chris, experienced air travelers, both felt a little uneasy at the speed of the plane making its final approach but tried to maintain a brave face for the kids. Chris gripped the armrest as the jet's wheels smacked down on the asphalt. The pilot hit the brakes and

CHAPTER FORTY-ONE

reverse thrusters to keep the aircraft from rolling off the end of the runway. They jolted to a stop, but the kids didn't seem to mind the bouncing.

"Welcome to Indonesia!" a flight attendant announced over the intercom. "The current temperature in Surabaya is thirty-two degrees Celsius."

The number was meaningless to Chris. He shrugged at Maria, whose homeland—along with the vast majority of the world—used the Celsius scale. "Just under ninety Fahrenheit," she said. "Not too bad."

The pilot maneuvered the plane closer to the terminal, where it was met by a stair truck. Chris couldn't remember the last time he disembarked on a mobile staircase rather than through a jet bridge. He and Maria took their time helping the kids gather their belongings and make sure nothing was left behind. When they stepped out of the fuselage onto the top platform of the stairs, they were shocked by the brightness of the sun and the intensity of the heat. After walking only fifty meters across the tarmac toward the immigration checkpoint, Chris was already sweating profusely. "Ninety degrees?" he asked Maria. "Are they kidding? Feels more like a hundred."

The immigration counter was on the ground floor of the terminal building, and all passengers had to pass through it before they could advance to other parts of the airport. The booths on the right side of the large room were designated for citizens of the Republic of Indonesia, while those who held foreign passports were directed to the left. By the time the Billings family reached one of the international windows, the Indonesians had all been processed. Chris was trying hard not to be annoyed by the leisurely pace of the agents behind the plexiglass. Maria slid the passports through a slot to an officer wearing what looked like a police uniform, complete with a badge, various colorful pins, and epaulets. He picked up the first passport, which belonged to Maria, and slowly flipped through the pages until he found the visa sticker that had been issued by the Indonesian Embassy in Washington, D.C. In this moment, Chris was thankful for the office staff at Every Tribe Mission, which had handled all of the necessary paperwork and communication.

"Wait here," the officer said. He slid his chair backward, stood up, and disappeared through the door at the back of his booth.

"It's probably nothing," Maria told Chris. "I don't think this guy sees a lot of American passports."

Unseen by the humans, Sword, Purity, Glory, Dew, and Bravery had formed a perimeter around the family. Light returned to the group from another area of the airport. "We might have some trouble at the next stage," he said. "Spirits of greed and corruption are everywhere. Looks like they have the run of the place."

"As expected," Sword said. "Go back and monitor the baggage. Make sure no one gets too close."

The immigration officer returned to his booth at that moment and settled onto his perch. He held up Maria's passport, comparing the photo to the woman standing before him.

"Where did you get this visa?" he asked.

"In the United States," she said.

"Consulate? Embassy?"

"The embassy in Washington, D.C."

CHAPTER FORTY-ONE

He flipped through Maria's small booklet once more and examined the visa yet again. At last, he stamped the page and moved the passport to the side.

Next it was Chris's turn. Just as the officer was ready to stamp the visa page, his phone rang. He answered, listened silently for about ten seconds, then hung up.

"I will return," he said. He got up and again exited his booth.

Chris turned around and saw that all of the other foreign passengers had been processed. Only his family remained on this side of the immigration checkpoint.

Five minutes later, the officer returned with a colleague wearing the same uniform. This new guy was going gray at the temples and appeared to have one extra stripe on his shoulder. Chris figured this was a big deal in the world of immigration officers.

"You are Billings Christopher?" the new guy asked.

"I am," Chris said.

"You have fourteen luggage?"

"Uh, no. We have fifteen pieces of luggage."

"Maybe one is missing," the officer said. "We have fourteen with your name. Why so many?"

"We are moving here. For two years."

"You like it here?"

"So far, yes."

"You have not been here before?"

"No. This is our first time."

"You have not visited, but you decide, I will move to Indonesia. With my family."

"Yes."

"This is odd, no?"

"Maybe a little."

The officer burst into laughter. "Well," he said, "good luck to you."

Chris got his stamp, and the agent whipped through the children's passports with barely a glance.

The family followed a corridor and emerged into a baggage claim area. Bethany was the first to spot their stuff, which had been placed in a mound off to the side. "There it is," she said.

Suddenly three porters materialized and started loading the Billingses' luggage onto carts. Chris tried to explain that he had no money, but of course they could not understand him. The porters pushed, pulled, and prodded the carts in the direction of the X-ray machine manned by a group of bored customs officers. Chris noticed that several of their bags were marked with a white X, probably written with chalk. As the mountain of luggage approached the officers, they grabbed several pieces from the carts — the bags and trunks that had been given the telltale X.

The officer who appeared to be in charge walked over to Chris. He pointed at the marked suitcases. "Open," he said.

Chris complied, and the other agents swarmed over the bags. It seemed to Chris as though they were looking for something in particular. One of the officers stood up after a minute and held out a bottle of multivitamins that Maria had packed.

The chief officer smiled at Chris and said, "No drugs."

Chris shook his head from side to side. "Not drugs," he said, pointing at the label. "Vitamins."

The officer now frowned. "No drugs Indonesia."

Another officer rattled a bottle of ibuprofen discovered in a different suitcase.

CHAPTER FORTY-ONE

"Not drugs," Chris said.

"Maybe you pay me a fine," the chief officer said.

Just then a distinguished older woman approached. She was wearing the same uniform as the customs officers, but with more badges and elaborate insignia.

She smiled politely at Chris and Maria. In a British accent, she asked, "What seems to be the problem here?"

"Thank God someone speaks English," Chris said. "I'm not sure what the problem is, ma'am. It seems these men want to take our vitamins and ibuprofen."

She nodded and addressed two of the young men who were still searching the luggage. She spoke in a language Chris could not understand, and the men stepped aside.

"You cannot bring medicine of any kind into the country," she said. "This is our law.... Where are you from?"

Chris hesitated because he'd heard Americans are not always treated well here. "The U.S.A.," he said.

"May I see your passport?" she asked.

He handed over the little blue booklet and said a quick prayer under his breath. The woman smiled slightly and began to turn the pages, searching for his visa sticker. "Oh," she said. "You are working with the church?"

Chris nodded.

The woman closed the passport at once and handed it back to Chris. She issued instructions to the officers standing around, and they began to close the Billingses' suitcases. She turned to Chris and Maria. "You are free to go," she said, "but be careful once you are through those doors. Do you have someone meeting you here?"

"Uh, yes," Chris said. "I think so. I hope so."

"Good. Your friend will have to call the airline regarding your missing suitcase.... I hope your stay here is fruitful." When she saw that all of the luggage had been replaced on the carts, she turned and walked away. The remaining officers followed her with their eyes and then looked at each other with puzzled expressions on their faces.

The porters guided the luggage carts toward the sliding doors, with Maria and the kids close behind. Chris rushed to catch up.

The Billingses could not believe the scene on the other side of those doors. Hundreds of people crowded around a waist-high steel barrier, waving, shouting, trying to get their attention. The cacophony of voices, car horns, airport announcements, and jet engines — not to mention the wall of heat — stopped them in their tracks.

"Hold up!" Chris shouted to his family while trying to grab the porters. "Let's make sure Orien and Harriet are here before we go anywhere." He hadn't planned on the possibility that no one would be there to meet them. From left to right he scanned the sea of humanity, but he did not recognize any of the faces staring back at him and shouting an endless stream of nonsense.

He turned to Maria. "Start praying."

42

ORIEN AND ASEP pulled into the parking lot across from the arrivals hall just as the Billings family passed through the immigration checkpoint. At his age, there were few things Orien disliked more than wasting time at airports. It's not that he had anything against airport runs, he just didn't want to be there any longer than was necessary.

That morning, Orien was driving his Toyota van, which had been provided by the mission eight years earlier. He would transport the Billings family back to his home for the night. Asep was behind the wheel of the Bible school's truck with the shallow box in back. He would haul the new family's luggage.

After they parked side by side, Asep hopped into the bed of the truck so he could view the sliding doors over the mass of people crushed up against the barriers. Orien sat in the driver's seat of his van and repeated his instructions: "You're looking for a man and a woman with three children, two girls and a boy," Orien said in the local language, Bahasa. "Their skin tone will be more like mine than yours."

Asep chuckled at the old man's joke. "Nothing yet," he said.

"When they come through the doors, hopefully they'll sit tight and wait for us to reach them. I assume the porters will have claimed the load by that point. Then we can blaze a trail back here and you can help them load up while I take care of the porters. We have to make sure no suitcases disappear on the way through the crowd."

"It sounds like you have experience in these matters."

"Ah, yes. Sometimes we learn things the hard way."

"So what do you know about this family?"

"Not much, to be honest," Orien said. "But I've known their pastor since we were students in Bible college a hundred years ago. He's a good man and a good judge of character. He told me they are teachable, they know how to work hard, and they know how to work with other people. And I said, 'That's good enough for me. I can work with that.'"

"The doors are opening," Asep said. "Three carts loaded with luggage. An American family. It's them!"

Asep jumped down from the truck, Orien eased out of his seat, and they started across the parking lot. As they approached the crowd, it was as though an unseen force was splitting the mass in two, creating a clear path right to the door.

A relieved Chris Billings spotted Orien, who barked orders to the three porters. They steered the carts around the barriers and followed the old man to the vehicles. A few men in the crowd made halfhearted attempts to snatch luggage from the carts, but they thought better of it.

Chris and Maria huddled with the children and followed in the wake of their baggage. The kids were jostled a bit by the movement of the crowd, but it seemed more invigorating than

CHAPTER FORTY-TWO

scary. By the time they reached the van and truck, the mob had forgotten about them and turned their focus back to the doors.

Asep and Chris worked with the porters to arrange the luggage in the box of the truck. When everything was in place, Asep used rope to secure the load. Meanwhile, Orien gave the men some cash and sent them back to the terminal. Chris was amazed at how efficiently the process had unfolded. Wasn't it just a few minutes ago that he worried Orien hadn't made it?

Orien bent over and introduced himself to the children one by one.

"It's nice to meet you, Mister Berry," Bethany said.

"What's this Mister Berry?" Orien said. "I'm not your principal. You can call me Uncle Orien, if that's okay with you." His glasses had slid down his nose, and he used a finger to push them back into place.

Chris and Maria still weren't sure who Asep was, and Orien recognized the potentially awkward situation. "Sorry, friends," he said. "This is Asep. He is a student at the Bible school, a mighty man of God. He speaks a little English, but you'll have to learn Bahasa to really communicate with him. And he's worth getting to know."

When everyone was settled in for the ride to the Berrys' house, Orien cranked up the air conditioning and turned in his seat so he could see the whole Billings family. "Welcome to Indonesia," he said, tears pooling in his eyes. "It's a beautiful nation that desperately needs Jesus. I hope you come to love it as much as Harriet and I have. I want you to understand something: Your family is an answer to prayer. My wife and I have been praying for coworkers for years and years, and the Lord has seen fit to meet our prayers with your obedience.... Now, you have had a long journey. I don't imagine you have slept well on those planes. If you fall asleep on our drive, I won't hold it against you."

Chris was determined to stay awake and soak in as much wisdom as he could from Orien, but his eyelids began to battle him before the Toyota reached the main highway. He stretched his legs, allowed his eyes to close, and dreamed about angels who appear as customs agents.

43

CHRIS AND MARIA remembered nothing from their two-hour road trip from the airport in Surabaya to the Berrys' home. There was good reason for this: They'd spent almost the entire journey in the deepest sleep they'd enjoyed in days. Only when Orien parked the van in the driveway and cut the engine did they wake up, slightly disoriented by their exotic surroundings.

The trees were different from those growing on their land in Pennsylvania. The scents drifting to them on the breeze were unlike any they were accustomed to. The quality of light felt more vibrant. Even the grass seemed greener.

Harriet Berry had prepared a light lunch of sandwiches and fruit, just in case Maria or Chris or the kids felt like eating. Mostly they felt like sleeping. One of the facts they confirmed was that this part of Indonesia was eleven hours ahead of Grapevine. The clock on the wall told them it was one in the afternoon, but their bodies were screaming at them: *Why are you awake at two in the morning?*

They each ate a bit of food and fought their exhaustion as long as they could, but they all succumbed to nature and went to bed.

"Don't feel bad about sleeping," Orien had said. "Some people look at jet lag like it's a character flaw, but there's a point where we can't fight our bodies any longer. Anyway, you'll probably be feeling normal in a week and a half or so. Everybody's different, but it usually takes me one day to adjust for every hour of time difference."

They slept for several hours in the afternoon, and now it was two in the morning and the whole family was awake. Chris thought it was an ideal time to update his journal.

> Today's entry is sponsored by... jet lag. That's right—jet lag, the price we pay for the ability to cross eleven time zones in a mere matter of hours. It's interesting to think about jet lag. It's a totally modern disorder. Until the invention of the airplane, and specifically long-distance flight, jet lag was impossible. No form of transportation was fast enough over great distances to cause such disruptions to our circadian rhythms.
>
> I wonder what it would have cost to take a ship from New York to Indonesia. Is it even possible these days to hitch a ride on a passenger ship and go halfway around the world? I'm guessing that form of travel would have been much more enjoyable than what we just experienced. We were in the air for a total of 23 hours. Add in the travel time to and from the airports. Going through security, customs, immigration. Sitting around the airports waiting for the next flight. Add it all up, and it's one loooong day. Or make that a long couple of days. Apparently we lost a day of our lives when we passed over the international date line.
>
> Orien said something about going to church tomorrow, and like a dummy I asked him, "Oh, you have church on Saturday?"

CHAPTER FORTY-THREE

He just chuckled and said, "No, today is Saturday. You lost count somewhere in the air."

So that's what it's like so far being a missionary. You lose entire days and don't know what happened to them. How will I ever figure out how to function in this place if I can't even keep track of what day it is?

Now, that would not have happened if we'd made this voyage on a steamer. Note to self: Look into booking return passage on a seagoing vessel.

In the old days, of course, that's how missionaries got to their countries. I have to admit that would feel much more consequential, much more permanent, than the way we do it. We have open-ended roundtrip tickets. Whenever we're ready to head back, we can call the airline and pick a good day to do it.

I heard a story—not sure if it's true—about some missionaries in the old days. Instead of buying a crate or trunks or whatever for the stuff they were taking with them, they would buy a coffin. That way, if they died on the field, their family and friends wouldn't have to go to the trouble of finding a box to bury them in.

As I said, not sure if that really happened. But it does make me wonder. How committed am I to this whole thing? I still own a nice house on ten acres. Still own a valuable company. Still have a good chunk of money in the bank. What's the difference between somebody like the Berrys, who have stayed in one place for close to forty years, and others who go home after two? Something to ask Orien in the days, weeks, months, years to come. I have a good feeling we'll be spending a lot of time together.

My prayer in this moment: Father, thank You. Thank You for calling me. Thank You for an amazing wife and kids. Thank You *for the privilege of serving You in such a spiritually dark place. Thank You for the promise of Your presence. We don't have to ask You to be with us. You're already here. Thank You for guiding and empowering us through your Spirit. We need You. Amen.*

44

BY THREE IN THE MORNING, the house was finally quiet. Maria and Chris lay in the bed in the Berrys' guest room, drifting in and out of sleep. Timothy sprawled sideways on a mattress on the floor next to them, tangled in a thin sheet. In a strange house in a strange land, he wanted to be close to Mom and Dad. Bethany and Hannah shared the pullout sofa down in the living room.

Chris decided to do what he always did when he was unable to sleep: He prayed. He thanked God for his family and asked for their protection. He prayed for the health of Orien and Harriet Berry, asleep now in their own room down the hall. He prayed for the week ahead, their first week in their new country. He prayed for his church family back home in Pennsylvania and for everyone who had committed to pray for his family. He allowed himself an ironic thought: He was praying that those who said they would pray, would remember to do so. Was his prayer a result of theirs?

Eventually Chris noticed that Maria's breathing had become steady. Frustrated with his own lack of sleep, he tried to match her peaceful rhythm, inhaling when she inhaled, exhaling when she exhaled.

He must have fallen asleep, because he startled awake at twenty past four. What was that? Had he heard something? Was someone in the house? Then his confusion cleared and he realized what it was. From the minaret at the local mosque, the Muslim call to prayer was being broadcast throughout the neighborhood. It was haunting and beautiful. This guy could really sing. Was that a requirement? Did they have tryouts for the job? The singer, he knew, was called a muezzin. He would have to learn the word in Bahasa.

Chris had watched a series of videos on Islam in the weeks before their departure. One of them explained the call to prayer, and Chris found one fact in particular to be humorous. The call to prayer was given five times a day, and each time the words were identical — except for the prayer at dawn. There was an extra line inserted in that one, the one he was listening to right now. The added line declared, "Prayer is better than sleep." When you want people to get out of bed to pray, that's exactly what you tell them.

As the muezzin finished the call, Chris was sobered by the realization that almost no one listening to his words had ever heard the true message of Jesus. And without receiving that message, they were forever separated from the God who created them and loves them. "We need Your power, God," he prayed. "Without Your help, there's no way we can do what You've called us to do."

After the call to prayer, Chris was unable to get back to sleep. He tiptoed out of the room and down to the kitchen. His body clock told him dinnertime was approaching, so he found some fruit in the refrigerator and ate while drafting a brief update for his family's prayer warriors. Around five, Orien shuffled in and started preparing a pot of coffee without saying a word. "Trouble sleeping?" he asked when he finally sat at the table.

"Yeah. The call to prayer woke me up. Do you ever get used to that?"

He pushed his glasses up his nose. "The first call of the day—I usually don't hear that one. I'm a pretty sound sleeper, and the hearing loss helps. You might want to try earplugs when you sleep.... But I hope you never get used to the call. My mentor, years ago obviously, was a missionary from London. Was with a different organization. But he took me under his wing and tried to teach me what he thought I would need to know. He said, 'Satan wants to keep these people in bondage by telling them lies five times a day. Well, we're going to turn it around on him. When we hear the call to prayer, what do we do? We pray. We pray that the truth of the gospel and the power of the Spirit will go out wherever those words ring.' And that's been my rule of life ever since. No matter what I'm doing when I hear the call to prayer, I stop and pray."

"When I heard it this morning, I had a sense that God was showing me that this is a hard place and we have no hope of making a difference without His power. Everything we do has to be soaked in prayer."

"And that's probably the most important lesson you'll ever need to learn here," Orien said. "You'll learn the language. You'll learn your way around town. You'll learn how to pay your electric bill and order food. You'll even learn how to preach. But without God's Spirit, those are just words.... Bob Hollins mentioned that he made you give him a list of prayer partners. How many are there?"

"He asked for two fifty. We ended up with over three hundred."

"Excellent. That's very good. I encourage you to think of them as true partners in the ministry. What they do is just as important as what you and Maria will do here. So when you ask them to pray, be specific. Tell them exactly what you need them to pray for."

Orien got up, poured two cups of coffee, and carried them back to the table. "In my spirit," he said, "I have a sense that we are living in the last days. And it's not just because I'm as old as the hills. The church is in the last days. The world is approaching the end of an age. Our priority now is getting the good news to all the nations, all the *ethne*, the specific ethnic groups that have never been reached. There are tribes on these islands that have never encountered a follower of Jesus. The enemy has held them in darkness. If I were a young man, I would seek out those places and go. We don't need to hear a 'call from God.' He's already told us that's His priority. I'm afraid my body is too old and worn out to do that kind of work anymore. But maybe... maybe my last assignment is to help you get there."

45

AFTER BREAKFAST on Monday, Orien and Harriet took the Billings family to the Bible school, a twenty-minute drive across the city. As Orien deftly maneuvered through the traffic, Chris reflected on how little he really knew about this nation. He had read some books and articles and watched a few videos, but even basic facts were just now being revealed to him. For one, the vehicles traveled on the left side of the road, which would take some adjustment on his part. He hadn't even thought to ask about that. The benefit of being self-funded was that the family was able to arrive in Indonesia just six months after first discerning God's leading. One of the downsides of this speed was that their pre-field learning process had been seriously truncated. Their learning curve would be steep.

Chris wanted to keep track of the twists and turns Orien was making but gave up after five minutes. There's no way he would be able to remember all of these roads and intersections. He and Maria spent the trip trying to decipher the meaning of signs along the route. Chris kept flipping through the

Indonesian–English dictionary he had purchased months earlier but never had time to study.

On the edge of town, traffic began to thin out and low-lying green mountains appeared to the west. Orien passed through a residential area and turned onto a road lined with neat palm trees. If Chris didn't know better, he might have thought he was driving up to a municipal golf course in Florida. Orien stopped in front of a small shack and waved to a young man seated inside. The guard hopped off his stool and came out to shake Orien's hand. They exchanged a few words, and Orien drove onward. "He's a second-year student," Harriet said of the guard. "Has the vision of an apostle.... Most of the students take part-time jobs on campus."

Chris noted a wall around the perimeter of the property, and Harriet identified the buildings they were passing: "That's the men's dormitory.... This is the administration building and faculty offices.... Most of the classes are held here on the left.... Behind there is the library and computer lab.... The women's dormitory is here.... This new building is the chapel. It has everything you'd find in a church sanctuary back in the States."

"A new church plant meets there on Sundays," Orien said. "It's led by a few recent graduates. They're seeing some miraculous things happen in that group."

"I'm not sure what I was expecting," Maria said, "but it wasn't this. It's beautiful."

The road curved around to the left, cutting through spacious and tidy lawns, and several smaller buildings occupied the back corner of the campus. Orien turned into a small driveway in front of the second-to-last structure.

CHAPTER FORTY-FIVE

"Welcome," Orien said, "to your new home."

The single-story house was painted a pale yellow to match the rest of the campus buildings. A concrete walk led to the front door, which was flanked by windows on both sides. Based on the construction sites they'd passed on the way over, Chris guessed the shell of the house was bricks and mortar with a smooth layer of concrete over the bricks. The pitch of the roof was about the same as their house back in Grapevine, but this one was topped with red clay tiles.

"I love it," Maria said. "This place is like a sanctuary in the middle of the city."

"This house was built for the first director of the school, a missionary from Canada," Orien said. "That man knew how to pray. And his wife was the best disciple maker I've ever known."

"No pressure," Chris said to himself.

When Orien unlocked the front door, the kids scattered through the house, scouting out the rooms they would like to claim for themselves. A corridor led from the entrance to a door in the back. All of the family's luggage sat in a pile in the living room, where Asep had deposited it two days earlier.

"So," Orien said, leading Maria and Chris into the kitchen and dining area. "As you can see, it's fully furnished. We replaced some of the appliances when we heard for sure that you were coming. And we had some plumbing work done that was just finished last night. Otherwise we would have had you in here earlier."

"Wow," Maria said, turning the water faucet on and off. "Thank you so much. It really is wonderful. I know you said we could consider finding another place off campus at some point, but I don't really see that happening. It's already beginning to feel like home."

"That's kind of you to say," Harriet said. "But we won't hold you to it. If you ever think something else might work better, maybe after you're more confident in the language, just say the word."

They drifted to the hallway and moved toward the back of the house. There were three bedrooms—the girls would share one—and the bathroom was more spacious and modern than Chris had expected. The back door led to a patio with a table and chairs and, beyond that, a small lawn with well-tended grass.

"I think I found my prayer closet," Chris said. "I can already picture this as part of my morning routine. Jesus, Chris, Bible, coffee."

"You'll notice," Orien said, "that there's no room for a study or an office. So we've already arranged an office for both of you in the administration building. It's on the second floor with some of the faculty. Right next to mine, in fact. And there's no charge. Our mission built most of this place, and we still contribute monthly to help keep the doors open. The goal is to become self-sustaining, but we aren't there yet."

Just then, Hannah stuck her head out the door. "There's someone at the front door," she said. "I think it's the man who took our luggage from the airport."

Chris and Orien went to the entrance and invited Asep inside. He and Orien had a brief conversation.

"Asep would like to know if you need anything at the moment," Orien said.

"Not at the moment," Chris said. "And please thank him again for going to the airport."

CHAPTER FORTY-FIVE

Orien relayed the message, and Asep spoke again to Orien, occasionally glancing at Chris. When he finished, Orien turned to Chris. "There's one other thing," he said. "Do you know the story in First Samuel about Jonathan and his armor bearer attacking a Philistine garrison?"

"Of course," Chris said. "Jonathan is my favorite person in the entire Old Testament."

"Okay," Orien said. "Asep said he had a dream last night about that very scene. Except he was the armor bearer—and you were Jonathan."

46

JIM TUCKER HUNG UP the phone and slapped his desk—Chris's desk—in celebration. He jumped up from his chair and jogged back into the shop where he found Tom Hansen.

"Great news, Hansen," Jim yelled over the screech of a bandsaw. "Just closed a huge deal with a regional wholesaler. Huge. A bit of everything. It'll keep us busy for months. As soon as I have the final paperwork, I'll get it back to you so you can order the material.... Who needs Chris, right?"

Tom shook his head and laughed as Tucker walked away.

Back in the office area, Jane Renfroe's door was open a few inches. Jim knocked, and Jane immediately answered, "Come on in."

Tucker leaned against her doorframe and passed on the news about the wholesale order.

"That's great, Jim," she said. "I know Chris put in a lot of time with the owners there over the past couple years. I'm glad you're around to close the deal. I wouldn't know the first thing about setting up something like that."

"Just happy to do my part.... Hey, not sure if you remember, but I'll be out of the office the next few days on a sales trip. Heading to New York to meet with some contacts Chris left for me."

"Oh, that's this week already? Well, good luck."

"One question. Do you want me to pay for everything myself and then submit receipts, or—"

"No, you should use a company credit card. It's easier that way. Then the bill comes straight to me and we don't have to deal with reimbursing you. But make sure you save those receipts."

"Got it. Well, see you Friday."

Jim crossed the hall to his office, where a spirit named Greed sat waiting for him. Jane glanced at the clock and saw that it was only three-thirty. Maybe he was just getting a headstart on his goodbyes? But two minutes later, Jim walked out the front door with his windbreaker on and his laptop under his arm. "Huh," she said.

As Jim and Elaine ate dinner that night, he said, "Got a surprise for you."

"Yeah, what's that?"

"We're going to New York this week—if you want to, that is."

"Really? Where in New York?"

"The city. Manhattan. We can leave tonight or tomorrow, whatever you want."

"I'd love to. What's the occasion? Is it for work?"

"Nope," he said. "Just want to get away with you for a few days. I've been putting in a lot of extra hours lately, getting up to speed before Chris left. I think you deserve to stay in a nice hotel, eat some good food."

CHAPTER FORTY-SIX

"Are you sure you can be out of the office that long?"

"Hey, I'm the boss of my schedule now. I decide if I can get away."

"I guess. You've worked many years for that privilege."

"You got that right. And it's not like they're paying me what I'm worth. He promised me...well, he led me to believe that I would be running the whole operation. But he didn't want to pay me a managerial salary, so he divvied up the job three ways."

"You put it that way, you deserve a few days out of the office.... I can be packed in thirty minutes."

"Sounds great." He looked at his watch. "We can be in the city by nine."

Greed sneered as Elaine left the table. "You deserve it," the spirit whispered to Jim. "They don't care about you and your health. You have to look out for yourself. They're cheating you, taking advantage of you. And it's not like you're stealing. You *will* be inspecting some fine furnishings, after all. The happier you are, the better salesman you'll be. This is an investment in the company, really. You deserve this."

Before he got into his car a half hour later, Jim pulled his wallet out of his pocket. The company credit card was right where he'd left it. He thought, *Thanks for the getaway, Chris.*

47

THE NEXT TWO MONTHS went by in a blur for the Billings family. It seemed that everything in their lives had been upended, but they were enjoying the honeymoon phase that many missionaries experience in a new land. They were adjusting to an equatorial climate, trying exotic new foods, taking excursions into the city. There were moments of stress, of course, but each new day was filled with opportunities for discovery.

Not long after the Billingses' arrival, Orien and Harriet sat down with Chris and Maria and laid out a plan for their first year in Indonesia. "I want you to get really good at saying no," Orien said. "Both of you are high achievers. That's clear. You're doers. But this is really important. You have three jobs right now, and only these three. First, tend to your spiritual lives. It's easy in a time of transition to allow our disciplines to slip. If anything, you'll need to spend more time abiding in Jesus than you ever have. That's the priority. Second, establish a homeschool routine for your kids. This is new for them and for you, so you'll need some time to figure out what works best. And finally, the rest of your focus is on language, language, and more language. Without language, you'll never learn culture. And without culture, you'll never really understand the people. If you want to have a lasting, fruitful ministry here, you need to learn the language."

And so, from their first week in the country, Maria and Chris dedicated themselves to full-time language learning. Five days a week, they had private lessons with a trained teacher in the city. They also met with Asep three nights each week to practice what they were learning. Chris was a little frustrated that his wife and kids seemed to be making better progress than he was, but that only motivated him to work harder.

One evening, as Maria, Chris, and the girls sat around the dining-room table sipping tea and practicing vocabulary with Asep, Timmy was playing with his band of new friends in a rice field a hundred meters away at the edge of the Bible school compound. His family's move to the tropics was a grand adventure for Timmy, introducing him to an array of new creatures, like the salamanders he was chasing this night.

Suddenly one of Timmy's friends cried out, "*Awas ular!*" The other boys immediately sprinted to safety, leaving Timmy alone on a footpath between the rice paddies. At first, he thought he was the victim of some kind of joke. But then he saw it. Blocking his path, coiled and preparing to strike, was a three-meter-long cobra.

Timmy froze in terror. He wanted to run, but his legs were concrete. All he could do was pray: "Jesus, help!" Timmy's guardian, Bravery, rose to his full stature, drew his sword, stepped in front of the snake, and called for the rest of the squad to join him at once. Bravery identified the demon attached to the cobra. It was not Sickness or Pain—but was Death itself.

CHAPTER FORTY-SEVEN

Ω

At that moment in Grapevine, Pennsylvania, Michael Lamb was sorting mail for his delivery route — a route he could walk with his eyes closed if necessary. Through two decades on the job, he had become a fixture in the community, a joyful public servant who knew every person on his circuit. Even though his official title was mail carrier, Michael saw himself as a full-time minister whose real work was intercession. He was paid by the U.S. government to deliver mail and pray all day. A member of Lakeside Community Church, he took a special interest in the Billings family and usually interceded for them when he made his delivery to Custom Clock and Furniture.

But this morning, a travel magazine caught his eye. The cover featured a stunning photo from Indonesia — and the Holy Spirit prompted Michael to pray for the family, and for Timmy in particular, without delay. "Lord," he prayed, "I don't know what's happening over there right now, but protect that family. I don't know what kind of danger they're in, but surround them. Place Your angels around Timmy. Keep that sweet little boy from harm."

Ω

Bravery and Death battled to a stalemate, but the angel suddenly felt his strength surge. Somewhere, he knew, the saints were praying. Death, sensing that the momentum was slipping away, made his move and lunged at Bravery's glistening sword. In that instant, Light arrived and nudged Timmy aside just as the cobra struck. Having missed its target, the snake recovered and spit a stream of venom into its victim's eyes. Timmy dropped to the ground, shrieking in pain.

The boy's screams pierced through the language lesson taking place in the house. Maria's maternal instinct told her at once that something was seriously wrong, and she started to rise from her chair. Asep, who understood the words the other boys were yelling, jumped up and beat her to the door. Chris followed immediately and sprinted toward his son. From fifty meters away, he spotted the snake. It appeared to be frozen in midair, hood opened like a sail, within easy striking distance of the boy. Timmy writhed on the ground rubbing his eyes.

"Oh, God, please help me!" Chris cried as he ran, gasping for breath. "Please! Not Timmy!" Maria, a few strides behind her husband, was praying in the Spirit, begging God to save her child.

Asep started clapping, stomping, shouting—trying to draw the snake's attention away from the boy. The cobra slowly backed away, and Chris approached cautiously. He bent over, eyes still on the snake, picked up his son, and took two tentative steps backward. Instead of striking, the cobra turned aside and slithered into the rice field. Chris carried Timmy back to the house, where Asep washed his eyes with water.

On their way to the hospital just minutes later, Maria composed a quick email on her phone. She explained the situation in a few sentences for their prayer partners. Her request was clear: "Pray for a miracle." The army of intercessors—including Michael Lamb—got to work, bombarding the throne room of heaven on behalf of Timmy Billings.

CHAPTER FORTY-SEVEN

Maria's update later that evening told the rest of the story: "Thank you so much for praying! By the time Timmy got to see a doctor, he was calm and had no pain. It's like nothing happened at all. The doctors are all amazed. One of them even called it a miracle.... Needless to say, we will all remember the meaning of the word *ular*."

48

BANDU LEANED AGAINST a tree in front of his hut and took a long final drag from his cigarette. He flicked the butt to the ground and exhaled slowly, watching his daughter strain to keep up with her thoughtless friends. He wanted to grab each of them by the shoulders and shake them until they understood how special Fatima was, how amazing. But all they could see was her legs that didn't work quite right. He knew that as they got older, they would leave her behind, physically and socially. But what could he do?

The amulet tied around Fatima's neck reminded Bandu of his father's power—both its reach and its limits. If his father's connection to Nyale was strong enough to save her life, why could he not also heal her?

Soraya had invited his son to participate in an all-night prayer gathering later that week. Only a select few were welcome. The *dukun* called it a channel to higher levels of power granted by Allah and Nyale. Until now, Bandu wasn't sure he would go. But watching his little girl struggle to live her life, he made his decision. He would do whatever it took to make his daughter whole again.

Ω

From his perch in the trees above the village, Nyale kept a close watch on Bandu, the spell caster's son. This young man was the key to his ongoing control of these people, but the demon simply did not trust him. What he would give for the power to read minds. What was Bandu thinking? What did he care about? Where was his soft spot? His love for his daughter was evident, but how could this be used against him?

A sentry appeared out of nowhere and bowed before Nyale. "Master," it said, "a visitor approaches from the west."

Within seconds, Lucifer's personal messenger stood before the ruler of Seora. He had not been back since the day of the outsiders' failed attempt to reach the village.

"Nyale," the messenger said, "the great prince sends me with a warning. The Enemy's forces are closing in. The count is down to five nations."

"Five!?" Nyale could not hide his alarm.

"Just five nations remain in total darkness. Our master wishes to know if you have noticed any unusual activity around Seora."

"Nothing," Nyale said. His perimeter scouts had heard rumors of the Most High's warriors farther down the mountain, but he did not see how sharing this news would help him. "Everything is under my control."

CHAPTER FORTY-EIGHT

"See that it stays this way. We have picked up increasing chatter concerning these islands. We suspect that some of these places and peoples are being brought before the Most High for the first time in human history. Even though the recent outsiders were unable to penetrate your defenses, it seems they have turned to their most powerful weapon. I don't need to remind you what this means."

"Of course not," Nyale said.

"Good. You must remain on alert."

The messenger unfurled his bat-like wings and flew back in the direction from which he had come. Nyale tried to keep a brave face for his troops, but dread washed over him like a downpour.

49

"Up for a trip back in time?"

Orien's question snapped Chris out of his vocabulary study. He'd heard somewhere that learning a new language was a simple matter of effort, so he worked at it every day until his brain and tongue could handle no more. Six months after arrival, he was finally seeing the pieces fall into place. He set his homemade flash cards on the desk and turned to face his mentor standing in the office doorway.

"Sounds intriguing," Chris said. "What do you have in mind?"

"Asep and I are heading into the mountains in a few days. Some former students of ours invited us for a visit. They're working with a tribe that's experiencing a great awakening. Hundreds coming to faith in Jesus. It's a miracle really. Ten years ago, there were no Christians there. A hundred years ago, they were still throwing kids into the volcano."

"Seriously?"

"True story," Orien said. "The enemy had controlled them from the beginning of time. He'd blinded them and convinced them their sacrifices were necessary for fertility."

"That's amazing. That really happened here? I've heard stories, but...." His mind struggled to comprehend human sacrifice.

"Well, you'll get to see the volcano with your own eyes. Our Indonesian brothers and sisters are doing the hard work in hard places, and God is moving. By the way, do you know how to ride a horse?"

Ω

Later that week, after a long, bumpy ride in the Bible school's van, followed by a final couple of tedious hours on horseback, Orien, Asep, and Chris witnessed an event that seemed impossible just a few years earlier.

One by one, more than two hundred members of the Sagi tribe waded into an icy mountain stream to declare their allegiance to Jesus Christ and be baptized by Orien's former students. The young pastors had asked Orien to baptize these new believers, but the old missionary was happy to remain in the background. "Thank you for honoring me with this request," he told them, "but this is not for me to do. The Lord has given you responsibility for these people. You are their shepherds."

Orien sat on the bank of the stream, overcome by the emotion of the moment. He'd prayed for this people group for decades, and now God was answering his prayers before his very eyes. "Thank You, Jesus," he said. "Thank You, Jesus. May this be just the beginning. Send more, Lord. Build Your kingdom in this place. Thank You for this glimpse of eternity."

CHAPTER FORTY-NINE

The three visitors spent the rest of the day praying for the sick and encouraging the pastors and other believers. Chris was struck by the simplicity and beauty of the people and their lifestyle. And he was surprised to realize that he was able to understand phrases in the conversations taking place around him.

Later that night, as the activity of the village quieted, Orien, Asep, and Chris settled into the hut they were sharing. "How gracious of our Lord to allow me to witness this day," Orien said. "Our time in this land has not been wasted. In His goodness, God has received our meager efforts and brought forth fruit." He translated his comments for Asep as he opened his Bible to Revelation chapter seven. He pushed his glasses up his nose and began to read: "After this I looked and there before me was a great multitude that no one could count, from every nation, tribe, people and language, standing before the throne and in front of the Lamb. They were wearing white robes and were holding palm branches in their hands. And they cried out in a loud voice: 'Salvation belongs to our God, who sits on the throne, and to the Lamb.'

"What a sight that will be," he continued. "Can you imagine? Individuals from every nation, tribe, people, and language. And the nations John is referring to here are not the countries on a map with their own borders and flags and currency. *Nations* means individual ethic groups with languages and cultures all their own—like the Sagi. They will all be represented around the throne.... And I believe Scripture teaches that the return of the Lord is connected to His gospel being preached among every nation and tribe and tongue. Jesus said that 'this gospel of the kingdom will be preached as a testimony to all nations, and then the end will come.' That day is not far off."

"How many nations, how many of these people groups are in Indonesia?" Chris asked.

"In total?" Orien said. "There are almost eight hundred groups throughout the country. Most of them have some gospel witness. But I suspect there are a few that have never been reached. They've never heard the good news in all of history. But it's hard to know for sure how many there are, or where they are. Some could be like the Sagi — they're being reached by other indigenous groups right on their doorstep."

Ω

The trip up the mountain rejuvenated Orien's spirit, but it took a toll on his body. Heavy rains and landslides washed out the mountain road in a couple of places, and the journey back to the city was twice as long as normal. The old missionary couldn't get out of bed the next day. Harriet sent a text message to Chris and Maria: "Please pray for Orien. He's exhausted, sore, and can't keep any food down. Please ask your prayer team to join us."

50

"As we suspected," Sword said, "we were followed down the mountain. We need to be prepared for an assault at any moment. What's our status?"

The squad of guardians, gathered outside the chapel of the Bible school, turned to face Light. "Our numbers are growing by the day," he said, "and we can all feel new strength through the prayers of the saints." The others nodded in agreement. "But we're still short. Our perimeter is not as stout as I would like. If the prayer coverage does not increase, I'm afraid we're vulnerable—especially outside these walls."

"The scouts are sending word every hour," Sword said. "There's more and more activity in the area. It's clear now that the enemy knows we're here, and probably why we're here. They will not tolerate our incursions into territory they've claimed for their master. We must hope the saints do their job."

Ω

Two days later, Chris and Asep traveled to a meeting of Indonesian pastors, accompanied by Sword and Mercy. Orien wanted to go with them but was still confined to bed. "Send greetings to the brothers and sisters," he said, "from a tired old friend."

After lunch that day, Maria and the kids piled into the Bible school's van for a trip just outside the city. Every other Thursday afternoon, they took a break from their homeschool studies and got together with other expat children—missionaries from Korea, Australia, and the UK. The kids enjoyed playing, and the parents looked forward to conversations in English.

A few kilometers from their destination, Maria was surprised to see a makeshift roadblock on a quiet stretch of highway. She slowed to a stop in front of the barrier made of tree limbs and brush and hit a button to make sure her doors were locked. A lean man stepped out from the shade of the jungle, and Maria opened her window just enough to hear what he had to say.

"Road closed," he said. "Detour this way." He pointed to a gravel track through the trees to the right. He smiled.

Something didn't feel right. Maria had seen detours before. The roadblocks always had official-looking signs, and the men always wore orange or yellow vests. This guy looked like he'd just rolled out of bed.

"Road closed," he said again.

As Maria contemplated backing up and turning around, another truck pulled up behind her. The man walked back, spoke with the driver, and pointed to the gravel road. After a few seconds, the truck maneuvered around Maria's van, turned onto the detour route, and disappeared into the jungle.

CHAPTER FIFTY

Maria pushed aside her doubts, waved to the man, shifted into gear, and steered right onto the gravel road. For the first two hundred meters, the track was straight and smooth. The canopy of limbs and leaves overhead created a tunnel cut off from direct sunlight.

Maria rounded a curve and immediately slammed on the brakes. The recent rains had flooded this section of road, and before her sat a pool of brown water at least fifty meters long. There was no way around it. Where had the other truck gone? One word crashed into her mind:

Ambush.

Before she could shift into reverse, two men burst out of the trees, one on either side of the vehicle. They pulled on the handles of the locked doors and began pounding on the windows.

Bethany, in the front seat, instantly started praying: "Jesus, help us! Send Your angels to protect us!" The guardians were already on site, engaged in hand-to-hand combat with demons of greed and rage.

Hannah began screaming, and Timmy froze, his eyes locked on the man outside his mother's window.

Maria gunned the engine, and the bandits leapt onto the vehicle, one on top and the other on the back bumper. She slammed the accelerator to the floor. Just before steering into the center of the muddy pool, Maria jerked the van to the left and the man on top tumbled over the edge.

The vehicle gained speed through the pool, now over a half-meter deep. Maria could only guess what the road looked like below the surface of the water, but she knew she couldn't stop. "Help us, Lord!" she cried. "Help us!"

The man on the bumper kept pounding on the back window. Maria couldn't shake him. Finally the van reached the edge of the pool and jostled up onto dry road. Maria floored the accelerator again and wrenched the steering wheel back and forth. Bethany called out, "Let go of our car, in Jesus' name!"

Maria glanced at her rearview mirror for a split second and didn't see the pothole appear out of nowhere. The front left wheel slammed into the hole. The rear of the van skidded around to the right as Maria fought to keep control. Hannah and Timmy crashed into each other. Maria pulled the steering wheel in the opposite direction. In the whiplash action, the bandit lost his grasp of the van and fell backward onto the gravel. Light made sure he stayed there.

Maria stomped on the accelerator. The jungle track eventually merged with a road she recognized, and she flew home in a daze.

Ω

Chris wrote in his journal that night:

> *The enemy attacked my family while I was away. He's trying to frighten us into running. I'm not so stupid to believe we can stand up to this in our own strength. But I know God brought us here, and He's able to protect us. If anything, this reinforces my resolve. We need to activate the prayer warriors to do battle like never before. We must not quit before the last nations are reached with the gospel.*

51

SORAYA STOOD AT THE door of the mosque, greeting the men of the village as they finished Friday prayers and went about the business of the day. He took pleasure in intimidating them, especially the younger men full of modern ideas. He liked to remind them that he was still in charge.

As Bandu approached the exit, Soraya pulled him aside. "Please wait, my son," he said. "There is something we must discuss."

When the last of the worshippers left the building, Soraya and Bandu sat in a corner.

"This is a momentous day in your life, Bandu," the old shaman said. "Nyale has shown me that your preparation must now begin in earnest, and the other elders have agreed. Next week, I will send you to Bilonga, where you will begin a course of study in a *pesantren*. If you are to fulfill your destiny and serve this village as its spiritual leader, you will need to learn Arabic like an expert, so you can someday teach your people the Qur'an and the sayings of the prophet."

"But I have a wife, father. And a young daughter. Will they travel with me?"

"Of course not. That is no place for a woman. Your mother and I will look after Sri and Fatima and ensure that all of their needs are met. That way, you will be able to fully devote yourself to learning. The *pesantren* in Bilonga is the very school I attended as a young man. The *kyai* there is a man I have known for years. He has assured me he will give you the very best education. And when you return, the people of this village will hold you in even greater esteem."

Soraya warned his son of the dangers of the city, from immoral lifestyles to violence to followers of false gods bent on the destruction of Islam. "Have nothing to do with them," he said. "Keep yourself pure. Someday you will make the pilgrimage to Mecca."

☧

Less than a week later, Bandu was in his new city, overwhelmed by his new world. He'd said goodbye to his wife and child, ridden in a van down to the coast, boarded a boat, crossed a stretch of sea, and arrived in Bilonga, home to more people and buildings and animals and vehicles and light and noise than he ever imagined.

If given an option, he would have stayed in his room all day. But that wasn't an option. Salahuddin, his father's old friend, made sure that Bandu was present for all prayers, meals, and lessons. Bandu was grateful for the respect afforded him because

CHAPTER FIFTY-ONE

of his father's reputation, but he would have preferred a bit more freedom.

One morning, as Bandu studied in his room, he was interrupted by a knock on his door. It was Abdullah, an experienced student who lived across the hall.

"You need a study break," Abdullah said. "Come, let's go for a walk. I know a place where we can relax and drink some tea. The books will not run off while we're away."

As they passed through the narrow streets, Bandu was amazed by what he saw. His friends back in Seora wouldn't believe it. He hardly believed it himself. Shiny vehicles, strange sounds, shops selling every product imaginable.

The pair turned a corner, and Bandu was drawn to a building on the opposite side of the street. Music emanating from inside both attracted and repulsed him.

"What's that?" he asked.

Abdullah just looked at him.

"What is that building?" Bandu asked again.

"It's called a church. It's a gathering of infidels. Worshippers of false gods, enemies of Allah. They wish to spread lies and deceive our people. They should not even be allowed to gather. You do not have one where you come from?"

"No," Bandu said. "But my father has spoken of this."

"Yes. Their day will come."

52

THE TEXT MESSAGE from Harriet arrived before seven the next morning: "Sorry, need to cancel our meeting today. Orien still not well. Asep will drive us to hospital. Please pray. Will update."

Maria and Chris set their phones down and called out to heaven on behalf of their mentor, then Maria dashed off an email to their prayer team back in Pennsylvania.

Just before lunch, Harriet called Maria with the news. Orien had dengue fever, which explained the fatigue and joint pain. The doctor ordered some tests but was optimistic. The next couple of days would be critical.

Ω

Orien's condition deteriorated overnight. His doctor was stumped. Dengue usually didn't present this way, but the tests indicated complications—internal bleeding, possible organ failure. The doctor talked about sending him to a better hospital in the provincial capital. He would make the arrangements.

Chris and Maria rushed to the hospital. Even if they couldn't do much to help, they wanted to be near Orien and Harriet, a couple that had grown to mean so much to them. They brought food for Harriet and Asep, who hadn't left the building. They carried chairs into a corner of Orien's room. They needed to be present but didn't want to be in the way.

Asep sat beside Chris and started praying for the old missionary. Tears streamed from the corners of his eyes as he pleaded with God. His words and tears eventually stopped flowing, and Chris wondered whether his friend had fallen asleep.

Asep then turned in his seat to face Chris. "This man is my father," he said. "Do you understand?" Chris nodded his head, grateful for the simple language Asep was using. The young man continued: "When I was sixteen, I had a dream. A man called to me, 'Asep, come, follow me.' I didn't know this man. I said, 'Who are you? Where are you going?' He said, 'I am Jesus. Follow Me, and I will give you life.' Then this man showed me a church in my town. I knew where it was. I passed it on the way to school. He said, 'They will tell you about Me.' And then I woke up. The next day, I went to the church. The pastor taught me about Jesus, and I decided to follow Him. When I told my father, he threw all of my things into the street and said don't come back. Then the pastor said, 'I will send you to my friend Orien.' Then Orien became my father."

CHAPTER FIFTY-TWO

"You're still here?"

Orien's voice was a weak rasp, but he was speaking for the first time all day. Chris and Maria got up from their chairs and stood at the side of his bed.

"Do you need anything?" Maria asked. "It looks like Harriet and Asep have stepped out."

"No, I'm fine for now. I know they're talking about moving me, but I'm not sure it'll do any good. The Lord hasn't told me what will happen to me — not that I expect Him to. But if He wants to take me now, I'm ready."

He paused to catch his breath. Chris couldn't say a word.

"For years," Orien said, "we prayed for more workers. Some came, but none lasted. I started to wonder if anyone would. Then you came — an answer to prayer. Some days are hard, as you've found out, but keep going. Focus on the big things. Proclaim the gospel. Make disciples. Plant the church. And never stop loving the people."

Sometime after two in the morning, with Harriet and Asep at his side, Orien breathed his last and entered into his eternal reward. At the end of the week, hundreds gathered at the Bible school to honor his life and ministry. Pastors, former students, colleagues, missionaries from a half-dozen agencies, brothers and sisters in Christ — all expressed shock at such a sudden and profound loss, but also gratitude for God's faithfulness in the life of His servant.

The director of the Bible school, a former student of Orien's, stood before the mourners and recounted his mentor's many roles: "Our friend was a husband, a church planter, a preacher, a disciple maker, a teacher, an ambassador of his King. But now, the mantle must be passed."

Chris wondered whether the speaker might mention his name as a successor to Orien's ministry, a recipient of his mantle. But the preacher continued: "The mantle now passes to each and every one of us. Each of our lives was touched by this one man and his commitment to the Lord, and now it is up to each of us to carry on this legacy." Chris, stunned by the pride in his heart that would raise its ugly head in such a moment, repented at once and asked God to use him in some small way.

After the service, Chris and Maria were amazed at Harriet's poise and patience as she greeted each mourner. Her life had been upended in a matter of days, but still she took time to make everyone feel welcomed.

Later, in a quiet moment, she found Maria and Chris. "My husband's death has not canceled my call," she said. "I'm going back to the States for a memorial and to spend some time with my sons and their families, then I'll be back. And I want you to know this as well: Orien's death hasn't canceled your call, either. This isn't what you signed up for, but we need both of you now more than ever."

53

WHEN CHRIS RETURNED to his office the following week, he found a note sitting on his desk. He recognized Harriet's handwriting immediately.

> *Chris and Maria—*
>
> *I'm not sure if Orien ever mentioned this to you, but he'd always hoped to write a book. Perhaps write is too strong a word. Compile would be more accurate. He wanted to go through his files and pull out some of his favorite sermons, devotionals, letters, journal entries, thoughts on living in Indonesia, et cetera. As you can imagine, he never had the time to do more than talk about it—as far as I can tell.*
>
> *Can I ask a huge favor of you? Would one or both of you be willing to start sifting through Orien's office while I'm in the States? My husband only recently started using the computer in his work, so most of what I'm looking for will be in physical files and notebooks.*
>
> *If you find anything that might be a good possibility for inclusion, just set it aside and I'll make the tough decisions when I return.*
>
> *Blessings,*
Harriet

What a job, Chris thought. *And what an honor.* He'd hoped to learn from this man for years to come, but Orien's unexpected death robbed him of the opportunity. Perhaps this task would afford him the chance to continue his education.

Over the following days, Chris set up shop in Orien's office, systematically working through desk drawers and notebooks. His glance occasionally drifted to the imposing file cabinet in the corner, and he wondered how many months it would take to catalog its contents.

On the third day, Chris opened a journal that he knew at once would alter the course of his life. Its spine had been salvaged by a strip of amber packing tape, and its green cover bore the scars of unspoken battles. The first page featured these words in Orien's neat printing: "The Never-Reached Tribes of Indonesia."

A crude, hand-drawn map of the major islands of the country spread over the next two pages. Each island on the map was assigned a number. As Chris flipped through the rest of the book, he discovered that each number was given its own page. Orien had included the name of each island followed by a list he identified as "tribes/nations." Some of these tribes had been written in blue ink, some in black, some in pencil. Some had been crossed out. Chris surmised that Orien returned to the journal as he gathered new information about the islands and people groups.

Chris stopped at a page titled "Small Eastern Islands." Orien had listed four tribes, three of which he had crossed out. The remaining name jumped out at him: Merapu.

Chris said the name aloud: "Merapu." Was this tribe still unreached? Had someone already carried the good news to

CHAPTER FIFTY-THREE

them? If not, what would it take to reach them? Sitting in Orien's office, Chris felt quickened in his spirit to pray for this people group. "Father," he said, "You love these people and desire for them to be in Your great global family. Send one of Your ambassadors to them with the good news of Your Son. Start preparing their hearts right at this moment to receive Your love."

Asep joined the Billings family for dinner that night, and Chris asked if he'd ever heard of the Merapu.

"Yes, I believe so," he said. "Very small tribe in the east."

"Do you know where they live?"

"I think I know the island," Asep said. "I have relatives on another island close by."

"Orien wrote in his journal that they had never been reached with the gospel. Is that still true?"

Asep shrugged. "One way to find out. Maybe we can go there someday."

"I think we should pray for them," Bethany said. "Right now. I think it's what Uncle Orien would want us to do."

And so they prayed for the Merapu that night. And every night after.

54

SEASONS PASSED, and life managed to go on without Orien. The counselor sent by Bob Hollins at Every Tribe Mission had helped Chris and Maria realize that Orien had been more than a mentor or colleague. He had become a father to them.

In the middle of his grief, Chris was able to thank God for the men who had invested in his life after his own father walked away. He thought of Granddad, Fritz Bernheim, Orien Berry—men he hoped to be like someday.

Chris had never been comfortable talking about his feelings, so he relied on his wife to walk the kids through their grieving process. The family faced life a day at a time and settled once again into a rhythm of homeschooling, language study, increasing ministry responsibilities, and dreaming about the future.

Harriet had returned to Indonesia as promised. She moved from her house in another part of the city to an apartment on the Bible school compound. She taught a class each semester on spiritual disciplines and took over Orien's office next to Chris and Maria's.

One evening about nine months after Orien's passing, Harriet knocked on the door of the Billings home. Maria, Chris, and Asep were just starting a lesson on Indonesian grammar.

"Sorry to stop by uninvited," Harriet said. "I was just out for a walk, and a thought popped into my head."

"You're always welcome here," Maria said. "Our home is your home."

"That's very kind." She joined them at the table. "I have an idea I'd like both of you to consider. As you know, your apprenticeship with the mission has an educational component. Most of the time, that means taking online courses through one of our affiliated schools back in the States. But I've noticed that your language skills are improving dramatically. Your hard work is paying off. So here's what I propose: Would you consider taking classes right here, at the Bible school? It would do wonders for your growth in the language, and you'd be able to develop deeper relationships with these amazing students, who will be your colleagues before long."

Chris and Maria looked at each other, eyebrows raised.

"I think it's a great idea," Chris said. "However, the thought of reading and writing in a second language makes me a little nervous."

"As well it should," Harriet said. "It'll be a stretch, but I'm confident you can handle it. Besides, I think it'll send a powerful message that the missionaries aren't above everyone else."

"Great point," Maria said. "I'm ready whenever you are."

"Let's do it," Chris said. "We can get started right after our trip out east."

CHAPTER FIFTY-FOUR

Ever since the Holy Spirit brought the Merapu people to Chris's attention, he couldn't shake the thought that he would have a part to play in reaching them with the gospel. If his task was simply mobilizing prayer support, he was content with that. But he had a feeling his role would be more.

As the months had passed, Chris, Maria, and Asep grew more serious in their plan to visit the islands in the east, in the region where Orien's book indicated the Merapu might live. Asep made the arrangements with his relatives in Bilonga: He and the Billings family would visit and explore, trusting the Spirit once again to guide their steps.

The morning of their trip arrived, and Maria inspected the kids' luggage one final time. Chris placed the plane tickets on the table and opened his laptop. He needed to check his email once more before disappearing off the grid for four days.

At the top of his in-box sat a message from Jane Renfroe, his office manager back at Custom Clock. Jane emailed on the first day of every month with a brief report on the company's business and confirmation of the wire transfer to Chris's personal account. But that update wasn't due for another week. The subject of this message read "bank accounts?"

Chris read:

> *Hey, Boss.*
> *I just got back into town after a weeklong vacation. I'm having trouble logging into the company accounts. The site is telling me my*

passwords are invalid. Did you happen to change the login info for some reason while I was out? Sorry to bother you with this, but I haven't been able to get through to Jim. Maybe he knows something. I'll check with him in the morning.

Jane

Chris's brain scanned through the potential reasons for this news, and none of the possibilities made sense. The growing dread in the pit of his stomach almost convinced him to postpone the trip until the situation was resolved, but he brushed aside his concerns. He wrote:

I haven't changed any of the login credentials. I'm sure Jim has a good explanation for what happened. Maybe the system prompted an automatic password update. Who knows? I'm heading out of town for a few days. Don't know if I'll be able to check in. But please update as soon as you hear anything. —CB

He closed the computer, picked up the plane tickets, and herded his crew to the van. *Okay, Tucker,* he thought. *What have you done?*

55

THE FLIGHT FROM SURABAYA to Bilonga lasted two hours. Chris had hoped to relax, but he couldn't stop thinking about Jane's email. Maria sensed her husband's unease and asked what was wrong. He told her what he knew, but not what he suspected.

When they landed, Asep took the lead. He'd arranged transportation to their homestay, a small, humble resort of bamboo huts overlooking the sea. The kids all agreed: This was paradise.

Before dinner, Asep and Chris headed into the surrounding neighborhood to find bottled water and other supplies. Even though there were restaurants nearby, Asep had encouraged them to prepare at least one of their meals over an open fire. He was certain they could find a passing fisherman eager to sell his catch.

The pair walked by a neat white building that featured wide windows on all sides. Chris stopped when he recognized a word on the sign next to the door. "It's a church?" he asked.

"It is," Asep said.

"Father," Chris prayed, "bless Your children. May they be fruitful witnesses to Your love and faithfulness in this city. May lives be transformed by the power of the gospel as it's preached in this place."

Asep and Chris meandered through the streets as though they were led by the Spirit. An ornate building set back from the road caught Chris's attention. Young men lounged in the shade of a small grove of trees.

"What is this?" Chris asked. "A school?"

"Yes. It's a *pesantren*. Like a Bible school, but for studying the Qur'an. There are some in our city as well."

Chris nodded and whispered a prayer that the students would encounter the Truth.

※

Bandu missed Sri and Fatima, but he'd adapted to life as a student. His skill in Arabic and knowledge of the Qur'an advanced by the day, and he made sure to get home every few weeks to be with his family. With each visit, his stature in Seora grew, and he looked forward to finishing his studies. Salahuddin would tell him when he was ready.

On this afternoon, he stepped away from his books for a moment, hoping that a breeze off the sea might clear his mind. In the courtyard of the *pesantren*, joking and smoking with his fellow students, he witnessed an unusual sight. Outside the gates, across the street, stood two men. One looked like an Indonesian. He might even be related to the Merapu. But the other man was clearly a foreigner, even though he dressed like a local. He was tall and lean — and had the palest skin Bandu

CHAPTER FIFTY-FIVE

had ever seen. He'd spotted foreigners in Bilonga before, but this man glowed.

The two men started to walk away, and Bandu decided to follow. What were these people doing here? He knew they were enemies of Allah. Perhaps he could convince them of their error. Or at the very least, he could foil their plans. He finished his cigarette and stepped into the street.

ω

Chris and Asep turned a corner and almost crashed into a vendor pushing a cart loaded down with fruit. A mob of small children followed the cart, begging its owner for a sampling of his produce.

In his mind, Chris flashed back twenty-five years to the streets and parks of Grapevine, Pennsylvania. But instead of fresh fruit, his gang had yearned for frozen desserts, drawn by the telltale bell of the ice cream man's truck.

"Is it okay if I buy some fruit for them?" Chris asked Asep.

"Only if you want friends for the rest of your life."

Chris handed a few bills to the vendor and started passing out slices of papaya, mango, yellow watermelon, pineapple, and banana to the delighted kids. As they ate, they organized an impromptu choir for Chris and Asep, quickly exhausting their repertoire of children's songs.

"Where are you from?" the bravest of the kids asked Chris when the concert ended.

"East Java," Chris said.

"I don't think so," the kid said.

"It's true," Asep said. "We were just there this morning."

Down the street, Bandu leaned against a tree and noted the tactics of these servants of Satan. *So typical,* he thought. *Go after the small and the weak.* He needed to warn the children to stay away from these outsiders, but he was not yet ready to reveal himself.

Later that night, Asep and the Billings family enjoyed a dinner of fresh fish and an array of fruit—a final purchase from the street vendor. Asep cooked the fish over hot coals of coconut husks, just as he'd seen his mother do when he was a boy.

After watching a red sun set into the ocean, the kids collapsed into their beds in the bamboo hut they shared with their parents. The three adults settled around the fire, talking about the sense of brokenness and desperation they felt around them—such a contrast to their physical surroundings. Their discussion soon turned to the tribes on these islands yet to receive the message of Jesus. Chris told Maria about the church he'd passed, just a kilometer from where they sat.

"Asep," Chris asked, "when you graduate, do you want to serve in a city like this that already has churches?"

"No, Chris. Like the apostle said, 'It's my ambition to preach the gospel where Christ has not yet been known, so that I wouldn't be building on another's foundation.' Like our brothers and sisters at work among the Sagi."

CHAPTER FIFTY-FIVE

"Or the Merapu," Maria said.

"Yes. Or the Merapu."

☙

As soon as Chris's head hit the pillow that night, he fell into a deep sleep. At once, he was reliving the events of the day through his dreams. He was on the plane. Then he was outside the *pesantren*. Then he was standing next to the fruit cart.

But instead of participating in these scenes himself, he was observing them from above. And it was no longer he who walked through his day. Now he saw Jesus hand money to the vendor. He heard Jesus joke with Asep. He watched as Jesus rubbed the head of a child.

Chris turned his gaze down the street and saw a strange man watching from the shadows. He drifted in the man's direction, but the stranger ignored him. He wouldn't take his eyes off Jesus. Finally, the man spoke to Chris: "Who is that man over there touching the children? I must know. Who is he, and why has he come?"

"It's Jesus," Chris called. "It's Jesus." But as soon as Chris spoke, the stranger doubled over in pain.

"I can't hear you," the man said. "If I could hear you, then I would know. Please tell me! Who is this?"

"It's Jesus!" Chris yelled. But the man did not respond.

Chris woke up in a sweat. He remembered every detail of the dream. He had no idea what it meant.

56

TWO DAYS LATER, Chris boarded a flight back to the States in circumstances he never could have imagined. He wedged himself into a window seat, opened his prayer journal, and poured his heart onto the page.

No one has died (yet), but this feels like a funeral. I'm heading back to Grapevine to see if God can raise my company off its deathbed. Maybe it's too late.

We still don't know all of the facts, but it looks like Jim Tucker emptied the bank accounts and disappeared. The police suspect he's planned this since I hired him 18 months ago. He slowly gained access to the login info and passwords, and now it looks like he's moved everything into offshore accounts. He could be anywhere by now. If that's not bad enough, Jane says Granddad's Eli Terry is missing.

Jane blames herself, but I know the truth. I never should have hired the guy in the first place. I don't want to think about what I'll do if I ever find him.

Timmy's too little to understand what's happening, but Maria and I talked with the girls in general terms, explaining that the company's in trouble. Bethany asked if this means we have to move back to Pennsylvania. We told her no, and she said, "Good, because I don't want to go. I could live with Aunt Harriet."

Is it a coincidence that this has happened right when we've started talking and praying about the never-reached tribes? When our language skills give us the ability to get out and do what God has called us to do? I don't think so. It feels like we're under attack in the spirit realm. I know some people think that's just mumbo-jumbo, but Scripture is clear. Just because we can't see it doesn't mean it's not there.

So, Lord, I need Your wisdom. I'm meeting with my employees, suppliers, bankers, not to mention the police. I'll get together with Fritz and Gloria and other friends from church. We need to hear from You, and we need You to do what only You can do.

But however this turns out, I'm going back to Indonesia. There's too much work to be done.

ꙮ

When Chris landed in Newark, Will was waiting for him. "Don't take this the wrong way, big brother," Will said, "but you look terrible."

"Love you too," Chris said, engulfing Will in a bear hug. "I think I've slept a grand total of twenty-three minutes in the last day and a half."

In the first hour of the drive west, Chris shared what he knew about the case. At the appropriate times, Will let loose with a stream of R-rated vocabulary directed at Jim Tucker.

CHAPTER FIFTY-SIX

"It's all my fault," Chris said. "I never felt completely comfortable with him."

"I'll stop you right there. There's one person to blame here, and it's not you." That was a kind thing for Will to say, but Chris didn't believe it.

Will asked: "So what are your plans?"

"The priority is to save the business, if possible. Worst-case scenario is we shut everything down and liquidate the assets. We have a lot of equity in the building and equipment, so we should be able to cover our debts and take care of the workers."

"So, long-term," Will said. "Are you moving back home, or—"

"Either way, we're staying in Indonesia," Chris said. He'd anticipated the question and formulated his response. "That's our life now. I know not everyone understands this, but we truly believe God called us there. And His call doesn't go away when our plan changes or when life gets hard."

"Good," Will said, blinking away tears. "That's what I hoped you'd say. I miss you and Maria and the kids like crazy—especially Maria and the kids—but God has shown me you're exactly where you're supposed to be. I don't want to get all emotional and everything, but you've helped me see there's more to life than being safe and comfortable and buying new stuff. You're making your life count."

"We're just trying to be obedient."

"I know. And I'm proud of you. And I'll do whatever it takes to help you get back there."

Before meeting with his employees the next day, Chris needed to get a clear picture of his financial reality. So he and Jane scheduled a visit with Greg, who'd served as the company's CPA going back to Granddad's days.

"Chris," Greg said, "this is a major blow, but there's no reason it has to be fatal."

"You don't know how reassuring that is," Chris said.

"Well, you have a long track record of success. That means something to your creditors and customers. And it sounds like you have several months' worth of orders yet to fulfill."

"That's right," Jane said. "About four months' worth of work."

"Right there," Greg said, "that should be enough to help you secure a short-term loan to cover payroll for a while. And then there's the insurance policy. You won't receive a payout right away, but that's a game changer."

"What's this?" Chris asked. "What insurance policy?"

"Your commercial crime insurance," Greg said. "It covers things like embezzlement."

Chris and Jane exchanged puzzled glances.

"If I remember correctly," Greg said, "your grandfather added that to his commercial policy a couple of years before his stroke. It's all one quarterly premium, so you might not have paid much attention to it."

"It does sound vaguely familiar," Chris said. "I'm afraid I don't have a lot of patience for the fine print."

"Of course, the business was smaller then, so it probably won't cover all of your losses. You'll have to talk with your agent, but it looks like Arthur managed to save his company after all."

CHAPTER FIFTY-SIX

Rather than the funeral he'd been preparing for, Chris's presentation to his employees turned into a celebration.

"You've no doubt heard some stuff about the business side of the operation," he said. "It looks like we've been betrayed by one of our own, and the police assure me they will do everything they can to get to the bottom of it."

More than a few of the workers chimed in with remarks that put Will's to shame.

"However," Chris said, "I have some great news. The work will go on, and you will not miss a single paycheck. Our banks and insurance companies are willing to work with us. Everyone who's placed an order with us still wants to see it fulfilled. Our suppliers are still on board. It'll take a number of months or maybe even years to get back to where we were, but here in the shop, nothing will change. Thanks to all of your hard work through the years, this company has a great reputation in our community, and they want to see us succeed." The outlook for the company was better than Chris expected but he knew that the next year would require even greater personal sacrifices. They had some savings but the monthly amount the company gave him would be put on hold for a while or at least until the insurance kicked in, Jim Tucker was caught or there was a significant rebound in the company. It felt like he had lost it all. Chris had a quiet moment in the parking lot and just closed his eyes and committed it all once again to the Savior he loved and served.

Ω

The night before he left for Indonesia, Chris asked Fritz Bernheim to call an impromptu gathering of the Billings family's prayer band. He wanted to see his old friends and give them an update on the work, but even more, he needed to impress on them the reality of the spiritual battle they faced.

"If you've been praying for us once a week," he said, "we need you to add a day. If you've been praying once a day, we need you to double it."

He revealed what he was sensing about the next phase of the ministry, that the Lord was guiding them to the never-reached tribes of the east. And he gave them a specific name to carry to the throne room of heaven: the Merapu.

57

NYALE SETTLED INTO his nest above Seora and rustled the trees with extra vigor. He could not allow the pitiful people below him to forget he was still there, watching and controlling everything.

One young man had the temerity to pass by with a smile on his face, not a care in the world. Nyale at once summoned a demon of fear. "Ruin his day," Nyale said. "Don't let him have a moment of peace until I command you otherwise." The demon drifted downward and landed on the man's back. His smile disappeared. He looked over his shoulder and picked up his pace.

A sentry suddenly arrived before Nyale and gave a perfunctory bow. "A visitor, my lord," it said. "With a report on the spell caster's son."

Nyale nodded. "The visitor may approach," he said.

A small, gray, bat-like figure appeared. Its eyes shifted from side to side. "Master," it said, "I return from Bilonga, where Bandu is studying the book."

"Yes, I'm aware. Continue."

"He is a diligent student. His teacher believes he will be ready to return soon."

"Go on."

"But I must report a troubling incident. Outside the school, we detected surveillance by two servants of the Most High. They are not from Bilonga. We understand they are from another island. One of these men, a man of prayer, is called Asep. The other man, a foreigner, appears to be his assistant. And they were accompanied by three of the Most High's warriors. Two of them, named Sword and Light, are well known among our troops for their great strength and intelligence."

"Surveillance. That is expected. Powerful angels. What else?"

"Well, master, it seems Bandu followed these men on the streets. He didn't tell anyone what he had done, so we are unable to decipher his motives."

"What!?" Nyale screamed. "When did this take place?"

"Almost one week ago, sir."

"Why am I just now learning of this!?"

"We wanted to monitor Bandu further before issuing our report, my lord. Besides, the outsiders appear to have received bad news and departed the island the next day."

"This is unacceptable! Any contact with servants of the Most High must be conveyed as soon as possible! Out of my sight!"

Nyale had to act decisively. He called a spirit named Fever to his side and gave his orders: "Find Soraya the shaman and attack him immediately. Afflict him with pain he's never before experienced, to the very edge of death. And spread the word: Make it known that I am not pleased."

CHAPTER FIFTY-SEVEN

That night, Bandu had trouble falling asleep. He told himself it was because he missed his wife and daughter. But he knew the true reason. He couldn't stop thinking about the two outsiders he'd followed through the streets the week before. The day after spotting them, he went back out, hoping to see them again. Maybe he could find where they were staying. Maybe he could find out who they were. He'd gone out every day, but his quarry had vanished.

When Bandu finally drifted off to sleep, he entered a dreamworld unlike any he'd ever visited. The visions inspired him and disturbed him. They drew him in and repulsed him at the same time. He saw his father and his wife. He watched as a man placed his hand on his daughter's head. Was that Fatima running through a rice field? He overheard the conversations of his *kyai*. He followed the two outsiders up the mountain to his own village. When he woke up before dawn, his heart was racing. He could not make sense of what he'd seen and heard. All he knew was that the pale man and his friend could give him the answer.

The next day, Salahuddin called Bandu to his office. "We have received word from your village," the teacher said. "Your father is gravely ill. No one can say if he'll make it. You must return to your people at once."

On his way to the boat that would carry him back to his island, Bandu took his time, meandered through the streets, peered into every cafe and shop. The outsiders were nowhere to be found.

58

BACK IN INDONESIA after his whirlwind trip to Pennsylvania, Chris felt renewed energy for the task ahead. He was relieved that his company had somehow survived, but the incident confirmed in his heart and mind that he was more than a clock maker. He was an ambassador of King Jesus, and he would go wherever his King sent him to proclaim whatever message his King asked him to declare.

On the voyage back, he sensed the Lord telling him that his family's mission would be inextricably linked to the Merapu. The lostness of the tribe weighed on him, and he felt God give him an urgency to see the people group reached with the gospel.

Chris couldn't envision exactly how it would happen, but he formed a rough outline. He and Asep would return to Bilonga and try to find someone — anyone — associated with the Merapu. They would gather whatever information they could learn about the tribe. Maybe the Billings family would even relocate to Bilonga to establish a base camp. Above all, they would dedicate themselves to prayer and fasting. Chris remembered the times Orien had talked about the overwhelming, all-encompassing task of reaching the never-reached. The enemy controlled these peoples for thousands of years and would throw every resource available into the fight.

When Chris shared his plan with Maria and Asep, they didn't hesitate. "I think this is why we're here," Maria said. "It seems like everything has been pointing to this moment."

"It won't be easy," Asep said, "but I will be at your side.... There's something I recently remembered. We think the Merapu are on an island called Turang. It's a short boat ride from the port of Bilonga. But their island has another name, an ancient name used by some of the old men. The ancient name is Ajansamar. It means fortress of the underworld. Powerful spirits rule that land."

"That makes sense," Chris said. "If it was an easy job, it would have already been done. I'll commit to praying for the Merapu by name each time the call to prayer goes out, and we can ask others at the Bible school to do the same. And I believe we should fast on Fridays. We have no chance unless we operate in the power of the Spirit."

As they talked, Maria started composing a message for their prayer partners in the States, enlisting them in the effort. "Join us in praying and fasting for the Merapu people," she wrote. "We don't know much about them, but we believe they have never in their history heard the message of Jesus. They are trapped in darkness unless we go. Pray that our God would break down strongholds, prepare men and women of peace who will give us access to their villages, and soften the hearts of the people to receive the truth. Ask for wisdom and protection as we make plans to travel to their island."

CHAPTER FIFTY-EIGHT

Within minutes of sending the email, Maria began receiving replies.

Gloria Bernheim wrote, "We are with you, dear friends. May the warriors of heaven prepare the way."

"I'm believing for a great awakening among the Merapu people," the letter carrier Michael Lamb wrote. "And I will join you in fasting every Friday."

Aaron Patterson responded from State College: "Penn State Christian Fellowship is standing (and kneeling!) with you. So proud to call you our alumni. I'm setting up a calendar so there's always someone praying for you, around the clock."

The angelic warriors in the room nodded their approval. "This is where the battle is won," Sword said. "Let's prepare for the reinforcements that are sure to come."

59

BANDU'S VAN REACHED Seora just after sundown. The return of the dying shaman's heir was big news, and word of his arrival spread quickly through the village. Sri picked up Fatima and rushed to the clearing near the mosque, where visitors parked their vehicles. She found her husband stretching sore muscles like a sprinter before a race.

Bandu wrapped his wife and daughter in his arms, grateful that their separations would soon be a thing of the past. "That journey," Bandu said, "has a way of making a young man feel old."

He took time to greet each of his friends who had come to meet him, then noticed a couple of the elders on the edge of the group. "Your mother is expecting you," one of the men said.

Bandu sent Sri and Fatima home and made his way to his parents' hut. The information he'd received had been spare, so he wasn't sure what he'd find when he got there. Was his father even alive? Inside the hut, a lamp burned in the corner and Djum kept vigil beside her husband's bed. Soraya, never a large man, looked shrunken beneath his blanket. His eyes stared, unblinking, at the ceiling. The odor of death hung in the air.

"Father, it's Bandu. I've come home. Can you hear me?"

Soraya gave no indication that he was aware of his son's presence. Only a slight and intermittent raising of the chest let Bandu know his father was still alive.

Bandu told his mother he would return in the morning and stepped through the doorway into the twilight. He took a deep breath of fresh air and exhaled slowly. He was glad Soraya was alive, wasn't he? For the first time, Bandu considered that the alternative might be for the best. With his father out of the picture, he could take his place among the leaders of the village. He was certainly ready.

ω

Nyale followed as Bandu walked the path from his parents' hut to his own. The ruler of Seora weighed conflicting pieces of evidence concerning the young man. First, Bandu possessed certain natural gifts. He was intelligent, and others were eager to follow him. He would make an acceptable *dukun*—if he fully gave himself over to Nyale. And that pointed to the conflict. Nyale still didn't trust him, couldn't trust him. Bandu was too unpredictable. Soraya would do whatever Nyale commanded, but Bandu... Bandu was another matter.

ω

CHAPTER FIFTY-NINE

Bandu startled awake in the middle of the night. A man was calling his name, but now he knew it was only a dream. As the fog of sleep cleared, he realized it was the same man from the dream he'd had in the city. *Who was this man? What did he want? How did he know my name?* Once again, he sensed that the answers were in Bilonga. Until he found the two strangers, he was in the dark.

Unable to go back to sleep, Bandu eased himself out of bed and tiptoed out of the hut. Under the glow of a full moon, he paused on the path to light a cigarette. Maybe this would calm his nerves. He wandered through the village trying to reconstruct his dream, but the details eluded him. He was left with impressions, feelings, vague desires. The man in the dream hadn't explained himself, but he gave Bandu something he'd never before experienced: a sense of peace.

♎

The days turned to weeks, and Nyale kept Soraya balancing at the edge of death. At last, he summoned his most trusted underlings to debate their options.

"I don't wish to prolong this matter any longer," Nyale said. "I could take the spell caster's life at any moment, or I could call off the fever and restore him to his position. What shall it be?"

The assembled demons remained silent. Nyale had given no hint of his preference, and they were reluctant to venture an opinion.

"I see," Nyale said. "Let's do it like this. What is the case for removing the old man and replacing him with the son?"

A spirit of deception spoke up. "The son," it said, "is a capable teacher. The elders at times have called on him to explain the book, and his answers have been acceptable to us. He has learned well at the distant school."

"Yes," Nyale said. "What else?"

"Master," another said, "the son already has a measure of influence. All of the young men follow him, along with many of the elders. He is seen as a leader. In addition, his child's affliction keeps him loyal to you."

Nyale asked, "What about the other side? Why should I consider restoring the old man?"

"For me," a demon of disease said, "it comes down to control. Soraya doesn't eat a papaya without consulting you first. He is the picture of loyalty. As the humans say, 'Better the devil you know.'"

Nyale chuckled at the irony. "Indeed," he said.

ω

Soraya emerged from his trance the next day stronger than he'd been in years. "It was Nyale," he told everyone within earshot. "Nyale has spared my life."

A few days later, when it became clear to Bandu that his father's health would hold, he brought up the topic of his return to Bilonga. "My studies are almost complete," he said. "The sooner I go back and finish my course, the sooner I can come home for good and learn alongside you."

"I will consult Nyale," Soraya said. "He will let us know."

CHAPTER FIFTY-NINE

That evening, as he'd done for decades, Soraya burned his incense and recited his incantations, anticipating a simple word from Nyale. When he heard nothing, he tried again the next day. But for the first time since he'd assumed the role of *dukun*, Soraya failed to hear Nyale's voice. Something had changed. Still, he granted Bandu's request.

"Nyale has given no answer," he said, "but you may return to the *pesantren*. If this was important to Nyale, he would have spoken."

60

ASEP TURNED OFF the toll road and pointed the van in the direction of the departures terminal.

"Let's find a place to park for a few minutes," Chris said. "We still have a lot of time."

When they pulled into the parking lot of an airport hotel, Chris twisted in his seat to face his family. "Kids," he said, "can you pray for Asep and me before we get on the plane?"

Timmy started: "Dear Jesus, help Daddy and Asep have a fun trip. Please keep them safe, and help the airplane to not crash. Amen."

"That's a good prayer," Asep said. "I agree with all of that."

Maria and the girls took turns calling on heaven on behalf of the travelers — and for the Merapu people. "We ask You to guide Chris's and Asep's steps in Bilonga and wherever else You might lead them," Maria said. "Help them to see with Your eyes. Send someone who can give them information about the Merapu. Lord, we pray for miracles on this trip. Work in ways that we can't even imagine. Do the things only You can do. May this trip lead to a great awakening among the Merapu and other never-reached peoples in the area. Place Your angels around them, and protect them from the schemes of the enemy."

Asep drove to the terminal and wedged into a spot along the curb. On the sidewalk, Chris hugged his kids, holding on a bit longer than usual, praying a blessing over each one. Everything was happening too quickly and he wanted to slow down, to make this moment last. There were so many unknowns surrounding this trip, including his return. Saying goodbye was always hard, but this was especially difficult, not knowing when he would see his wife and children again. *If I see them again*, he said to himself. *Wait. Where did that thought come from?* His throat tightened as he embraced Maria and lifted her off her feet. *If this is the last time…* he dismissed the idea and set her down.

After sharing one final kiss with her husband, Maria herded the kids into the van. She grabbed the keys from Asep and maneuvered the vehicle back into traffic. All three children jumped into the backseat and waved until they were out of sight. *What a privilege*, Chris thought, *to be their dad*. He picked up his bag and turned to Asep. "Let's do this," he said.

As the pair worked their way through security, the heavenly guardians gathered off to the side — Sword, Light, Mercy, and three newcomers. The prayers of the saints had been bombarding the throne room of the Most High, and He'd responded by sending more troops.

"Enemy forces are everywhere," Sword said. "They're not even trying to conceal themselves."

"That's to be expected, right?" Mercy asked. "This has been their domain. They might be surprised that there are so many of us, but I'm sure they're as cocky as ever."

CHAPTER SIXTY

"Be on guard," Sword said. "Expect an assault at any moment."

When Asep and Chris saw their plane, they couldn't believe their eyes. It was a Fokker F27, a turboprop at least forty years old. Chris had no idea the plane was still in active service. An agent at the gate noticed their nervous glances and tried to be reassuring. "It's perfectly safe," she said. "We use these occasionally when our newer planes are down for maintenance. No need to worry."

I'll worry if I want to, Chris thought.

Twenty minutes later, as the plane rumbled down the runway, Asep leaned over to Chris. "Hey, brother," he said. "Let's hope your prayer team remember that we're traveling today." Chris forced a smile and closed his eyes.

The first two hours of the flight passed uneventfully. As they approached Bilonga, the captain gave the standard instructions about landing procedures, and the two flight attendants went about their routine. But as the craft began its descent, the captain noticed a problem with the landing gear. The wheels at the nose and on the left side extended as designed, but the gear on the right locked halfway down.

The plane was falling rapidly, but the gear wouldn't budge. At the last possible second, the pilot pulled the plane up out of its descent and roared past the runway. Over the next ten minutes, the craft circled the airport in a wide holding pattern. The captain tried to retract the landing gear, and the apparatus at the nose and on the left operated properly. The gear on the right, however, stayed locked into place. After several more failed attempts, the captain's voice came over the intercom: "Ladies and gentlemen, we're experiencing a slight problem with the landing gear, and it doesn't look like we'll be able to resolve it in the air. So, we'll have to attempt a landing with what we've got. Two of the three landing gear legs appear to be functioning properly, so we'll make some adjustments accordingly. Sit tight. It could get a little bumpy."

Pilots, Chris thought. *Masters of understatement.*

Chris knew that some people who go through near-death events talk about seeing their life flash before their eyes. As the F27 floated toward the runway, he didn't experience a flash. For him, it was more like a leisurely highlight reel of his life. He saw moments of his childhood, pictures of his mom and brothers, his grandparents, Maria walking down the aisle, the births of his children. He never imagined it would end this way for him, that he would never see his wife and kids again this side of heaven, but he was grateful for the life God had given him. He whispered a short prayer.

The wheels screeched on the runway, and the plane pitched dangerously to the right. But almost immediately, it bounced back up, all of its weight balanced on the nose and left side. The captain guided the craft to a stop as quickly as possible. Fire engines and ambulances raced down the runway to the ancient plane, its passengers finally able to exhale.

61

"WHAT'S WRONG, my friend?" Abdullah asked. "You seem distracted since coming back to us. Still worried about your father?"

Bandu looked up from the breakfast he hadn't yet touched. Could he dare tell anyone about his troubles? What would Abdullah think?

"Yes, of course," Bandu said. "Father is old, and his recent illness came on so suddenly. It could happen again. And I'm thinking of my daughter and my wife as well. I look forward to being with them.... But there's something else."

Abdullah leaned across the table. "You don't have to tell me anything," he said. "But your secret is safe with me."

Secret? Is that what Bandu had been doing—keeping a secret? He realized he had to tell someone.

"I've been having dreams," he said. "They started the night before I went back to my village. I'm not sure exactly what they mean, but I can't stop thinking about them. They follow me through my day."

"That's wonderful," Abdullah said. "It could be that Allah is speaking to you. The prophet said to thank Allah for good dreams and share them with others."

"Well, I'm not sure they're *good* dreams. I can't figure out what they are."

They hustled to the classroom for their morning lessons and made plans to talk again later. In class, Bandu debated what to tell Abdullah. He had trouble deciding, mainly because he was so unsure of the details. How could he talk about dreams made up not of actions but of feelings? How could he describe the mysterious man calling him by name?

After lunch, Abdullah suggested they skip their afternoon classes and find a tea stall in the neighborhood. There, they could talk openly without fear of being overheard by nosy classmates or teachers. Bandu was desperate to discover the meaning of his dreams, so he readily agreed. When everyone else was occupied, they left the *pesantren* and found a quiet *kios* on a side street. They claimed a table in the corner, and Bandu sipped pensively from his cup. Abdullah allowed him time to gather his thoughts.

"I'm not sure what to make of these dreams," Bandu said. "Yet I feel they're important."

"It's a great honor to receive dreams from Allah," Abdullah said. "Perhaps if you tell me about them I can help you interpret what they mean."

"Perhaps. But I'm afraid there isn't much to tell. I see a man, and he is calling out to me. He knows my name. He invites me to follow him."

CHAPTER SIXTY-ONE

A demonic messenger whispered in Abdullah's ear. "It could be the prophet," Abdullah said. "He knows of your desire to be a teacher, and he calls you to submit to his path."

"I'm sure it's not the prophet," Bandu said. "I don't know how I know this, but it's not. In the dream, I want to go with him. I feel a great peace whenever this man is near. It's like a warm shower washing over me. He doesn't say these words, but he makes me believe my daughter will walk again."

"What does this man look like? Do you recognize him at all?"

"That's one of the strange aspects of all this. I don't recognize him, and in the morning I never remember what he looked like."

"This is a very confusing riddle. I've never heard anything like this. If you have a dream again, write it down immediately. If you remember more details, maybe we can find the answers."

A spirit sent by Nyale to follow Bandu rose from the next table. *The master*, it thought, *needs to hear about this.*

62

EARLIER THAT MORNING, Chris had closed his Bible and prayer journal and placed them on the small table next to his bed. The room he and Asep were renting for the week was nothing special, but at least the bed had sheets.

"Now that was interesting," Chris said. "You ever notice in the Book of Acts, Paul and his companions are totally dependent on the Holy Spirit? Not just for the power to do miracles and preach the gospel, but even where they're supposed to go? They ask God where to go next, He tells them, and they obey. And when they get there, He leads them to specific people and places. A lot of the exciting stuff just happens out in the streets."

"Orien always said Jesus' ministry was like that too," Asep said. "He'd be walking somewhere with the disciples, and He'd notice someone. Or another person would come up to them and ask a question. They were on the way somewhere, but Jesus would always stop and have deep conversations and heal people. What did Orien call them? Divine interruptions—that's it."

"I like that," Chris said. "When we head out today, let's pray for divine interruptions. We can walk and pray and ask God to guide us down the streets He wants us to see. Maybe we'll run into someone who's ready to have a conversation."

"Maybe," Asep said, "we'll meet someone who can point us to the Merapu."

On their prayerwalk through the streets of Bilonga, Chris and Asep tried to discern and follow the Spirit's leading. They prayed silently for every individual they passed, asking God to reveal himself to them. They prayed for grace and peace upon homes, schools, and places of business. They both sensed the Lord guiding them to the southwest, so they followed the streets in that direction. Eventually, they realized they were in the neighborhood where Chris had bought fruit for the children during their previous visit.

"I don't believe in coincidences," Chris said. "Let's find a place to rest and pray. God has led us to this part of town for a reason. Let's ask Him to show us what He's up to."

Asep pointed out a *kios* down the street where they could get out of the sun and drink some tea. At that moment, two young men stepped out from under the makeshift roof of the *kios* and turned left.

ω

Bandu spotted the two outsiders across the street and quickly looked away. There was no question about it. They were the same

CHAPTER SIXTY-TWO

men he had seen with the children weeks ago—the men who could tell him about his dream. His heart raced, but he tried not to alert Abdullah.

"You see that?" Abdullah asked. "I wonder what he's doing here. Not too many foreigners in this section of the city."

Bandu pretended not to have noticed. He made a show of peering over his shoulder as he walked. "That's a good question," he said. "The resorts are some distance away." Before he and Abdullah turned the next corner, he saw the two strangers duck into the *kios* they had just left.

Bandu couldn't let the men get away, but he also couldn't let Abdullah know what he was about to do. He needed to formulate a plan quickly, something plausible that would allow him to break free. About a block from the *pesantren*, he started frantically patting his pockets. "Did I leave my wallet there?" he asked. "Did you see it on the table? I think it might have fallen."

"I don't remember seeing anything. Should we go back and look for it?"

"No, we're almost home. Why don't you go on ahead and I'll rush back there."

"I'm happy to go with you," Abdullah said. "I don't think I'm capable of studying more today anyway."

"I insist. You shouldn't have to pay for my mistake. It won't take long."

"Okay. But let me know when you find it."

Bandu rushed back to the tea stall, but when he arrived he thought he was too late. From the street, he couldn't see the men anywhere. Then a voice grabbed his attention: "Are you looking for us?"

Ω

The young man was stunned by Asep's question. Chris could tell he wanted to approach, but he stood in the street for ten seconds before moving. He cautiously approached their table in the back corner and asked if he could sit. Asep gestured toward an empty chair. The young man sat and studied the faces of Chris and Asep without speaking another word.

"Why have you come back?" Asep asked.

"I need to ask you some questions."

"What would you like to know?" Chris said.

"The foreigner speaks Bahasa!?"

"I do."

"Who are you?"

"My name is Chris. This is Asep. What's your name?"

"My name is Bandu. Where are you from?"

"I'm from America. Asep is from Surabaya in East Java. And you? Where is your home?"

"I am from a small village on a small island not far from here."

Chris and Asep exchanged a glance. Asep asked, "What is the name of your people?"

"We are the Merapu."

A chill ran down Chris's spine. He said, "Bandu, we know why you're here. You followed us one day. Then God sent you a dream, but you don't know what it means."

"How can you know that? I've never told anyone—except Abdullah. Has Abdullah been talking to you?"

"No," Asep said, "we don't know Abdullah, but we know about you."

"But how?"

"God told us you were coming back," Chris said. "And He told us about the dream."

"What if I said I don't believe you?"

"That's your choice," Asep said. "But you're the one who came to us with your questions."

"But how can I trust you? How do I know you speak truth?"

"What if we told you what else we know?" Asep asked. "We know you have a daughter who is not well. And we know there was a man in your dream—a man who knew your name."

Bandu forced his chair backward, but he could not make himself stand. "Are you prophets?" he asked.

"In a way," Chris said. "We speak the message of God in the name of Jesus the Savior."

"I should have known," Bandu said. Then he launched into the standard Islamic criticism of Christianity—words he'd memorized since arriving at the *pesantren*. Point by point, he attempted to refute the virgin birth, the crucifixion and resurrection, the Holy Scriptures.

"We're not here to argue with you," Asep said. "But Jesus appeared to you in a dream and called you by name. God sees you. He knows you desire to serve Him. He is showing you that Jesus is the way."

"But these are lies," Bandu said. "How can you expect me to believe them?"

"Can I tell you my story?" Asep asked. "Jesus spoke to me in a dream as well, when I was sixteen years old. I eventually believed, and He made me a new man." For the next ten minutes, as Asep explained how Jesus had changed his life, Chris prayed silently. Bandu didn't say a word.

"You might think this is foolishness," Chris said. "You might think it's hard to believe. But can we meet again tomorrow? I know you have many more questions."

Bandu considered Chris's proposal in silence. His face betrayed no emotion. At last, he replied: "Yes. Let's meet again. I would like that."

63

THE NEXT DAY, the three men met in a park far from the shadow of Bandu's *pesantren*. They claimed a bench along a walkway tucked behind a stand of trees. Despite the privacy, Bandu remained alert to the possibility that he would be seen by someone who could report on him.

For the first hour, they talked about their families and their hometowns, comparing life in Seora, Surabaya, and Grapevine. Bandu seemed especially interested in Asep's tale of abandonment. "Your family threw you into the street," he said, "but the followers of Jesus adopted you?"

"That is the Jesus way," Asep said. "He offers adoption to all who have been shamed and abandoned."

Soon the conversation turned to ideas about God, and Chris noticed a shift in Bandu's attitude. It wasn't hostility as much as discomfort. The beliefs Asep and Chris shared directly contradicted everything he'd ever been taught, and Bandu was quick to recite the typical arguments. He even tried to get the two outsiders to repeat the shahada, the prayer of conversion, but Chris sensed the young man's heart wasn't into it.

Chris and Asep understood that intellectual arguments were not going to change Bandu's mind. It would take something supernatural. The dreams had started him down the path, but he wasn't there yet.

"I must get back to the school," Bandu said at last. "If I'm gone too long, they will start to ask questions."

"We understand," Asep said. "Shall we meet again tomorrow? Perhaps you'll succeed in converting us then."

This lighthearted acknowledgment of their dance brought a smile to Bandu's face. "I will see you tomorrow," he said. "Please, friends, be patient with me."

That night, Chris called with an update for Maria, who reported everything to the intercessors back in the States. "Please pray for divine favor," she wrote. "Tomorrow, Chris and Asep will ask this young man if he will take them to his village."

In the park the next day, the men picked up where they'd left off. Bandu seemed to have a memorized rebuttal to everything Chris and Asep shared. But the Holy Spirit gave Chris an idea.

"Bandu," Chris said, "I think you believe what we're telling you. Not in your head, but in your heart. You know this is true. But you're also thinking about what this would mean for you, what it would mean for your family. Am I right?"

"This is very difficult," Bandu said, trembling with emotion. "I believe that Jesus is a great prophet, and I believe He came to me in my dreams. But is He the Son of God? How could that be?"

"And what would happen if you decided to follow Jesus?" Asep asked. "You're wondering about that as well."

"I can't imagine. I would be banished from my village — or worse."

CHAPTER SIXTY-THREE

After a moment of silence, the Spirit prompted Chris to ask the question: "Speaking of your village, Bandu, we have a request of you. It's a big request. Do you think it would be possible to take us to your island, to your village? We would like to meet your family and your people." He stopped talking and started praying in silence.

"I don't see how that's possible," Bandu said. "Not many outsiders have visited my village. It's like a fortress." A contingent of heavenly guardians surrounded the men, keeping the demonic influences away from Bandu's ears. At last he spoke: "Okay. I will take you there. We will leave in two days."

☾

"He invited them here!?" Nyale screamed. "To my village!? This is a disaster. Bandu is too clever for his own good. I should have stricken him instead of the girl."

"There is more, my lord," the messenger said. "The two outsiders are surrounded by powerful warriors of the Most High. Their number is growing by the day. We should assume they will be coming as well."

Nyale turned his gaze to the distant horizon and said nothing. *So this is how it ends*, he thought.

"My lord?" the messenger asked after an uncomfortable silence.

"Summon Rephan," Nyale said, "and tell him to bring whichever army he deems appropriate."

64

THE FERRY LADEN with vehicles, animals, produce, and a few dozen people left the port of Bilonga within an hour of its scheduled departure time. Over the crackling PA system, the captain apologized for engine trouble—but said the problem was now fixed. Bandu, Asep, and Chris settled into their seats for the three-hour trip to Turang. That was the new name, Chris told himself. He couldn't recall the ancient name Asep had mentioned, but he did remember its meaning: fortress of the underworld. As the boat churned through calm seas in a gentle rain, Chris and Asep prayed for the power and protection of the Holy Spirit.

When the ferry reached Turang, Bandu led his guests through the narrow, winding streets of the port city to a cramped bus terminal. He left Chris and Asep on a hard plastic bench and returned minutes later with the tickets they needed for the rest of the journey. A bus took them inland, and then they boarded a crowded van that would carry them up to Seora.

"I'm sorry," Bandu said, "but the comfortable parts are now behind us. My village is only thirty kilometers up the mountain, but it could take four hours. The road is not good, and the rain will make it worse."

As soon as the vehicle pulled away from the station, the clouds opened. The deluge pummeled the van, and the windshield wipers couldn't keep up with the downpour. The driver slowed his progress to a crawl.

Two other travelers were residents of Seora and recognized Bandu, the son of the *dukun*. They inquired about his studies in the city as well as the two outsiders traveling with him. He politely engaged them in conversation, but soon the rocking and lunging of the vehicle was too much. The passengers focused on the road and asked for protection from whichever gods could hear them.

After an hour, the van reached the end of the pavement. From this point on, the road would be gravel, if they were lucky. Thirty minutes later, the driver stopped at a crossroads and half of the passengers got out and marched toward a village up the ravine.

The rain continued, washing out sections of the road. The driver inched his way through sharp ascents and switchbacks like a soldier crossing a minefield. Most of the route featured thick jungle on either side, but in some places the road narrowed and cliffs dropped off in one direction. Chris was amazed by the vistas, and by the absence of guardrails. One little slip and… he didn't want to imagine what could happen.

Up ahead, the mountain rose sharply on the left side of the road and fell away just as drastically on the right. At that point, the road took a hard left. The driver tried to maintain a safe speed while hugging the cliff, but the rear of the van fishtailed to the right in the slick mud. Chris braced himself, and the cabin filled with screams of terror. The driver overcorrected, and the back of the vehicle whipped in the opposite direction, slamming into the exposed rock on the left side of the road. The rear wheels spun in the mud and at last gained traction. The driver maneuvered the vehicle to a flat stretch of road, hopped out of his seat, and inspected the damage.

Chris exhaled slowly and tried to calm his racing heartbeat. Asep and Bandu were equally shaken. "It looks like someone doesn't want us to reach that village," Asep said.

"I have a feeling the angels are working overtime today," Chris said. He turned to Bandu, who was clutching his backpack on his lap. "Bandu," he said, "you look as pale as I do." The young man almost managed a smile.

Ω

They reached Seora at dusk. Even though Bandu had tried to send word of his visit, his arrival was a surprise. And when Soraya realized the outsiders were there because of his son's invitation, he lost it. He pulled Bandu into the mosque.

"How could you be so stupid?" he asked. "How could I have been so stupid to allow you to go to the city? How could I have thought you would ever be more than a field hand, like your grandfather? You know nothing about these men and their schemes. You know nothing about how the world works — despite all of your study at that *pesantren*. They've tricked you. They found the weakest man in all of Bilonga and fooled you into trusting them."

Soraya met with the village elders to debate what to do about the foreigner and the other outsider. Some suggested sending them away immediately, but Asian hospitality eventually won the argument. They sent Bandu to deliver the news.

"The elders would like to welcome you for the night," he said, "but you must leave in the morning. A place is being prepared for you. You will stay in the guest room of my father's home. But first, we will share a meal."

Chris and Asep sat at the table with Soraya, Bandu, and some of the other leading men of the Merapu tribe. Even though the villagers said the appropriate words, the outsiders sensed they were not welcome. And when their drinks were placed before them, their suspicions were confirmed. The coffee was only mildly sweet. Asep understood this for the insult it was. In their culture, the sweetness of the coffee was proportional to the affection for the guest.

As they feasted on a fish called lele, young bamboo, and singkong root, Chris and Asep silently interceded for their hosts. They asked the Spirit to help them speak about Jesus when the opportunity arose. Out of nowhere, one of the elders turned to face Chris.

"You are a Christian, yes?" he asked.

"Yes," Chris said, "I am a follower of Jesus." In that moment, he sensed the Holy Spirit speak to him. He continued: "And so is Asep. We are both disciples of Jesus."

This revelation went off like a grenade in the room. The men had assumed that the foreigner would follow the foreign religion, but not their fellow countryman.

"Is this true?" Soraya asked Asep.

CHAPTER SIXTY-FOUR

"It is," Asep said. "When I was sixteen years old, Jesus appeared to me in a dream and called me to follow Him. I would like to tell you my story, if you want to hear it."

Soraya scanned the faces of the other men at the table. Each gave silent assent to Asep's offer. "You may speak," Soraya said.

The wave of intercession on behalf of the Merapu over the previous weeks empowered Asep, Chris, and the unseen warriors of the Most High who were posted around the house. The armies of darkness could only stand at a distance and guess what was being spoken inside. Asep told his story, and the Merapu elders were engulfed in a sensation of warmth and peace they had never before experienced. Soraya was unconvinced, but the others departed that night with one overwhelming question: Could this possibly be true?

Ω

Soraya still could not believe his son had invited these infidels into their village. This could ruin everything he had worked for. He'd devoted his life to keeping these lies from reaching his people, and now his own son had opened the door. At least the outsiders were close, sleeping in the guest room of his home. At sunup, he would send them on their way.

Sometime before four that morning, Soraya rose from his bed to sound the first call to prayer of the new day. As he passed by the guest room, however, he heard a soft sound coming from the other side of the curtain. It was the one called Asep, speaking to someone. Was he plotting with the foreigner?

"Father in heaven," Asep whispered, "I ask for Your blessing on this entire household. I beg You to give them the greatest blessing of all—eternal salvation and a place in Your family. You do not wish for any to perish but want all to find eternal life, so I ask that You grant Soraya and Djum good health. Preserve their lives until that glorious moment when they see Your great love for them and surrender all that they have to Your will. May Soraya's influence then expand to new heights, and may he become a true spiritual father to this tribe."

Nyale and Rephan acted at once. They summoned a spirit of death and released it upon Soraya. The old man felt the illness overtaking him in a matter of seconds. He vomited on himself, collapsed to the floor, and started shaking uncontrollably. The noise awakened Chris, and he and Asep found Soraya on the floor outside their room. "He's burning up," Chris said. "Let's get him to the bed." They carried him to his room, where his wife was beginning to stir. Chris prayed, "In the name of Jesus, release this man!" The demons fled immediately, and Soraya sat up in bed, fully healed.

Djum turned to Asep and Chris. "Who are you," she asked, "and what do you want with us?"

65

"THE ELDERS ARE TROUBLED by your presence," Bandu said as he served breakfast to Chris and Asep just after sunrise. "They say you have brought a bad spirit into the village. You must leave as soon as the driver is ready. I'm sorry I let you come."

On their way to the van, they attracted a crowd of curious children, eager to catch a glimpse of the pale outsider. In the clearing beside the mosque, one of the bolder boys kicked a ball to Chris. He passed it back, and soon several others joined in their game. Bandu, alerted to what was taking place, hustled over and sent the children away.

"You must wait in the van," he told Chris, Asep, and the few villagers who would ride with them down to the coast. "The driver will be here soon."

When the driver arrived, however, the van would not start. He played with the ignition, tested some wires under the hood, and threw his arms up in exasperation. "This can't be happening," he said. "Wait here. I'll be back soon." He shuffled toward the center of the village.

About ten minutes later, there was still no sign of the driver—but the children had returned. They kicked their ball back and forth, glancing occasionally at the strange man in the van. Chris watched them and was overcome with the compassion of Jesus. He felt the Father's love for them and dreaded the thought that they would face life—and eternity—apart from their Creator.

Chris and Asep stepped out of the vehicle, and the kids cheered, gesturing to the outsiders to join them. As he kicked the ball, Chris prayed silently for God's blessing on each of the children. His thoughts turned to Bethany, Hannah, and Timmy, amazed that God's love for them was somehow so much greater than his own.

The ball escaped the circle of kids, and Chris chased it down. For the first time, he noticed a little girl off to the side. She was on the ground, and he was afraid she'd fallen. But then he saw that she was using her hands to propel herself, dragging her body and legs behind. She beamed up at Chris, and he knelt in the dirt beside her. He sensed a word from the Spirit: "I want to heal this girl today."

Ω

The village elders gathered at the edge of the clearing, wondering why the infidels were still there.

"It's a problem with the van," Bandu said. "The driver is working on it, and then they'll be gone."

"Young man, you've brought great shame on us all," one of the elders said. "There will be consequences. If you cannot fix this,

CHAPTER SIXTY-FIVE 339

the council might see fit to banish you—along with your cursed child. And your father is not blameless in this either. *His* actions will be called into question as well. Perhaps it's time for a *dukun* with better judgment than he has shown of late."

Another man called out: "What's that foreigner doing?" They turned to see Chris kneeling next to Bandu's daughter, his hand on her head.

"This must end at once," an elder said. He handed Bandu a *kris*. Bandu felt the heft of the dagger in his hand and looked confused. "Wave it at him," the man said. "Scare him. Make him see that you're serious."

Bandu started walking toward the outsider, one halting step at a time. He still wasn't sure what he would say to Chris, or what he would do when he reached him.

But dark spirits suddenly attacked his mind with thoughts of hatred and violence. *How dare he lay hands on your daughter? What vile act is this animal planning? Is it not bad enough that he has brought shame on your family? There is only one thing left to do: You must end this.* The rage welled up within him, and he picked up his pace. Soon he was sprinting toward Chris.

The heavenly warriors, obeying new orders from their commander, stepped aside. Out of the corner of his eye, Asep caught sight of Bandu streaking toward his friend, the blade of the knife glinting in the sunlight.

"Chris!" Asep yelled. "No!"

Startled by his friend's warning, Chris began to rise and turn, but he had no chance to defend himself. Bandu, under the control of unseen forces, was upon him. He plunged the dagger deep into Chris's back, directly through his heart.

Chris collapsed to the ground. Bandu stood over him, slowly emerging from a trance. Several of the children who witnessed the attack ran from the clearing, screaming their confusing news throughout the village. The shock paralyzed Asep for a moment, then he sprinted to Chris's side.

"Jesus, save my friend!" he cried. "Save him! Save him!" He pulled the knife from Chris's back, and a villager handed him a shirt. The elders rushed to the scene and encircled the dying man, spewing vitriol at Bandu and shouting incoherent instructions to Asep. He worked frantically to stop the flow of blood, but the wound was too severe. There was nothing he could do.

After minutes of futile effort, Asep slowly rose to his feet. *This can't be happening*, he thought. *It's only a bad dream.* In the bloody dirt beneath him, his friend Chris Billings — husband of Maria, father of three amazing children, man of God — lay dead.

Sword, Light, and Mercy surrounded Asep and bathed him with words of comfort. Just meters away, the village elders closed in on Bandu, shoving him, jabbing him with accusative fingers, yelling about curses, shame, and banishment.

Asep staggered to their circle and faced the killer. "What have you done, Bandu?" he asked.

At that moment, a little girl's joyous laughter arrested their attention. As one, the men turned to witness a sight they never thought they would see. Fatima, the cursed child of Bandu, was running and leaping and giggling with her astonished friends.

"What have I done?" Bandu said, staring at his little girl. "I've killed the man who healed my daughter."

Nyale watched from the tree line, seething with rage as his world collapsed around him. "Stop her at once!" he screamed to his troops. "Attack! Attack!" But when the demons tried to move forward, they discovered they were frozen in place. A sense of dread washed over them as they realized their time was short.

ω

News of the murder—and healing—shot through Seora. A crowd soon gathered in the clearing, most not believing that such a thing could happen in their village. Someone found a blanket to cover Chris's body, and Soraya pulled Asep aside.

"You must leave this place," the *dukun* said. "I command you."

The warriors of the Most High established a wide perimeter around Asep, forcing the enemy's spirits into the jungle surrounding the village. Even Rephan and Nyale were limited in the face of the heavenly soldiers, who had grown in size and brilliance.

Asep stood before Soraya, who was aging before his eyes. "After everything you've seen and heard," Asep said, "do you still believe you control what happens here? The rule of the ancient spirit has reached its end."

Asep returned to Chris's side, the crowd parting as he passed through. He spoke in the anointing of the Holy Spirit:

"Friends, what you've witnessed this day is a miracle. The bondage you've been under has been broken. The spirits of darkness that imprisoned you have been defeated. This man and I came to you with a message of freedom. God sent us to you, the Merapu, with His good news: You can be free of shame. You can be free of guilt. You can be free of the chains of sin. You no longer have to live in fear. You can have peace with God through Jesus Christ, who has revealed His power by restoring this child. You can see it with your own eyes. The blood of my friend — which has been spilled on this ground, which is even on my hands — is crying out to you. God offers His forgiveness and freedom to each of you this day. Jesus is calling you to follow Him, to submit to Him. If you are ready to lay aside your chains and follow, come forward and I will pray with you."

Without hesitation, Bandu stepped before Asep and fell to his knees. "I am ready to follow Jesus," he said. "I need His forgiveness." As Asep prayed, Bandu felt the peace of God wash over him.

Some of the villagers gasped when they realized Soraya's son had declared allegiance to the outsider's God. Then Sri, holding Fatima's hand, walked through the crowd and knelt next to her husband. Seven others joined them that day, the first followers of Jesus in the history of the Merapu people.

Rephan lingered as long as he could tolerate the scene. Then he departed to break the news to his master: *The last nation has fallen.*

66

"BANDU, I WILL BE BACK as soon as possible," Asep said. "Is it safe for you to stay here?"

"My father is displeased," Bandu said, "but he informed the elders he will protect me for now. He thinks I'll change my mind and everything will go back to the way it was before."

The young men, now brothers in the family of God, embraced as the driver leaned on his horn. "Let's go," the driver called to Asep. "I don't want to be stuck on this dreadful mountain one more night."

"Take care of the Book I gave you," Asep told Bandu. "It's the story of Jesus. Read it to the others. Ask God to show you what it means."

"I will do as you say. Come back soon."

Asep boarded the van and closed the door. He rode down to the port city with Chris's body in complete silence. When he found a phone, he called Harriet. Between sobs, he managed to relay the tragic news. He couldn't imagine facing Maria and the kids. Harriet said the Lord would give her the strength to tell them.

The sun rose over Seora the next morning, and for a moment Nyale imagined that life hadn't changed much. He knew the majority of the villagers remained under his spell, and he still had a bag of tricks he could unleash on these traitors.

But Nyale's confidence evaporated the second Bandu opened the door of his hut. Two immense warriors of the Most High led the way—a pair that had arrived with the outsiders a day and a half earlier. The intensity of their brilliance forced Nyale to avert his gaze.

"Fear, come at once!" he shouted to the spirits of his realm. When no one appeared, he called again: "Fear, I command you, come! Doubt, I have an assignment for you!" Again, there was no response. His annoyance gave way to dread. What was happening to his army?

Nyale followed Bandu, Sri, and Fatima at a safe distance. The angels had spotted him but elected not to engage. The family entered the village mosque, and the demon thought—hoped—that they might renounce their actions of the previous day. But he would not be able to hear for himself. A squad of the Most High was positioned around the structure, and none of Nyale's subordinates had yet arrived to support him.

Bandu's boldness took the villagers by surprise. Not even twenty-four hours after declaring allegiance to Jesus, he strode into the mosque carrying the Book of his new God. He left his wife and daughter in the women's section of the building and marched to the base of the mimbar. Rather than mounting its steps, he stayed on the main floor and turned to face the men.

"The God I now serve," he said, "has left a Book to help His people know Him. The Book tells the truth that we all witnessed yesterday. This God is a healer. He restores broken bodies. He opens blind eyes. For centuries, our people were blinded by Nyale. Our fathers made pacts with him, but he only deceived them. Now our eyes are open. Jesus has removed the scales, and we see for the first time. I don't know everything about this Jesus, but He appeared to me in my dreams and I believe in Him and His power. If you want to study this Book with me and learn what it means to follow Him, come with me today and we will seek together. This God invites us to know Him, and He is powerful enough to teach us."

Bandu walked out the door into the light of day with thirty more Merapu in his wake. Nyale could only watch.

67

A DAY AFTER ASEP'S return to the Bible school, Maria and the Billings children boarded the first of three planes that would carry them back to the States. They were numb with shock and grief. Maria had decided to tell the children the same incomplete truth Asep had reported to the authorities: Their father's death was the result of a tragic accident. In time she would share more details, but the priority now was getting Chris's remains back to Grapevine for a memorial service. The paperwork required to transport a body, miraculously, sailed through in record time.

At the airport in Surabaya, Asep waited for the Billingses' plane to take off, then he made his way to a domestic terminal. He had a church to plant in Seora.

ꭥ

Around the same time the Billings family landed in Newark, Asep's van pulled into the Merapu village. The sun was setting over the western hills, and activity in Seora seemed to be winding down for the night. Asep followed the path to Bandu and Sri's hut — and he suddenly found himself in the Book of Acts.

Three men were passing Bandu's hut when Asep arrived. "If you're looking for the teacher," one of them said, "he's not here. He's at his father's home. Join us. We're going that way."

As they walked, the men described life in the village in the few days since Asep had left. Bandu was boldly teaching from the book of Jesus morning and evening, and more people were believing every day. So many were interested, in fact, that the group outgrew Bandu's hut. They prayed and asked God where they should meet, and Soraya of all people offered his home as a gathering place.

The previous day, Bandu had read a story about Jesus healing a blind man. A villager asked whether Jesus still did such things, and Bandu said, "I don't know. I know He healed my daughter, but she wasn't blind. Shall we find out?"

One of Asep's companions filled in the details: "So we all got up and walked down to the hut of a woman who's been blind for ten years. Bandu said, 'Can we pray for you and ask God to heal you?' She said, 'You can if you'd like.' So we gathered around and prayed for her healing in Jesus' name — and she could see! That woman is my father's sister. They now both follow Jesus."

Asep couldn't believe what he saw when they reached Soraya's home. A hundred people sat in and around the hut as Bandu read from the Book. They eagerly listened, asked questions, and discussed what the stories meant for them.

Bandu spotted Asep at the edge of the crowd. He called out, "My brother, we've done what you said."

68

FRITZ BERNHEIM'S EYES lingered on the casket, and he tried to imagine the joy Chris Billings was experiencing at this moment. What a juxtaposition. *We mourn*, he thought. *We weep. We suffer. And you, my friend, are in the presence of relentless, unending joy and love.*

The pastor scanned the stunned faces of the mourners in front of him. What could he ever say to bring a measure of comfort to Chris's family and friends? He prayed that the Holy Spirit would infuse his simple words with the peace that only God can offer.

Fritz cleared his throat and spoke: "The psalmist writes, 'Precious in the sight of the Lord is the death of his saints.' Let's contemplate this truth. Chris's life — and yes, even his death — is precious to the Lord. On your way in here today, you saw the news vans in the parking lot. As our community has learned about the final days of Chris's life, they've become curious. They have questions. They want to know what happened. They wonder why a man who had everything he ever wanted would give it up and go with his family to the other side of the world.

And so the reporters are out there, doing their jobs, asking questions, trying to learn more about our dear friend, and we welcome them.

"But I am troubled by some of the comments I've been hearing in the community, and even in this place. Many are saying, 'What a waste. What a tragic waste of a life.' Maybe you've heard that as well. Maybe you've thought it. Maybe you've even said it. Friends, may we grieve this loss, but may we never think of Chris's life as a waste. Let us choose to believe the truth of Scripture—that Chris Billings's life and death are precious to the Lord.

"And why is that? Because Chris lived a life of complete surrender to his God. He heard God's word. He believed God's word. He obeyed God's word. The Lord told His people to carry His good news to everyone everywhere, to the ends of the earth. And Chris, being Chris, obeyed. That kind of obedience, that kind of surrender, is precious to God."

Fritz shuffled his notes and opened a small book. "A couple of years ago," he said, "Chris started keeping a journal. He wrote about the process of becoming a missionary. He wrote about prayer requests and answers to prayer. He wrote about his insights gleaned from Scripture. He wrote about his love for the people of Indonesia. He didn't write every day, but he did record an entry the day before he died. Maria has given me permission to read a portion of it. This is what he wrote: 'I dreamed of heaven last night. Orien was there. Granddad was there. Bandu was there. He's the young man from the Merapu tribe who will take me and Asep to his village. You know who else was there? I was there. I'm not sure what all of this means,

CHAPTER SIXTY-EIGHT

but it's a reminder of why we do what we do. We work hard and sometimes we suffer, and sometimes we sacrifice so that Jesus can receive His reward: people from every tribe and nation and tongue gathered around the throne, so that we can help people get into heaven, and help get heaven into us.'"

He closed the book and set it aside.

"We mourn our loss," he said, "but the apostle Paul reminds us that we don't mourn as those who have no hope. All who call on the name of the Lord will be saved, and we will see Jesus face to face. Paul wrote to the Thessalonians, 'For the Lord himself will come down from heaven, with a loud command, with the voice of the archangel and with the trumpet call of God.' This is our hope."

The Spirit's presence was palpable in the church, and Fritz closed with a simple invitation: "Chris Billings died while sharing the good news of Jesus with the Merapu people. Maria informs me that several members of that tribe have received Christ as their Savior—and we praise God for this wonderful news. What about you? Are you ready to surrender your life to Jesus Christ? Are you ready to declare your allegiance to Him?"

Dozens across the sanctuary raised their hands, indicating their commitment to Jesus. "All of heaven is rejoicing with us," Fritz said. "Let's go in the peace of Christ."

At the end of the service, a spirit of celebration led Chris's family and friends through the doors of the church. Maria huddled with the kids as the pallbearers carried the casket to the waiting hearse.

Suddenly, the heavens rumbled, a brilliant light flashed overhead, and a trumpet blast resounded across the atmosphere. All eyes lifted to the skies. The mourners' sorrow at once turned to shouts of joy.

"What is this!?" Maria asked, embracing her children. The kids started jumping up and down in anticipation. Timmy pointed to the sky. His question caught in his throat:

"Is that who I think it is?"

Maria lifted her arms to the heavens. Her answer confirmed what they all were seeing:

"My Savior and my God!"

EPILOGUE

SONGS OF PRAISE rang out across the eternal city as the children of the Most High basked in His presence. Finally, the people of God were gathered as one, doing what they'd been created to do, free from sorrow, pain, sickness, disease, worry, fear. They represented every nation, every tribe, every tongue, every era of human history, and they filled the air with endless worship of the victorious King.

Chris Billings knew the riches of the new heaven and new earth could never be exhausted, and he reveled in the thought of spending eternity exploring the depths of God's love and creativity.

Every moment was a celebration. Through tears of joy, he had welcomed Maria and the children to their reward. He had greeted Bandu and Sri and Fatima. He had reunited with Asep and Orien and other co-laborers in God's mission. He had met long-departed family members and heroes of the faith.

One day as Chris stood alone, surveying the multitudes of worshippers and reflecting on God's goodness, Asep and Bandu approached, accompanied by a third man.

"Brother Chris," Bandu said, embracing the man whose life he'd ended. "This is Elang. He has something to say to you."

Elang grasped Chris's hands and peered into his eyes.

"Chris," he said, "you do not know me. I grew up in Seora and lived there my whole life. Until the day you and Asep came to our village, I did not know God. But because you obeyed Jesus, because you came to tell us about Him... I am here and we are now brothers."

Every moment was a celebration.